Call of the Whisperwind

Jeffree Wyn Itrich

Published by Milagro Mountain Press
P.O. Box 34131
San Diego, CA 92163

ISBN-13:978-0-9896991-0-5
ISBN-10:0989699102

Acknowledgements

Much appreciation to Debra Kain, Linell Maloney, and Canda Williams for their thoughtful comments on the manuscript. Special heartfelt thanks to my husband Earl Itrich for his assistance and support throughout the writing and publication of this book.

Author's Note

Call of the Whisperwind is Book Two of the Bradshaw Family Saga, which began with Destiny at Oak Valley.

Chapter One

1883 Santa Fe, New Mexico

The day dawned with its usual indigo brilliance, shards of blue puncturing the sky. The quiet of the early morning ebbed as the light cast its glow. Watercolor rays radiated down on the crimson earth, where the vast desert wilderness meets the sky. Warm dry breezes carried the scents of chaparral and sage, floating down the town's streets and through windows open in the early autumn air, the last vestige of summer.

Rachel Bradshaw tosses and turns in the shadowed morning light; a cold, clammy sweat covers her, making her nightgown stick to her pale skin, plastering her dark brown hair to her scalp; she bites her lip fiercely and lets out a muffled scream. She sees her husband, Matt, lying in a dank pool of his own blood. Nausea roils in the pit of her stomach. Bile creeps up and burns her throat as her heart races frantically. Suddenly she can't breathe and gasps for air.

Matt reached over and shook her shoulder. "Wake up, Rachel, wake up."

She opened her eyes to see Matt leaning over her, his eyes pinched with worry, his brow furrowed.

"Same dream?" he asked, running his hand over her damp hair, pulling it off of her face.

She nodded, blinking herself awake. "It was so real." She swallowed hard. "You were dying." Tears of terror filled her emerald green eyes, turning them the dark shade of a forest at dusk.

He took her in his arms and stroked her head to calm her down.

"It's all right. I'm fine. It was only a bad dream."

Rachel buried her face in the center of his broad chest and breathed deeply until her racing heartbeat returned to normal.

As the first daylight seeped through the soft white curtains, she inhaled the scent of wild sage wafting in the window. It worked like a narcotic, sending her back into a deep sleep, this time peaceful. She woke up an hour later to find Matt watching her, a faint smile across his wide, generous mouth, his chocolate brown mustache curving over the edges of his lips

"How long have you been awake?" Rachel asked.

"I never went back to sleep after your nightmare."

Rachel frowned. "I'm sorry."

"Doesn't matter. Wanted to make sure you were okay. No harm done."

She stretched up and lightly pressed her lips on Matt's, which was all he needed to sweep down and kiss her back with the passion usually reserved for new lovers. Rachel felt her body instinctively respond, pressing up against his as though it had a mind of its own. Matt ran his hand down her hip and began to gather up her nightgown.

"A-r-r-rg-h!"

Rachel and Matt instantly froze and pulled apart, simultaneously turning their heads toward the open doorway. Matt let go of Rachel and fell back on his pillow. Rachel turned her body around and sat up. Their infant daughter, Maddie, had awakened in the room across the hall and wanted up, or breakfast, or both.

"Sorry, hon," Rachel said. "Somebody's hungry."

"Ugh!" Matt moaned.

Rachel got up and walked across the hallway. Little Maddie lay in her crib, her arms stretched outward, tears cascading down her round little cheeks.

"Mama's here," Rachel said reassuringly. "No need to cry." She picked up Maddie and carried her across the hallway to their bed, lay down with her nightgown pulled up and allowed Maddie to nurse. Maddie fell asleep before she finished. Matt too fell back asleep, however Rachel stayed awake, thinking, as she often did before rising.

Was it really only three years ago that she took that fateful hot-air balloon ride in the 21st century that brought her back to 19th century New Mexico? Yes, she nodded to herself, three years. And in that time she had left her old life behind and begun a new one unlike anything she thought possible. Not long after marrying Matt, they returned to Oak Valley to live in Dr. Bradshaw's house, the house that Matt and his brother James built for their father, and the stately home where Rachel met Matthew.

After living in the grand home for a couple of years, they ultimately decided they needed a different type of house, a more suitable home in which to raise family. They bought another piece of property and began plans to build a new home. With Oak Valley in boom-town mode it did not take long to sell Dr. Bradshaw's home, but the logistics of building the new home were a bit more problematical. They decided to move back to Santa Fe to live in Matt's house, plan out their Oak Valley home with a Denver architect and have the architect oversee the building of their new home. Matt went down to Oak Valley every couple of months to gauge the progress and make any decisions needed on site. Unfortunately, a multitude of problems delayed the construction, first by a few weeks, then a few months. It seemed as though the house would never be built.

Rachel felt an odd desperation to return to Oak Valley. She tried to explain it to Matt. Told him how she learned in the 21st century that the town leaders would refuse to allow the railroad to build a railroad line into Oak Valley and how that pivotal decision would ultimately be the town's demise. Oak Valley was now a thriving mining town growing at a quick pace. Although Matt found it hard to believe that a decision as simple as refusing to bring in the railroad would ultimately turn the flourishing community into a ghost town, Matt had come to respect Rachel's knowledge of the future and take her advice. She finally convinced him that they had to be living in Oak Valley when the town leaders began meeting about the railroad's request. If they weren't physically living there to persuade the officials otherwise, that their time and money spent on the house would be wasted. And the town would die.

Meanwhile Matt and Rachel settled into a comfortable life in Matt's home in Santa Fe until they could move back to Oak Valley. Rachel was beginning to doubt that the house and their move back down south would ever happen and that doubt contributed to her growing sense of unease. She sensed that she was the only one who could save Oak Valley, yet she also realized that she couldn't very well do it living in Santa Fe, a world away in the 19th century. It wasn't like she had any choice. Building a home in the 19th century in a place as remote as Oak Valley had its challenges. What could easily be done in months in her former time often took years in the 1880s.

Compounding that sense of a mission delayed, there were days when she thought about her former life in the 21st century, her job and her family, all of which she missed terribly. She knew she had never been happier than being married to Matt and raising their infant daughter. Still, it wasn't enough. In the 21st century she had studied microbiology at the University of New Mexico and had a prestigious position at a pharmaceutical company. She enjoyed working in medicine; she felt that she was contributing to society and making a difference, even if it was a small one. And as much as she loved her new role, she wanted more out of life. It wasn't a matter of money; they had enough with Matt's security business doing exceptionally well. It was more than that – deep down Rachel felt she was not living up to her potential. It was a dreaded feeling she woke with every morning, and which she shared with no one. Maybe it was time, she mused, to broach the subject with Matt. He had proven himself to be her best friend and well understood her challenges of adapting to the 19th century, even if occasionally he found them bizarre.

"Matt, when do you have to be at the stagecoach this morning for your trip to Oak Valley?" Rachel asked her husband as she placed a cup of coffee down in front of him at the breakfast table.

"9:00, why?" He looked her up and down in her silk robe, her thick chocolate brown hair tumbling down her shoulders. When he met Rachel, her exotic, almond-shaped eyes, framed in dark thick lashes, perfectly formed rosy lips, and glowing, porcelain skin mesmerized him. He could never get enough of her, even three years later. "You thinking we have time to go back upstairs?" He wiggled his brows at her.

"No," she grinned. "There's been something on my mind that I want to talk to you about. Maybe you can help me think through it," she responded as she sat down next to Maddie and began to spoon bits of pureed food into her mouth.

"I am already packed and don't have to leave for an hour. What's on your mind?" he asked, creasing his brows together.

Seeing his reaction, Rachel reached over and squeezed his hand. "Oh it's nothing serious. Well it is, but serious only to me." Rachel flashed her emerald green eyes at Matt who saw the worry in his wife's eyes.

"If it's serious to you, then it's serious to me. What's bothering you?"

Rachel spooned the last of the porridge into Maddie's mouth. The little girl yawned and was obviously ready to take her mid-morning nap. "Let me put Maddie in her crib. I'll be right back." Rachel picked up her daughter and carried her upstairs where she settled her down for the morning. Rachel returned to the kitchen and stood near him. Matt looked up at her inquisitively, a question mark across his face.

"Matt, I've told you what my life was like before, before I traveled."

Matt rubbed his chin, shook back his mane of chestnut hair, folded his muscled arms across his broad chest and concentrated on Rachel.

"I wouldn't trade this life for anything. I love being your wife and a mother to Maddie, but there's something missing," she began hesitantly.

"More children?" Matt asked, the right side of his mouth curling up, and the right eyebrow rising.

Rachel tossed her head and chuckled. "Now, why did I know you were going to say that?"

"Well, is that it?"

"No, it's not more children. We'll have to wait and see if God decides we should have more. But it's a different matter, one about me. You know I want to get back to Oak Valley for the town's sake, but it's more than that. I want more out of life. I have more to offer."

"This reminds me of the conversation we had a long time ago when I asked you to marry me and you said you wanted a career. I told you then that you could do my books, but that didn't seem to be what you wanted." Matt looked down at his large hands spread across his powerful thighs, then back up at Rachel.

"True, it wasn't then and it's not now." She stepped over to Matt, lifted up one of his hands to her lips, and kissed it gently, her face aglow. "It isn't that I don't want to help you if you need assistance with your business. It's that I want to feel fulfilled. I want to feel as though I'm contributing to the betterment of society. I want to do more."

Matt slowly nodded his head, trying to understand. "And when you were working in the 21st century, you felt fulfilled?"

Rachel nodded. "Yes, I did. And I want that feeling again, but I don't know how. I keep feeling as though I've lost a part of myself --- that place inside where my heart knew the way. Not my romantic heart; that I found in you and I'm grateful." She brushed the back of her fingers over his cheek. "I'm out of my element, so to speak."

Matt took Rachel's hand, turned it over and kissed her palm. He looked up and held her gaze for several moments.

"I'm not sure what I can advise, Rachel. I had hoped that being a wife and mother would be enough for you, as it is for other women. I know that you are not of this time and what fulfills women in our time plainly does not satisfy you."

"Thank you for understanding, Matt," Rachel responded quietly, running her hands around his neck. "That is exactly what I mean. I'm lost. I don't know how to find a way to fulfill myself. I don't even know how to start thinking about it. I've thought and thought and thought; I can't see my way forward."

"I don't have an answer for you, however, I do have a suggestion," Matt began, his words low, nearly a murmur. Rachel looked at him, wide-eyed, encouraging him to continue. "Pay a visit to your friend the jeweler who brought you back to the 19th century. After all, he got you into this; maybe he has an idea or two on what you can do here."

Rachel felt a comforting warmth coursing through her veins. Matt got it; he got her.

"I will be eternally grateful to the man for practicing his magic or voodoo or whatever it was that he did to force your time travel," Matt continued. He stood up and cupped his hands on her shoulders. "Now he should put a bit of that into practice to help you with this dilemma."

Rachel rolled her lips inward and played with a strand of her hair. "Hmm, that's an idea," she mused. "I hadn't thought to talk to him. Oh heck, I don't even know if he's still there. I haven't been back to the shop since we took Maddie to meet him after she was born."

Matt smiled at the memory. The curious jeweler took to the little girl like a grandfather seeing a grandchild for the first time. "He's still there. I've seen him around town from time to time and you've got a few more pieces of his artistic efforts since the last time we were in his shop."

Rachel blushed, knowing full well that Matt had showered her in more jewelry than she could ever dream of owning. She wasn't sure where he bought the pieces, and then realized they were probably made by the magical jeweler.

"Besides," Matt added, "that odd fellow seems to have an uncanny way of popping up when you most need him." He reached over and played with one of her curls spilling down the front of her robe.

Rachel began nodding her head. "Yes, he does. I don't understand the man, but you're right, he did get me into this, thank goodness. I had no idea what an extraordinary life lay ahead of me, but he did."

Rachel glanced to the side and eyed a bowl of peaches she had picked from the backyard tree. "I know," she brightened, "I'll bake him a pie and take it to the shop."

Matt blanched. "A pie? One of your pies?"

"Oh come on, Matt," Rachel admonished him, her lips turning downward into a frown. "My cooking has really improved. I can even make biscuits now."

Matt nodded, trying to be serious. "Yes, your cooking has gotten better but, um, your baking still has a ways to go."

Rachel's face burned bright red. She wasn't sure if she wanted to hit him or laugh. She knew that he was right. Cooking in a 19th century kitchen without the benefit of gas or electricity and modern conveniences like mixers and food processors and microwave ovens had proved to be a constant trial, one she lost as often as she won.

"Perhaps take him some peaches instead?" Matt offered, glancing at the bowl of peaches, and then added teasingly, "I mean, you do want him to help you, right?"

Rachel bunched up a napkin and threw it at Matt. "You are bad, really bad!" Matt ducked the napkin, reached down and picked up his traveling case.

12

"Gotta go, Rachie. You'll work it out," Matt murmured as he bent down, ran his hand around the back of Rachel's neck, pulled her close and kissed her deeply. "Give Mr. Magic my regards," he called as he walked down the hall and out the front door.

* * *

When she awoke from her blissful nap, Rachel dressed Maddie in a pink dress, sweater, hat and matching shoes topped with little ribbon bows. She placed her in a buggy and headed over to the home of her brother and sister-in-law, James, Catherine and their niece Emily.

As they meandered down the streets, Maddie wanted to stop and smell every flower she saw in every yard. This wasn't the first time Maddie had exhibited such curiosity. Rachel thought that if she lived in the 21st century her daughter would probably study botany or landscape architecture in college. In the 19th century she wasn't sure what options she would have, nevertheless she did not want to limit her possibilities. While she and Matt both agreed that Maddie should attend college, they were not quite of the same mind when it came to what she would study.

Matt said she should pursue subjects that would better train her to care for a household. Rachel completely dispelled that notion, saying that if Maddie showed an interest in other subjects – regardless of their being in the traditional male domain – that she should be encouraged, not dissuaded. Matt had tried to reason with Rachel pointing out that women did not have many career options in the 19th century. Rachel pointed out the many societal changes the country would undergo in a few short years, including the higher education of women.

One of the courses Rachel had taken at the University of New Mexico in the 21st century was a history of women in medicine and the sciences. It was a subject about which she was passionate nearly to a fault. She told Matt about women such as Elizabeth Blackwell, the first woman to earn a medical degree in the United States; Clara Barton, who founded the Red Cross; Madame Curie and countless other early female pioneers in medicine. Nevertheless, he suggested that rather than argue or make a decision at Maddie's young age that they wait and see what talents and interests she developed. Rachel concurred, knowing that her daughter was already showing signs of inquisitiveness that she exhibited herself when she was small. Soon they arrived at the home of James and Catherine.

"Hi Maddie!" a cheerful young voice called.

Maddie looked up to see her cousin Emily, now 11 years old, standing on the front porch waving at her. Rachel ushered Maddie into the front yard as Emily ran down the stairs, scooped Maddie up in her arms and began kissing her bright little cheeks. Maddie giggled incessantly and clutched onto Emily's long, golden braid, swinging to and fro down her back.

"What's all the commotion out here?" Catherine Bradshaw, Rachel's sister-in-law, appeared at the open door. Seeing who had arrived, she grinned at Rachel and the girls. The tall woman with shiny, jet-black hair pulled up into an elegant chignon at the nape of her long neck, stepped down and took Maddie from Emily's arms. "What brings you this way?" Catherine asked.

"Well, I was hoping you wouldn't mind if I left Maddie with you for an hour. Would it be okay?" Rachel asked.

"Oh yes!" Emily squealed. "We would love to take care of her."

Rachel looked up at Catherine to whom she posed the question, raising her eyebrows.

"Of course," Catherine answered graciously. "Emily, can you give Madeleine your undivided attention? Will you keep your eye on her every moment that your Aunt Rachel is gone?"

"Yes, ma'am," Emily nodded.

Catherine turned to Rachel. "Where are you going?"

"Just need to go on a few errands is all. Maddie is so curious now; she wants to touch and smell everything. It takes forever to get down the street much less conduct business in a store. It would be a huge help if she could stay here. I could finish more quickly."

"Of course," Catherine nodded her head. "Take all the time you need. You know how much we adore having her to ourselves any chance we get."

"Thank you, Catherine." Rachel leaned over and kissed her daughter. "Maddie, you stay here and play with your cousin Emily while I go on an errand, okay?"

Maddie looked at her mother, then turned back to Emily, clearly mesmerized with her cousin's braid. Rachel looked over at Catherine. "I won't be long." Rachel turned and walked back out of the garden toward the center of town as Catherine, Emily and Maddie watched her leave.

Rachel headed for the town's center, a mere ten minutes away. Coming around a corner she found herself in front of a jewelry shop, a wooden sign hung in front: *Cornelius August, Jeweler at Your Service*. To Rachel it was not just any jewelry shop. It was owned by the man who made the cameo Matt gave her when he proposed, and the very man who was responsible for bringing her to the 19th century.

Rachel opened the heavy wooden door and stepped inside. The small, squat jeweler sat at a work bench buffing a small gold ring. What little hair he had shot off the sides of his head, giving him a peculiar, clownish appearance. Wrinkled from years in the desert, he sported the softness of a satisfied man aging gracefully.

"Rachel, how good to see you!" the jeweler called out, delight gushing through his voice.

She beamed, strode over to the work bench and set her basket down on a counter. "It's nice to see you too, Cornelius."

"And to what do I owe this pleasure?" he asked, grinning his typical smile, his mostly bald head gleaming in the morning light. "Need a new piece of jewelry?"

"Oh goodness no, I have more than enough jewelry."

"Then what brings you here today?" he inquired, watching her face as intently as a cat facing a new conundrum.

"Well, I'm not sure where to begin."

"It is not of a jewelry nature I assume?"

"No, no, it isn't," Rachel responded.

"You're getting antsy is it?"

Rachel looked up, her mouth slightly hanging open. She nodded in agreement.

"How do you do that?" she asked.

"Do what?"

"Read my mind." She paused and raised her hand to her throat encircling it like a necklace. "You've done that as long as I've known you – able to figure out what I'm thinking before I say a word."

Cornelius smiled much wider. "Now Rachel, why do you even ask? You know that I took you under my wing when I brought you back to the 19th century, even though you fought it every bit of the way. I will always be here, ready to assist. Since I brought you here I feel a special responsibility for you."

"Okay, well, now I need you again. Not for anything big, just some suggestions on how to, how to, how to…."

"How to find that something beyond your marriage and child that will make you feel, how shall I say it, essential, that you are doing something significant that matters?" The man's eyes twinkled as he spoke.

"Yes, that's exactly it!" Her eyes brightened.

"So I thought," Cornelius sighed. "I truly believed you would visit me much sooner. I knew you would never rest easy in the role of wife and mother."

"But I love being married to Matt. And a woman couldn't ask for a better behaved or sweeter child than Maddie. I adore her. I never expected I would love motherhood so much," Rachel protested.

"This has nothing to do with love, Rachel. You know that." The jeweler looked at Rachel with an air of compassion.

Rachel nodded.

"You are an uncommon young woman, one who is not easily satisfied with what satisfies others. That has always been my challenge with you," Cornelius declared. "More than most you need for your life to have a higher purpose." He returned to buffing the ring.

Rachel nodded; there was nothing more that she could say. The jeweler accurately identified what had been aching in her heart. He paused buffing the ring and looked back up at her.

"Rachel, my dear, have you considered pursuing your love of medicine that excited you so in the 21st century?"

"Here, now?" Rachel's eyebrows shot up. "How would I do that?"

"Now really, Rachel, you are much more creative than that. Think about it. You have always been interested in science, in particular the sciences that help people. Medicine," the man leaned toward Rachel, emphasizing his point. "I always thought it a little strange that you didn't go into the healing arts and chose instead to be a microbiologist and later work in pharmaceutical marketing."

"It was a job. I'd considered going to medical school, but it didn't work out," Rachel professed.

"What do you mean it didn't work out?" Cornelius objected. "You were a lot smarter than that old philandering boyfriend of yours who you supported through his medical school education. You could have gone to medical school. You simply made a lousy decision."

A wrinkle formed across her brow. "How do you know about that?"

Cornelius simply smiled.

Rachel nodded, knowing he was right. "Okay, so what do I do now?"

"Your predicament is that you cannot control the world in which you now find yourself living, but you can control how you live in it."

"Haven't I been doing a pretty good job of that, Cornelius? What more can I do?"

"Take what you know and apply it to this century. For example, the healing arts. You are good at it," Cornelius responded. "Think about that long wagon trip you took with Matt and Emily. Your healing skills came in handy numerous times. And of course there was your heroic triumph at saving Matt from the gunshot wound. That man wouldn't be alive today had it not been for you."

Rachel bit her lip, knowing that what he said was true.

"Collect into one your destiny. Follow your heart, Rachel. It won't steer you wrong."

Rachel looked up at Cornelius, a hint of a smile darting out the sides of her mouth. He was right and she knew it. For the first time in weeks and months she felt better, as though she finally found some direction out of a complex maze.

"Thanks, Cornelius. You're absolutely correct and you've given me great advice. Why couldn't I see this?" Rachel asked, looking up as though the heavens should have enlightened her. She looked back at him. "It makes perfect sense." Rachel stepped over and gave Cornelius a big hug. When she let go his entire shiny head glimmered red as a strawberry, his Cheshire-cat grin in place. She turned to leave, then turned back.

"Oh, I almost forgot!" Rachel reached over to the counter and picked up the basket of peaches. "These are for you, from our garden," Rachel said as she handed the jeweler the basket. He bowed his head in appreciation.

A moment later, Rachel exited the shop and stopped on the sidewalk. She looked one way, then the other. As though a light bulb had gone off in her head, she turned quickly and headed down the street, strutting like a woman on a mission. She decided to make one more stop before she went back to her in-laws' house to retrieve Maddie. Rachel strode straight for the plaza, where she traveled down West San Francisco Street and took a right on Guadalupe. She stopped when saw a shingle hanging in front of an office that read '**Dr. Charles Horgan**'. She opened the door and stepped inside.

A painfully-thin, somber woman with an overly tight bun drawn up to the top of her head, sat at a desk and looked up when Rachel entered. The unforgiving hairstyle accentuated her sharp, angular features and long narrow nose. "May I help you?" she inquired dryly, her face devoid of compassion or interest.

"Yes, I'd like to see Dr. Horgan," Rachel said.

"What is the nature of your ailment?" the woman asked sternly.

"Actually, none," Rachel answered honestly. "I'd like to speak to him about another matter."

"Pertaining to?" the woman persisted.

Rachel swallowed and met the woman's hard eyes dead on. "It's a personal matter."

22

The woman stared at Rachel with a blank look for what seemed like a rude length of time. Finally she got up and went into the back of the office, her skirts whipping around her. A moment later a tall, bearded man in his fifties stepped out into the waiting room. He towered above Rachel at a basketball player's height. His shirt sleeves were rolled up exposing his arms covered in thick mats of auburn hair. Red-haired with flecks of gray and freckled, fair skin, his razor thin lips made him sport the same severe expression as the woman who greeted Rachel.

"Hello Mrs. Bradshaw," the doctor welcomed Rachel, wiping his hands on a towel. "What brings you into my office today?"

Rachel looked over at the woman who had now reseated herself at the desk, and back at the doctor.

"Do you have a few minutes to speak privately?"

"Why yes, of course. I only now finished my last patient before taking lunch. Please, follow me."

The doctor led Rachel through a milk-glass door, down a long, wood-paneled hallway and into an office in the back. He indicated a wooden chair in front of his large wooden desk for Rachel to sit. She looked around his office, noting the many medical texts lining his book shelves and various medical instruments sitting

23

on shelves. Instruments that in Rachel's opinion looked almost barbaric. *This isn't the 21^(st) century,* she reminded herself.

The man folded his hands together in his lap and looked inquiringly at Rachel. "How may I help you?'

Rachel smiled sweetly, sat up straight and looked the doctor in the eye. "Before I came to Santa Fe I worked in medicine, and now that my daughter is old enough to be cared for by others in my family, I would like to return to work. And I would like to work in medicine once again. Would you consider training me in order that I could learn from you?"

He traced each feature on Rachel's face with his eyes, studying her like a specimen. The doctor rocked back in his chair. He grinned ceremoniously and chuckled as though Rachel had just told him the funniest joke he had ever heard. Rachel did not see an ounce of compassion in his mocking facial expression.

"Why in heaven would you want to do that?" he asked, the lilt of amusement in his voice irritating Rachel.

"Why?" Rachel responded, blinking her eyes for emphasis. "Why not? I am educated and want to work in medicine again." She attempted to keep her voice calm, without revealing her annoyance with his reaction. She smiled at him, trying her best to convey her sincerity.

The doctor leaned forward, placed his elbows on the desk and put his fingertips together, forming a tent. For the first time Rachel noticed the protruding blue veins channeling across the back of his hands; she realized he was older than he looked. He regarded her over the tops of his fingers, watching her intently.

"Is your husband not providing well for you? Do you need the money?" he pressed, a twitch cascading across his dense, auburn mustache.

"Of course not!" Rachel snapped, and then realized that she was a bit harsh. She swallowed and started again in a more congenial tone. "I simply want to utilize my skills and assist those in need."

She gazed straight into his eyes, leaned slightly forward and laid her hands gently on the edge of his desk. He looked down at them and creased his brows in disapproval. She removed her hands immediately and sat up straighter in her chair as though someone pressed a hard plank against her spine.

"I am even thinking of attending medical school. Perhaps if I could train with you and show that on my application record to medical school it would increase my chances of being accepted."

The doctor leaned back and let out of howl of laughter. "You, a woman? Attend medical school and become a doctor?"

Rachel felt her face and neck burn. She knew she was flushed red and felt a storm gathering in her eyes, but couldn't help her body's reactions. "And why the hell not?!" Rachel fumed at the man, arching her brows in shock. She felt her voice quiver, but didn't think enough that he would notice.

The man bent forward. Her language and the anger in her voice surprised him. His face turned to one of mockery and disdain. As he spoke his nostrils flared slightly, matching the ridicule in his voice. "Well, Mrs. Bradshaw, first and foremost because you are a woman and women do not become doctors."

That was it, the tipping point. Rachel could not hold her practiced composure any longer, nor did she want to. "Have you never heard of the Woman's Medical College of Pennsylvania or the New England Female Medical College in Boston? They're training women to be doctors!" she spewed.

The man held his head back slightly and looked condescendingly down at her, down his long, straight nose. "Of course I have, but the one in Boston didn't last," he started, his voice rising. "They ran out of money and had to merge with Boston University some years ago. Clearly it was a bad idea that no one wanted to financially support and it still is," he snapped back, matching Rachel's tone of exasperation.

Rachel tried to keep her calm, but couldn't. She felt herself splitting down to her core. "Seriously, you don't think women can or should be doctors?" She stared at him straight on, holding her gaze with all the tenacity of a lioness.

The man shook his head vehemently and stared back at Rachel as though she were a stupid child. He sneered as he spoke. "Women lack the intellectual depth to understand the practice of medicine."

Rachel left out a very audible groan. "You are unbelievable! Never mind that it was I, not you, who saved my husband's life from that gunshot wound three years ago. You were going to let him die. I demonstrated plenty of *intellectual depth* then!" she spat back at him. Now she didn't care what he thought of her, she was fighting mad and not about to let this 19th century chauvinist get away with treating her like an idiot.

"To this day I do not understand what it is that you did," the man spoke haltingly, annoyance laced through his voice. "But undoubtedly you did not employ common, approved medical practices."

"What does it matter what I employed? I saved his life, which was a lot more than you did!" Rachel shouted.

Rachel and the doctor sat still glaring at one another, neither saying a word for a full minute.

"I believe our conversation is over, Mrs. Bradshaw. I have made up my mind on this matter. I urge you to forget this nonsense and concentrate on being a good wife and mother, your only true vocation."

Rachel rolled up her eyes, let out another groan, stood up and marched out of the office without saying a word. The woman at the front desk attempted to rise and tell Rachel goodbye, then saw the expression on Rachel's face, sat back down and watched her leave. Rachel stepped out of the office and shut the door, none too quietly. She stormed toward James and Catherine's house, thinking how on her way to the doctor's office she was full of anticipation and excitement, only to have the feeling replaced by searing anger and dejection. She knew Cornelius was right. Healing would be a good profession for her; however, figuring out how to do it would be her biggest obstacle.

* * *

"I can't believe that our dear Dr. Horgan would say that to you," gasped Catherine after Rachel told her the story of what happened at his office. She looked at Rachel with great empathy, her doe-like brown eyes searching Rachel's face. "Are you sure you heard right?" Rachel looked at her with such conviction, her green eyes smoldering, that Catherine quickly added, "Yes, I'm sure you heard correctly." A few moments passed and Catherine asked, "Is it really so different in your time? For women, I mean?"

Rachel nodded, taking deep breaths and trying to calm down. "Absolutely. Women do everything that men do. They work full time, yet still marry and have children. With a few exceptions they hold pretty much the same jobs as men."

Catherine's eyes widened. "Go on," she urged Rachel to continue. She could see that conversation was having a calming effect on Rachel. The patchy redness was leaving Rachel's face.

"The common complaint now is that women have two jobs, the one where they make money, and the job of being a wife and mother when they get home. Of course they have many modern conveniences to help them with their chores at home and work but still, a lot of my married friends with kids worked. It's a different society. I must admit, all my friends found it hard and crazy at times to juggle both work and home responsibilities."

"And you want to do this too, in our time?" Catherine pressed, a look of sisterly sympathy embedded in her expression.

29

"No, well yes, I do," Rachel professed, "but not in the consuming way of the 21st century. I want to contribute. Cornelius is right. Helping people get well would be a good way to use my background. However, without Dr. Horgan's help I don't know how to make that happen. He's given me a huge stomach ache. I'm all twisted inside."

Catherine smiled at Rachel, reached over and laid her hand on Rachel's. "I'll brew some tea; I have some ideas for you to consider."

As Rachel sipped her tea, Catherine told her about growing up in northern New Mexico, before there was a conventional doctor in the region, a time when they relied on traditional medicine.

"Traditional medicine?" Rachel asked. "What do you mean?"

"My dear Rachel, how do you think people recovered from illnesses and injuries before modern medicine came to this region?"

"Hmmm, I'm not really sure." *How quaint that Catherine considered 19th century medicine to be modern,* Rachel thought.

"Certainly you know that long before the Spanish came to this area the only people who lived here were the various tribes?"

Rachel nodded.

"They had their own healers, medicine men and medicine women," Catherine continued, stopping to take a sip of tea. "The Spanish came years later and brought their own healers who came to be called curanderos. Most were men but some were women as well, called curanderas."

"I recall reading a little about them in college. I don't know much," Rachel acknowledged. Not sure where the conversation was headed, but intrigued, she listened intently.

Catherine poured herself and Rachel more tea and sat back in her wingback chair. From the upstairs came giggles from Emily and Maddie, busy at play.

Catherine ran her long index finger around the edge of her china cup, producing a high-pitched hum. "The practice of curanderismo is an ancient tradition that incorporates many elements of faith, prayer, herbs, ceremony and sometimes items of nature. It varies from town to town. In many small villages, it is the curanderas and curanderos who treat illness and injury," Catherine explained. "They are highly respected members of their communities. Often the village people consider their powers to be magical," Catherine said quietly, as though it was a secret not meant to leave the parlor. Her dark brown eyes lit up as though stoked by some internal fire. "The people believe that their injuries and illnesses are caused by curses, lost wicked spirits, or other malevolence. The curanderas and curanderos frequently are called upon to dispel the evil eye that the villagers hold responsible for their illness."

Rachel watched Catherine speak with a fortitude and passion she had never witnessed before in her sister-in-law. In the years that she had come to know Catherine she could not ever recall seeing her show much excitement. Her normal mannerisms and character were much more subdued. Talking about history and curanderismo seemed to open a passionate vein in her.

"How do you know so much about curanderismo?"

Catherine smiled demurely and looked at Rachel directly. "My family has been in this region hundreds of years," she began, setting her teacup down on the table, straightening up and looking back at Rachel. "They came from Spain; they left during the Inquisition and slowly made their way to this area. All the women in our family for as many generations as anyone can remember have been curanderas, healers."

"I had no idea," Rachel said.

"Our family settled in Moralito, a small mountain village outside of Chimayó. Life hasn't changed much there over the last few hundred years. Each generation's curandera has trained the next. Once mother was old enough, grandmother taught her to become a curandera and still is."

"Did you train to be a curandera?"

Catherine grinned, a sweetness rolling across her face. Talking about her family obviously gave her great joy. "I learned quite a bit simply by growing up in my mother's household but no, I did not seem to have the gift. Not like my sisters, who became very talented curanderas, just like mother and grandmother," she sighed, rubbing her fingers over her heart.

"Okay," Rachel nodded, taking another sip of her mint tea, and drawing her brows together. "And what does this have to do with my dilemma?"

"Is it not obvious, Rachel? I am suggesting that you consider training to be a curandera," Catherine stated matter-of-factly, an excited flutter in her normally calm voice. "This form of healing has helped many people over hundreds of years. It may not be modern medicine, as you know it, but it is medicine nevertheless. If you are interested, I could write to my family on your behalf. Maybe you could train with them," Catherine offered and leaned back in her chair.

Rachel sat still, stunned, staring at Catherine.

"Is this such a peculiar idea?" Catherine asked, leaning forward again.

"Um, no," Rachel began slowly, trying to collect the thoughts rapidly swirling through her head. "It's just not an option I had considered, only because it never occurred to me. From my time I think of the only legitimate medicine as Western or modern medicine, but that's pretty narrow-minded, isn't it?"

Catherine nodded her head, and took another sip of tea.

Rachel looked around the room then back at Catherine with an expression nothing short of revelation, her eyes wide with wonder, like a child seeing a rainbow or a shooting star for the first time. "Catherine, your idea is brilliant!"

The edges of Catherine's lips curved upward, her face radiated with joy.

Rachel suddenly blinked repeatedly. "Do I have to be Catholic to train with a curandera? Because you know, I'm not."

Catherine broke out in a wide grin. "My family is not what you would call conventional Catholic, and they have been healers for generations. They are devout, yet still practice many of the old customs from Spain, as do many of the villagers. It may be worth exploring," Catherine tendered. "There is much to learn about herbs and their medicinal values. For example, earlier you complained of a stomach ache after you met with Dr. Horgan. How do you feel now?"

"Much better, why?

"Because you are drinking yerba buena, a spearmint tea, a time-honored remedy for stomach upset." Catherine answered confidently.

"I think my stomach feels better because you offered me an alternative to Dr. Horgan," Rachel responded, mirroring Catherine and easing back into the comfortable living room chair.

Catherine slightly nodded her head. "Possibly, but one of the tenets of traditional medicine is that you have to let go of your modern way of thinking and open your mind to the possibilities of local medicine and the old ways. It is as much about faith as anything else," she said, a wise look etched on her face. "Not everyone can be a curandera, Rachel."

"What makes you think I can be one?" Rachel asked, draining her cup of tea and looking over the top at Catherine.

"It takes a special kind of talent and I think my mother, grandmother and sisters will agree that you have it," she answered softly, her voice a low, soothing timbre. She reached over and again took Rachel's hand in hers. "This is a gift that either you are born with it or not. I don't believe you are aware of the healing impression you carry with you, but others feel it. I certainly do."

Rachel let go of Catherine's hand and leaned back in her chair. "Wow, I've got to give this some serious thought. None of this dawned on me. Oh heck, it wasn't even on my radar."

"Your radar?" Catherine cocked her head to the side.

Rachel laughed. "Oh, just an expression from my time. I really need to work on not using terms from the future; it confuses people here."

"Don't stop," Catherine chided her sweetly. "I find them endearing, if not amusing."

Rachel let out a chuckle and threw back her head. "I'm happy to provide a little entertainment. Seriously Catherine, I'm really excited about this possibility. I can't wait to talk to Matt about all of this, get his feedback, you know?" Catherine nodded her head. "He's my best friend and always has the most perceptive instincts. He thinks of aspects that I don't."

"Didn't you say he comes home in a couple of days?" Catherine asked. Rachel nodded. "Then you will get what you call your 'feedback' very soon. If you decide you want to learn more about curanderismo or simply wish to speak with my family before you make a decision, let me know and I will write to them and arrange a visit."

Chapter Two

Rachel walked into the front parlor every five minutes to peer out the front window overlooking the street to see if Matt was coming up the walk. Finally she saw him, and instead of waiting for him to come into the house, she ran out the front door and met him on the walk, throwing her arms around his neck.

"What's all this?" he asked, a grin seeping out from under his mustache.

"I missed you and I have something very exciting to discuss with you."

Matt set down his traveling case, bent down, ran his hands around her neck and kissed her deeply. "Where is Maddie?"

"Taking her afternoon nap. Why?"

"Then let's resume where we left off a few mornings ago. As long as we have some time to ourselves let's take advantage of it. Will your news wait?" Matt asked, his eyes twinkling with an impish delight.

Rachel grinned. "Of course," she whispered into his ear, running her arm through his and leading him into the house. "Wait, what about the house? Will it be done soon?"

"No," Matt sighed as he led Rachel up the stairs to the second floor. "I had to fire the architect; his design isn't working. I stopped the construction and will look for someone else to redraw the plans. I'm afraid it will be awhile before we can move back to Oak Valley."

He ran his hand across her cheek and through a strand of hair, then guided her into their bedroom and closed the door. Rachel felt a sense of dread at another delay in building their home, but understood there wasn't anything that could be done until a new architect was found.

"Then, for the time being we'll stay here, sweetheart. I can think of worse places to be than Santa Fe," she smiled bravely.

Matt bent down and lightly kissed her on the forehead, picked her up and carried her over to their bed where he proceeded to undress her, one exasperating garment at a time. Rachel broke out in laughter as Matt fussed with all the buttons and hooks, his patience waning.

"What's so funny?" he asked, clearly becoming annoyed with her dress.

"I think you'd like my century."

"How so?"

"Our clothes come off much more quickly, like in under a minute," she grinned devilishly.

"Then let's go back to Oak Valley and fly that balloon of yours to your time. Your fandangled dresses will be the death of me!"

* * *

An hour later Rachel lay in Matt's arms taking in the deep brawny smell of him. Lovemaking with Matt was like no experience she had ever known with anyone else. Every time her body responded with a mind of its own, taking her to greater and greater heights. How he managed to keep their lovemaking new she could not fathom. Even though she had been with Matt for three years she never tired of his attentions to her, the way he made her feel like the world was hers and that anything was possible. He was also the sexiest man she had ever met; she still couldn't believe she was married to a man as handsome as Matt. His smoldering eyes, his strong jaw line, his perfectly muscled physique. In her own century she surmised he would have been a well-paid model on the front of GQ magazine. Indeed she felt she was the lucky one, but to hear Matt's side he would assure anyone who would listen that he was the more fortunate one in the marriage.

"So Horgan treated you like you were an inconsequential woman, did he?" Matt grinned while running his fingers through her thick mane of hair. Rachel leaned up on her elbows and stared at Matt, not sure of his meaning. "Bad move on his part," he chuckled, scratching the two-day beard stubble on his chin. "Too bad I didn't warn him." Rachel's eyes widened in astonishment. "I'm kidding, I'm kidding," he laughed.

"It was humiliating," Rachel murmured.

"And now you're wondering if going into a healing profession is a good idea?"

"Actually, no, I'm not reconsidering at all. I think Cornelius is right. I don't know why I didn't think of it before. It's a pretty natural transition considering my background."

"Darlin', it's not much of a transition at all. On that wagon trip, you saved us. That trip would have been much more difficult without you and your medical skills. Emily and her rattlesnake bite? You know she would have died if you hadn't given her that, that, that stuff."

"Anti-venom injection," Rachel cut in, brushing it off as trivial. "What do you think about Catherine's suggestion of my training to be a curandera, provided her family would be willing to train me?"

"Smart," Matt said quietly, leaned over and kissed Rachel on the neck. "My brother didn't marry Catherine just for her fine looks, she's one of the sharpest women in town," Matt told her. "If her mother or grandmother or sisters would be willing to train you I think you should do it." Matt ran his finger over his mustache and creased his brows together with concern. "Rachel, if Catherine's family is willing, I would hope that you would not be gone for long periods." Matt lifted Rachel's chin to look her straight in the eye. "Maddie and I need you."

"That's a given, Matt." Rachel ran the back of her fingers across his cheek and held his jaw in the cup of her hand. "Although I toyed with the idea of medical school for all of seven minutes, even if I could get in – which is doubtful considering I have no school records in this century – I couldn't, I wouldn't leave the two of you. I love the two of you more than my own life."

Matt watched her soft pink lips as she spoke. When she was done speaking, he gently pushed Rachel back onto the bed, kissing her along her jaw line and down her neck.

"Again?" Rachel asked, a lilting surprise in her voice, a grin dancing across her face.

"Why not?" Matt mumbled as he ran his lips down her body. "The baby is still sleeping."

When Matt's lips reached her stomach Rachel arched her hips and momentarily forgot she had a single worry.

* * *

Matt was fixing a window on the front of the house when Catherine stepped through the front garden gate. She wore a favorite silk green hat, perched on the top of her head like an elegant cake decoration. It made her even taller than her usual grand height of nearly six feet.

"Hello Matthew," she called to him when he turned around. He set down his tools and walked over to Catherine, giving her a gentle kiss on the cheek.

"What brings you to our fair street this afternoon?" he asked, leaning back against a porch balustrade.

Catherine smiled primly, reached into her pocket and took out an envelope. "I received a letter from my mother about Rachel," she began, but there was no recognition on Matt's face. "You know Matthew, about her learning curanderismo from my family."

Matt nodded. "Of course," he said unexpectedly, nodding. "I wasn't, as Rachel is so fond of saying…..connecting the dots."

Catherine grinned cheerfully. "Yes, I have heard her say that too, and while I now understand its meaning, it certainly is an odd expression, is it not?"

Matt shrugged sheepishly. "Rachel has a unique way of speaking. It's a wonder people in the 21st century can understand one another."

"Well, I suppose that if everyone speaks that way, like any language, they would understand their vernacular use of the English language."

"One would certainly think so," Matt agreed. "Come in the house," he waved her up the stairs. "Rachel will be happy to see you."

They no sooner stepped into the house than Rachel came down the hallway holding Maddie in her arms.

Maddie squealed, holding her arms out toward Catherine. Rachel handed her over and Maddie immediately planted a wet kiss on Catherine's cheek, causing her to chuckle.

"Can we offer you something? Tea?" Rachel asked.

"Thank you, but no," Catherine responded. "I only wanted to tell you that I heard back from my mother regarding teaching you." She held out the letter.

Rachel's face lit up with a mix of surprise, anticipation and joy. "What did she say?"

Catherine nodded reassuringly. "She says that we can come anytime and they will all meet you and explain what the training would entail, giving you enough knowledge to make a decision on whether you want to learn the art."

"We? Really? You would go with me?" she asked, an excited high tone in her voice.

"Why of course, my dear. I would not send you up to my village alone," Catherine told her. She turned her head toward Maddie and nuzzled her nose-to-nose, making Maddie giggle. "I was thinking that we could take Madeleine and Emily too."

"Great!" Rachel replied, almost squealing. "When should we leave?"

Matt cleared his throat to remind the women he was still standing there. They both turned and looked at him.

"I have to insist that you take the stage," Matt interjected.

"Why?" Rachel and Catherine asked together.

"For safety. You both know how I feel about my family being safe."

"Yes, Matthew, I understand your concern, but there is no stage line to Moralito," Catherine stated. "The stage goes to Chimayó and it stops there only twice a week."

"Good enough" Matt nearly barked, then lowered his tone, "I'll speak to the station master and make arrangements for your trip."

"My dear sweet Matt, that is very kind of you to go to all that trouble," Rachel began a distinct cooing in her voice. She could tell he was going to dig in his heels. She hoped that injecting some sweetness might make him see reason. "But is that really necessary? Couldn't we just take the buggy? I mean, how far is Moralito?"

Matt looked down at the floor and rubbed his chin. "Less than a day's ride, but still a ways. What is it Catherine, five or six miles from Chimayó?"

"Five miles," Catherine responded. "From here to Chimayó by stage it usually takes about four hours. My family will pick us up at the station, and then it is another hour by wagon to the village. That is the only way to get there."

"If Catherine's family agrees to train me I will be going up there on a regular basis, right Catherine?" Rachel turned to her sister-in-law who nodded. "I will need a regular form of transportation." Rachel heaved a small breath and thought *'boy, if only I had my old jeep I could drive myself and be up there in a half hour.'* "We could manage the buggy ourselves and later I could go on my own."

"Go alone?" Matt asked, his eyebrows rising up his forehead. "Absolutely not, Rachel. It's too dangerous. The stage that has one of my men protecting it is the only way. If you need a more flexible schedule then perhaps I could spare one of my men to accompany you in the buggy."

"Seriously, Matt?" Rachel asked, trying not to become annoyed. She knew Matt was only looking out for her well-being, but it felt as though he was being overly protective, something he often did, something she frequently told him irked her.

Matt gave her one his stone looks that told her not to push his patience on the subject.

"Fine," Rachel let out a huge sigh as though she conceded a major contractual clause. "We'll take the stage and when my training requires my being there more often your man can accompany me. Ok?" Rachel shot Matt a look of frustration as she defensively crossed her arms across her chest, meeting his eyes with defiance.

Matt nodded, but continued staring down at Rachel, a troubled frown on his lips.

"I will let my family know to expect us in a week," Catherine piped up cheerfully to settle the tension in the room. "Would that be all right?" She looked at both Rachel and Matt. They both nodded. "Then I need to go and write them a letter to go out with the next post. I will see you both very soon."

Catherine bent over and kissed Rachel on the cheek while giving her a gentle squeeze of the hand, and handed Maddie back to her. She headed toward the front door. Matt followed and accompanied Catherine down the front path with her.

"Matthew, do not worry yourself so," Catherine tried to comfort him. "We will be fine. I have traveled these roads all my life."

Matt nodded. "I know. It's just she is so innocent of our times. In her world it seems the roads were safe. She forgets that in our world they are not."

"I realize you are very protective of Rachel and are only concerned for her safety. Remember that she is grown woman and I will be along." Then lowering her voice she said softly, "Do you remember that I am quite competent with a gun?"

Matt grinned his characteristic smile, the one that carved playful dimples deep into his cheeks. "Yes, I do," he answered, "and I hope you never have to use your God-given marksmanship talents, but it wouldn't be a bad idea if you took your Winchester along."

"Consider it done," Catherine responded, a gleam in her eye. She turned on her heel out the garden gate, toward home.

Chapter Three

A week later the sharp smell of piñon wood burning in hearths permeated the morning air throughout Santa Fe. Although a scent that Rachel usually found calming, this particular morning she was so excited it had no effect on her at all as she and Matt walked to the stagecoach office. The crisp air and slight dampness from the previous night lingered. Matt carried Maddie, who giggled most of the way pointing out animals and plants and people she knew, as though standing at a ship's helm directing the course. Shortly, they arrived at the line office where they saw Catherine and Emily waiting, wrapped in shawls, travel hats securely pinned on their heads, luggage at their side. Maddie squirmed when she saw them, stretching her arms toward Emily.

"Are you ready, Rachel?" Catherine asked.

"Of course," Rachel grinned glancing down at the long rifle Catherine held at her side. "Let's board, shall we?"

Emily boarded first, followed by Catherine. Rachel gave Maddie to Catherine to hold in her lap. She stepped back and slipped her arms around Matt's neck. "We'll be okay, you know."

Matt gazed steadily into her eyes. "Yes, I do know. Between Baca guarding up top with the driver and

Catherine inside with her Winchester, anyone stupid enough to stop this stage will be taking his life into his hands." Matt bent down and gently pressed his lips against Rachel's, oblivious to the many people watching them. "Safe journey," he whispered as they parted.

Rachel stepped up into the stagecoach, and settled herself between Catherine and Emily, taking Maddie onto her lap. But, the baby barely noticed; she was fully immersed in a game with Emily. After a couple more passengers boarded, the stage took off. Rachel leaned out the window waving at Matt who stoically watched them fade down the street.

"So, what's with you and the gun?" Rachel asked, looking down at Catherine's rifle. "Matt made you sound like you're a sharpshooter or something."

"Well, I suppose you could say that," Catherine cracked a small smile.

"So?" Rachel prodded, raising her eyebrows in question.

"There is not much to tell particularly," Catherine began slowly. "As you know my parents had only girls, my two sisters and myself. Our father wanted a son and decided that since my sisters were following in our mother's craft of healing and I was not, that I would be the son he wanted."

"You? A son? What do you mean?" Rachel shook her head, not understanding.

"He taught me some of the skills he would have taught a son. I did not do well with fixing wagon wheels or breaking horses but very early on I showed an aptitude for shooting. When he realized this he trained me to be a decent marksman."

"What is considered decent?" Rachel inquired, slightly tilting her head. "Although you'd think I'd have learned after living here awhile, I still don't know that much about guns."

"Are you familiar with the Winchester rifles?"

"Of course. They're the rifles that won the West," Rachel replied confidently as though she answered a test question correctly.

"Where did you hear that?" Catherine asked.

Rachel bent her head close to Catherine's ear and whispered. "It's an expression we use in my time. The Winchester rifles are highly regarded as helping to win the Western expansion."

Catherine bowed her head proudly. "I shoot a Winchester, an 1873 model. Father gave it to me years ago. Before that I practiced on his Winchester 1866. I think he got tired of not having his rifle when he needed it. He said I was good enough to have my own and that I should for protecting the family whenever he was away."

"Are you in fact a sharpshooter?" Rachel asked, looking Catherine straight in the eye.

"Well, yes," Catherine responded demurely. "I don't miss much."

"How far can you shoot?"

Catherine broke out in laughter, reached over and squeezed Rachel's hand. "Let us just say that I can hit pretty much any target, any size, at any distance -- within reason, of course."

Rachel slumped back in her seat, grinning at Catherine. "Wow, my own sister-in-law is a sharpshooter. Annie Get Your Gun, watch out!"

Catherine and the passengers sitting across from them looked over at Rachel trying to understand her meaning. Rachel shook her head grinning. "Never mind, it's a compliment," she responded. "No wonder Matt wanted you to bring along your rifle."

Catherine beamed, reached down next to her leg and patted the Winchester. "Yes, indeed. And hopefully there will be no need for Lillian's services."

"Lillian?" Rachel asked, a look of puzzlement on her face.

Catherine glanced at her rifle again. "That is her name, Lillian."

The two women smiled congenially, no explanation necessary. Catherine laid her head back and closed her eyes, her hand on Lillian's barrel. Rachel turned and gazed out the stagecoach window. Hawks floated in graceful loops across the pale tint of the sky, the air filled with their whistling cries. One hawk gripped a small squirming rabbit in its talons carrying it to certain death. Rachel grew restless for them to reach their destination; for the next juncture of her life to unfold. A few hours later the stagecoach pulled into a small village built of unassuming adobe and wooden buildings. It looked no different than most small towns throughout the state with its humble homes and children playing in the streets. Rachel immediately recognized it as Chimayó. In 130 years it had not changed much.

"There they are," Catherine pointed to a couple of young women standing next to a wagon and horses. Each was tall, slender and statuesque, like Catherine, with similar dark brown hair tucked into braids hanging down their backs. They grinned happily and eagerly waved their hands at the coach.

As soon as the horses stopped moving the small group descended the stage. Emily carried Maddie while Rachel and Catherine carried their bags. The two young women rushed up to Catherine and threw their arms around her. They all broke out in tears simultaneously.

"We have missed you so!" exclaimed one, the second agreeing with a nod of the head. Catherine held the young women tight, closing her eyes. She let them go and swept her arm up, waving Rachel and Emily forward.

"Rachel, Emily and Madeleine, I am pleased to introduce you to my sisters, Louisa and Sarah."

The two sisters looked astonishingly like Catherine with their dark sleek hair, fair skin and large chocolate-brown eyes. The sisters smiled and bowed their heads slightly. Watching the two sisters for a brief moment Rachel's eyes watered, remembering her own dear sister, Lauren. In the 21st century they too were inseparable.

Sarah stepped forward and clasped Rachel's hand. "We are very glad to meet you, Rachel, and so pleased you are interested in healing. We have much to talk about."

"Thank you, Sarah," Rachel nodded her head, "I'm glad to be here and very grateful that you and your family have taken the challenge."

"The challenge?" Sarah asked, not understanding, looking from Rachel to Catherine.

"She means training her, if you all agree," Catherine responded.

Rachel felt her face going red as once again she was caught using a 21st century term that did not fit in

19th century colloquial speech. *'I have got to stop doing that,'* Rachel admonished herself silently.

"Is that a term you use in your time?" Louisa asked cheerfully.

Rachel blanched, feeling every ounce of blood draining out of her face. She quickly turned to Catherine, her eyes wide. "Did you, did you…." she stammered.

Catherine nodded. "Yes, they know," glancing at her sisters, then back at Rachel. "They needed to know about your time travel in order to understand you. In addition, to study the healing arts you must be honest and forthcoming. Do not worry. Your secret is safe with my family. We are very good at keeping secrets."

Louisa and Sarah nodded in agreement, smiling reassuringly.

"It is part of our culture, as you will learn," Sarah confirmed, a slight glimmer in her eye that she shared with both Louisa and Catherine.

Rachel looked to Catherine. "You've been keeping secrets from me?" she asked with a slight grin, her eyes dancing.

"Yes, and you will understand why later. If you think your secret is big, just wait until we tell you about ours. It will astound you."

Rachel laughed, "I can't wait!"

The group climbed into the wagon and began the uphill journey to the town of Moralito, rapidly talking the whole way. As they entered Moralito, a small, sparse village of rustic adobe homes in the hills above Chimayó, Louisa steered the horses toward what appeared to be a cemetery. Rachel looked over at Catherine, and hunched her shoulders as to ask 'why?'

"I have not been home in a long time," Catherine stated. "I must pay my respects to my father and grandfather."

The wagon stopped outside the cemetery's front gate. The two sisters, Catherine, and Rachel got out while Emily stayed with Maddie. Catherine walked over to the gate, reached into a basket set to the side and took out two small stones. She headed to the cemetery center, her skirts rustling as she walked, followed by her sisters and Rachel.

Quiet cast its shadow on the sparse land, silence lying like morning before the first rays peek over the horizon, waiting breathlessly for daybreak. Throughout the cemetery wild grasses sprouted everywhere, except on the graves themselves which had been lovingly tended. The only sound was the rustle of the women's skirts and their light footsteps as they moved between the headstones.

Catherine stopped in front of two gray headstones carved with the names of Samuel Medina and Benjamin Medina. Below the names were etched years of birth and death followed by a diamond with what appeared to be a flame inside. Below each diamond was a small cross and a six-pointed star. Very gently Catherine placed a stone on each of the headstones, where other stones lay neatly in a row. She bowed her head, closed her eyes, clasped her hands and silently said a prayer. She stepped back and wiped away a silent tear, then turned and led the group out of the graveyard. A sudden breeze blew across the graveyard, quickly churning into a strong wind, whipping a resonating hiss around the group. Thunder began to rumble in the distance like the daunting beat of an ancient drum.

After exiting the gate, Rachel came up alongside Catherine. "May I ask why you placed rocks on the headstones?"

Catherine glanced at Rachel and murmured, "It is our way of showing respect for our family who has left us. It shows that they are remembered and much loved. We are the keepers of their memories, just as those who follow us will be the keepers of ours."

"I don't think I've ever seen this custom," Rachel said loudly trying to be heard above the piercing wind. "I noticed that several headstones had similar rocks on them. Is this a practice particular to this area?"

Catherine and her sisters nodded silently.

"It is our family tradition," Sarah responded, "but many families in our village honor their deceased the same way. It is a ritual that came with our ancestors from Spain."

"And when was that?" Rachel asked.

The three sisters grinned.

"A very long time ago. Around 1598," Louisa answered.

Rachel's eyes flew wide open. "Really? Your family must have been some of the earliest Europeans to set foot in this region. How was it that they came here so early?

"Dear Rachel, you are so inquisitive," remarked Catherine, the edges of her lips turned up in amusement. "Our ancestors came with Juan de Oñate."

"THE Juan de Oñate?" Rachel asked, astonishment spiking her voice.

"Why do you say it that way?" Sarah asked.

Rachel blinked, a little flustered. "I mean no disrespect. It's just that he's a pretty famous guy in New Mexico history. He was the governor in the early years as I recall."

Sarah nodded. "Yes, he was, and he brought a large entourage with him, including some of our ancestors. And that is how our family came to be in this area."

Rachel started to ask another question but Catherine held up a hand and slightly bowed her head.

"Enough history for now," Catherine interjected, waving the three of them toward the wagon. "We need to go home. Madre and Abuela are waiting for us."

The group got back in the wagon and traveled a short distance to an adobe house at the edge of town. They no sooner disembarked than an elderly woman and a middle-aged woman who appeared to be in her fifties stepped out of the doorway. The women looked remarkably like one another and Rachel immediately saw where Catherine and her sisters got their striking looks, -- pale skin, dark brown hair, large, deep-set brown eyes and expansive smiles.

"Welcome, welcome!" the younger of the two called to Rachel, Catherine and Emily. She stepped over to the wagon and took Rachel's hand. "I am Rebecca," and gesturing to the older woman, "and this is Leah, our matriarch."

Rachel slightly bowed her head, "I'm pleased to meet you. Thank you very much for having me and my family to your home. I can't tell you how excited I am to learn about curanderismo."

She looked up hoping she adequately conveyed her sincere gratitude. Leah stood to the side watching little Maddie in her arms.

"Would you like to hold her?" Rachel asked the older woman who broke out in a wide smile and bowed her head in return. Rachel handed the baby to Leah who cradled her gently.

"Hello Madre and Abuela," Catherine said, bending over to kiss her mother and grandmother on each of their cheeks. "I have brought you vegetables from our garden. Emily, can you get the basket out of the wagon?"

Emily, who was all but forgotten, stepped to the back of the wagon and retrieved a large basket full of squash and tomatoes and herbs. She handed them to Rebecca.

"You did not need to bring food," Rebecca admonished Catherine, "but it is much appreciated. Come now, bring your bags. It is nearly time to light candles." Rebecca, Leah, Sarah, Louisa and Catherine filed into the house, followed by Rachel and Emily.

They no sooner stepped foot in the door than the savory aroma of a chile stew greeted them. They set their bags on the floor and walked over to the table. Rebecca had set up a bassinette for Maddie. As soon as Leah laid her down, Maddie yawned and closed her eyes.

"My, what a good baby," Leah remarked. "Is she not hungry?"

Rachel laughed. "Oh, don't worry, when she's hungry she'll let us know!"

"I imagine that all of you are tired from your journey and wish to wash up. Please…" she gestured toward rooms down a hallway.

Rachel, Catherine and Emily made their way with their bags down the tile hallway where they found fresh linens on beds, towels and cool water in pitchers with porcelain bowls. After hanging their clothes in armoires, washing up and freshening themselves, the two women and Emily returned to the dining area, where they found everyone sipping on cups of tea. They handed each of them a teacup and they waited as Leah and Rebecca readied the meal. Rachel noticed two candlesticks with candles on a sideboard, and a platter of braided bread.

"Come, it is time," Sarah said softly. Following their example Rachel and Emily stood in a circle around the candles and bread. Leah lit the candles, circled the candles with her hands, and covered her eyes. Everyone bowed their heads. Very quietly Leah murmured a prayer. Rachel could barely hear the words; she was sure it was not Spanish as she knew it, nor was it English. She looked over at Catherine who mouthed, "later". When she was done, Leah gestured toward the table, indicating everyone should sit.

Rachel sat closest to the bassinette in case Maddie awoke. They were no sooner seated than Leah ladled stew into bowls and passed them to everyone. Rebecca sliced the bread and passed it on a platter. When everyone began eating Rachel joined in. She supped a spoonful and exclaimed, "This is wonderful! What is it?"

Rebecca smiled. "This is our family recipe for green chile stew."

"But this isn't pork, is it?" Rachel asked, scooping up a bit of meat in her spoon to inspect it.

Everyone shook their heads. "No," Catherine answered, her words low. "We do not eat pork."

Rachel blinked as though to clear her head. "Really?" then caught herself realizing her comment might have been disrespectful. "This is chicken, right?

"Yes," Louisa answered, looking Rachel in the eye. "This is how we make it."

"Well, it's delightful," Rachel glanced around at everyone. "As Catherine and Emily know, I'm not much of a cook, but I'm learning. I'd love the recipe if you're willing to share it."

The women broke out laughing and covered their mouths with their napkins to cover up their mirth.

"What's so funny?" Rachel asked looking around, not understanding why her statement should elicit laughter.

"We do not mean to laugh at your expense," Louisa chimed in, reached over and laid her hand over Rachel's. "We do not use recipes. Our cooking is handed down generation to generation."

"Really?!" Rachel responded surprised.

"When we return to Santa Fe I will show you how to make it," Catherine said. "It is not very hard."

"Even I can make it," chimed in Emily, taking pride in her cooking skills. "Right, Auntie Catherine?" she looked over at Catherine who nodded and smiled.

"Yes, and very well I might add," Catherine responded affectionately to her niece, "as good as mine."

Emily beamed at the compliment and lowered her eyes demurely.

For the remainder of the meal the group ate their soup and chatted amicably until Maddie woke up and made it clear that she too was ready for dinner. Rachel reached over, picked up the unhappy baby and started to head to the bedroom to nurse her.

"No need to hide yourself, Rachel," Rebecca called to her. "We are only women here. Make yourself comfortable in the sitting room," she indicated with a brush of her hand toward the large comfortable chairs. Rachel nodded and did as told, settling into one of the oversized chairs, edged in wood and leather. As soon as she began nursing Maddie, silence fell on the room. The group removed their dishes to the kitchen and joined Rachel. Leah walked over to the large fireplace at the end of the room, and stoked logs of cedar wood, causing them to crackle and send off a sweet, aroma that filled the room. As Maddie nursed, the group watched the orange flames furl playfully around the logs.

Rachel looked around at the group. "May I ask a question about your customs?"

"Of course," Rebecca responded.

"Well, when I was growing up I had a Jewish friend. Occasionally I spent dinner with her and her family on Friday nights, just like tonight. I remember that they lit candles and said a prayer, followed by a meal with similar braided bread. It was called challah, and it was egg bread as I recall. I remember it being a little bit sweet, just like the bread you served tonight." Rachel looked around at the group of women who merely watched her. "I see similarities is all, and was wondering about your traditions."

The women all looked from one to another, as though trying to determine who should speak. Finally

Catherine cleared her throat and spoke up, though tentatively at first, and quietly.

"In Spain our family was known as marranos. Here we are called conversos," she began, watching Rachel's face for any trace of understanding. Only seeing a blank expression on Rachel's face she continued. "The prayer that Abuela said tonight was in Ladino." Again, Rachel showed no comprehension. "This is a language very much like the Castilian Spanish our ancestors spoke in Spain."

"But what about the candles and the bread? Those are Jewish traditions I think," Rachel responded.

The women all looked from one to another. "Are you familiar with the term 'conversos', Rachel?" Rebecca asked. Rachel shook her head.

"People have called us crypto-Jews, as well as New Christians," Rebecca began. She glanced at the other women and back at Rachel. "Our family lived in Spain for centuries until 1492, when Ferdinand and Isabella decreed that all Jews must convert to Catholicism or leave or be killed if they stayed and did not convert. Surely you have heard of 'The Inquisition'?" Rachel nodded, her eyes wide, and Rebecca continued. "Even though our family was forced to convert to Catholicism, they continued to practice Judaism in secret, as did many Jews in Spain. When the authorities found out, our ancestors fled to Portugal, hoping for safety. The Inquisition came to Portugal soon after and they fled again, to Mexico. Ultimately the Inquisition reached Mexico too. That is when our family and many other converso families came north with Juan de Oñate and settled here. Their language was Ladino, also known as Judeo-Spanish or Judezmo."

"You're Jewish?" Rachel asked louder than she intended, her mouth hanging slightly open.

Catherine held her finger to her lips, speaking softly. "Yes and no. Although we no longer practice Judaism, we keep the traditions alive, such as what you saw here tonight and placing small rocks on the headstones in the graveyard. These are customs our family has practiced for generations."

"We are not even sure why we practice some of the things that we do. They are our traditions, so we continue them in honor of our family before us," Louisa added.

"Yes, and we attend church and outwardly we are good Catholics," Sarah interjected.

"This is amazing!" Rachel said. "Have you sought out other Jews? Tried to return to Judaism?"

The women all shook their heads and creased their brows, looking down. "No, no, it would be dangerous for us," Rebecca responded.

66

"Why? Rachel asked.

"People still do not accept Jews," Catherine responded. "It is safer and better for us to live as Catholics, but we remember the old ways and honor them."

"Do your neighbors know? Have they caught on?" Rachel prodded further.

Rebecca jumped back into the conversation with a knowing smile on her lips. "Most of our neighbors are also conversos. All of our families settled here a very long time ago. The mountains are filled with conversos just like us, Rachel," she murmured quietly, "this is our way of life, however it is not one we share with anyone outside of our immediate family. And now you are family too, through Catherine."

Rachel looked a little stunned, trying to comprehend what she had been told.

"Is this the big secret you hinted at earlier?" Rachel asked looking at the sisters, stroking Maddie's head as she began to slow her feeding.

Catherine and her sisters all nodded.

Rachel smiled and looked around at all of them. "Your secret is safe with me. You know my history of traveling here from the future. If people heard about it they would probably lock me up for being crazy,"

Rachel nodded. "Don't worry; I am quite capable of keeping your secret as well."

The women let out a collective sigh of relief as Catherine reached over and squeezed Rachel's hand in gratitude.

Rachel grinned and piped up, "so I guess this means we're not having bacon and eggs for breakfast tomorrow?"

The group of women broke out in congenial laughter. "No, no, we are not," Sarah responded. "But do not worry, you will be well fed," a tear of laughter seeping from the corner of her eye.

* * *

The next morning Rachel woke before the rest of the household. She lay in bed thinking of what she heard the day before, and listened as the nighttime quiet faded with the light of day. It wasn't long before everyone woke up and voices filled the halls.

After a breakfast of porridge, apples, eggs, cheese and coffee, the group of women headed to the back of the house and through a door into a large room filled with shelves of jars, each full of what looked like dried herbs and roots.

"Por favor," Leah said, indicating that Rachel should sit in a wooden chair opposite where she settled herself. Using a gesture Leah indicated that someone else should hold Maddie. After Rachel handed the baby off to Emily, she settled back in the chair. Everyone sat in similar chairs in a circle. Emily held Maddie in her lap, who watched the women with wide-eyed baby wonder.

"This is where we treat people who are sick or injured," Leah began. "We treat many kinds of illness and physical injuries."

Rachel nodded and urged her to continue.

"Curanderismo is an old form of healing. It uses faith, it uses herbs, physical manipulation, and it uses ceremony in some cases," Leah began.

"Yes, that's what Catherine told me," Rachel responded.

"For many people the source of their illness is a reaction to an event," Leah continued. "If the source of the illness or injury is not immediately apparent we have a heart-to-mind talk with the patient to discover the source of the suffering. This is called a platica. As we talk to the patient we find the susto, the physical reaction to the event."

"Sometimes it is espanto, loss of spirit," Rebecca added.

"And sometimes it is mal puesto or mal de ojo," Sarah broke in. Rachel looked blankly at Sarah.

"A curse, or literally, the evil eye," Sarah explained. "Another person can inflict it upon an unsuspecting victim. Many believe that the curse is inflicted by a bruja, a witch."

Rachel's eyes widened with surprise or doubt or both. She wasn't sure what to think and figured it was best to keep her thoughts to herself.

"It is the curandera's job to cleanse the spirit of the person afflicted, and remove the source of the suffering," Leah resumed her explanation. "A skilled curandera helps patients to turn on their own ability to heal themselves."

"This is where the role of faith comes in, right?" Rachel asked.

"Exactly," Leah nodded. "Patients must accept the source of the pain or illness and have great faith in both God and the curandera's ability to help them heal themselves. Without faith, it is nearly impossible to help a patient get well."

"Rachel," Rebecca interjected, "at the heart of our healing is our belief that healing can occur only with God's help. Nothing less."

Rachel slumped back in her chair, taking in the whole conversation. She looked to each of the women. "And you think I can do this?"

Leah smiled and took Rachel's hand in her own, enveloping her old boney fingers around Rachel's. "Most curanderas have specialties. Very few try to practice all aspects as it is a great deal to learn and sometimes difficult to practice," Leah continued. "For example," Leah waved her hand toward the sisters, "Louisa is a partera. She helps women with their pregnancy and childbirth."

Rachel quickly interjected. "In my century, parteras are called midwives. Many women want to have their babies the natural way with a midwife, without medicines to mask the pain of childbirth."

Louisa raised her brows in surprise. "We have herbal medicines to help the pain, but they do not mask it. How much do your medicines cover the pain?"

"Completely, but only if women want it and many do. The upside is that they don't feel anything, and that is the downside as well. A woman does not feel herself giving birth to her child."

The women all looked at one another in surprise. "To be honest, when I had Maddie, there were a couple of hours when I wished I had one of those medications.

She took her fine time leaving the pouch!" The women chuckled.

Leah swept her hand toward Rebecca. "My daughter is a sobradora. Do you know what that is?"

Rachel shook her head.

"I use massage to heal," Rebecca said. "Sometimes people hurt because they have a blockage that is making them sick. I use different oils, depending on the blockage, and massage to release the obstruction." Rebecca got up, walked over to a long shelf and took down a dark, glass bottle. She walked back to Rachel and uncorked the bottle to let her smell it. Rachel took a deep whiff and blinked her eyes at a strong aroma that stung her eyes.

"What is it? Rachel asked, looking up at Rebecca.

"Oil infused with herbs, ruda mostly. You know it as rue," she answered. "But I have many oils, each for different blockages." She turned and swept her arm toward the shelves of bottles.

"And this works?" Rachel asked inquisitively.

"Yes," Rebecca answered, turning back to her, "if the sick person believes. If the person does not, I can massage until the end of days and I still would not be able to open the blockage."

Rachel looked over at Catherine. "This is what you were explaining to me that day in your parlor about curanderismo being as much about faith as practice?" Catherine nodded.

"And now for Sarah," Leah continued, looking over at her other granddaughter. "She is a yerbera, an expert in the use of herbal remedios. You know them as remedies. We are very proud of our Sarah. I have taught her all that I know; it has been easy because she has a natural instinct for knowing what herb works best for which ailment, when to harvest herbs, how to store them, prepare and administer them. She is young, yet very experienced. Her soul carries the knowledge of generations of curanderas." Sarah beamed listening to her grandmother describe her skills. "Even though we do not know you well, we can see that you have *el don* and would do well with herbs."

Rachel looked around to each of them then back to Leah. "What is *el don*?"

Leah nodded. "It is the gift of healing."

"Catherine wrote to us about you," Rebecca interjected. "She told us of many instances when you used your medical knowledge to assist others in pain."

"Yes, but I used 21st century medicine," Rachel said. "That's not the same as having a natural talent."

73

"You are correct," Rebecca responded. "However, it is plain to us that you have the gift. Either you are born with it or you are not. And only another curandera can detect if you have it. We talked late into the night and we all agree that you do. Your gift is much like love."

"How so?" Rachel blinked her eyes, as though it would help her better understand.

"Love is not confined to time or boundaries and neither is *el don*. You were able to find your dear love despite your living in different centuries. *El don* is the same. If you have the gift, and we know you do, there are no limits. It is not confined to one time or place. Now Rachel, it is up to you if you want to undergo desarollo, an apprenticeship, to learn our craft or not. If you do, we are willing to teach you. It will take time and you must be patient."

Rachel leaned forward in her chair and looked around at the group of women, all of them smiling at her. She grinned. "Okay, if you think I've got what it takes, then let's do it. When do we get started?"

Everyone stood up and embraced Rachel, one at a time.

"Sit down everyone. Let us begin with our first patient then," Leah instructed. "Catherine, please sit on the bed."

Rachel looked over at Catherine with a look of surprise. "What's wrong, Catherine? You never said you were sick."

Catherine rubbed Rachel's shoulder. "It is not a conventional illness," she said sadly. "I have a cold womb and cannot get with child. They are going to help me."

"You can do that?" Rachel asked, as she looked at all the women. "You can treat infertility?"

"We have done so successfully before and we hope to help our dear Catherine," Louisa answered. "Maddie needs a playmate and we are determined to make sure she gets one."

"What will you do?" Rachel prodded further. "Do you perform surgery?"

Rebecca shook her head. "First I will massage Catherine with oil infused with cuachalalate. You may know it as juliana," Rebecca responded. "Meanwhile, Sarah will make a tea." Rebecca walked over to a counter, poured a small amount of oil in a bowl, added a pinch of powdered bark, stirred with a wooden spoon and returned to the bed, where she indicated Catherine should lie on her back. She pulled up Catherine's skirt and lowered her undergarments, revealing her belly. Rebecca spooned the oil into her hands and using the palms of her hands and her fingers, she began gently massaging Catherine's lower abdomen, using her fingers to press against her internal organs. Going slowly, she massaged with stronger and stronger movements.

Rachel watched with fascination, never taking her eyes off of Catherine and Rebecca. "What exactly are you doing?" Rachel finally asked, no longer able to keep her curiosity at bay.

Louisa stepped to Rachel's side. "Madre is manipulating Catherine's womb. She is trying to correct her belly by massaging her womb into the correct position. This will help her get pregnant."

Rachel continued to stare at Rebecca massaging Catherine's belly. She had never seen anything like this and was pretty sure this was no longer a 21st century practice. In her time she had heard of surgery to correct womb conditions that prevented pregnancy, but never using massage. Finally, Rebecca ceased her manipulations, and toweled off the excess oil. She indicated to Catherine to pull up her undergarments and pull down the skirt. When Catherine finished, Rebecca helped her daughter sit up on the bed. Sarah, who had been in the corner brewing some kind of tea, walked over to the bedside and handed Catherine a cup.

"What is that?" Rachel asked, her nose wrinkling at the strange aroma wafting from the infusion.

"Damiana and the bark of cuachalalate, the same as what Madre used in the massaging oil," Sarah answered. "They enhance a woman's fertility by warming her womb. It is best sweetened with a little miel, honey." Sarah laid a small cotton bag next to her sister. "Make a tea twice a day and infuse for 10 minutes before you strain and drink it. You have enough for seven days. Take for no longer than a week."

A question mark crossed Rachel's face. "Why can't she take it for more than a week?"

Sarah turned to Rachel, "because the damiana herb is not good for the baby. Should she get pregnant, damiana could do harm to the child."

"Seems to me that's dangerous," Rachel responded, concerned.

"Yes, you are correct," Leah interceded. "That is why we tell Catherine not to take it longer than a week. If she becomes pregnant within a week, exposure to the herb will not hurt a baby so tiny. It is simply best not to continue it as the child grows."

Rachel nodded; she understood the thinking, as she knew that in her time many drugs worked in the same way.

A knock on a side door attracted everyone's attention. "And so our day begins," said Leah. Louisa walked over, opened the door and invited an older man into the room. He ambled slowly over to a chair, sat down and removed his broad hat. He held the hat in his lap and fingered the rim.

"What is the problem today, Señor Baca?" Leah asked, sitting down on a chair opposite him and visually examining his face.

The man rubbed the front of his neck and grimaced. "Sore throat," he responded in a gravelly, hoarse voice. "Started yesterday; hurts a lot, like I swallowed broken glass."

Leah reached over and gently fingered his throat. "Hurts here?' Leah asked placing her fingers in the center and slightly rubbing with her thumb. The man grimaced and nodded.

"Have you encountered a bruja or do you think someone has looked at you with mal de ojo?" Leah asked. The man shook his head. "Have you felt a loss of spirit, been sad?" Leah prodded further. Again the man shook his head. "Then it is probably natural. Sarah, please make Señor Baca an infused tea of osha and yerba mansa."

Leah stood up and placed her hands on Señor Baca's head, closed her eyes and slightly bowed her head. Just above a whisper she prayed. "Dear Lord, bless this man in need of healing his body; mend and renew his spirit. Amen."

Sarah stepped over to the counter stacked with dark brown bottles. She took two bottles off of a shelf, sprinkled a small amount from each onto a board and crushed the leaves, roots and stems with a rolling pin. She scooped up the mixture and dropped it into a teacup, pouring boiling water over the blend. As the tea infused she placed several more leaves, roots and stems in a cotton bag, closed it tightly and, using the roller, crushed the ingredients inside the bag. Sarah brought the teacup and cotton bag over to Señor Baca. She handed him the teacup.

"Drink it slowly," Sarah instructed. "As many times a day as you can, make yourself a tea with this," Sarah pointed to the bag. "Your throat should feel better by tomorrow."

The man began sipping the cup of tea and nodded his head in appreciation. "I know it will work," he said. "The last time I had a sore throat and you gave me this tea, I was well in two days."

Sarah blushed; he could not have given her greater praise.

"What was in the tea?" Rachel asked after the man left.

"Like Abuela said, osha and yerba mansa," Sarah answered. "They are herbs that work very well for sore throats."

"Amazing!" Rachel remarked.

A moment later they heard another knock on the door. This time when Rebecca answered the door a young woman stood there carrying a small girl who was crying and holding her ankle. "She fell," the mother said. "She may have broken it." Rebecca ushered them into the room and pointed to the bed, to where the mother should lay her daughter down. Rebecca leaned over the child and as she lightly touched her ankle the girl gave out a cry. "I am so sorry, mi niñita, but I must feel if it is broken." The little girl nodded, tears seeping out the edges of her large tawny eyes. Rebecca felt gently, nodded and raised her head. "It is not broken," she announced. "Only sprained, but obviously painful." She looked toward Sarah.

"I will make a poultice of sueldo and cancerina," Sarah responded on cue looking at the mother. "It will help with both the pain and healing." She no sooner spoke than she took down another set of bottles and began making a poultice. Sarah smashed the plant materials in a bowl, adding a small amount of hot water from the tea kettle and a few drops of oil. She continued mashing until it softened into a paste. She grabbed a few pieces of muslin and walked over to the bed. First, she placed a large piece of muslin under the girl's leg and very gently applied the herbal poultice on her ankle. As

80

carefully as she could, she wrapped a long, thin piece of muslin around her ankle, completely covering the herbs and tucking the end into the wrapping. When she was done she looked up at the mother.

"Do not let her stand on this foot for at least 24 hours," she instructed. The mother nodded. "If she stays off the ankle the swelling will go down and she should be fine in a couple of days. If you can, make her elevate her foot onto a low table or chair or bed. I know it is hard to keep a little one from moving around, but it is important."

"She hurts too much to walk," the mother responded. She reached over and picked up her daughter. "Thank you from my heart," she said looking at all the women, then turned and left.

As soon as the woman left the group of women turned and looked at Rachel. "Questions?" Sarah asked.

"A million," Rachel answered. "Do you have a book with all these remedies? I don't know how I'll remember them all."

"We all felt the same way when we began and we all have our own journals. You need one too," Rebecca said. She walked over to a desk, reached inside and pulled out a thin book and a pencil. She handed both to Rachel. "It is blank, and for you to write down the remedios, however you best understand them."

"Thank you, this will help enormously," Rachel said. She sat down immediately and wrote down the remedies for infertility, a sore throat and the sprained ankle. As soon as she finished they heard another knock at the door. And so the day went, nearly non-stop, one ailing resident after another. It was dusk when they finished and headed back into the main house to begin preparing dinner.

After a simple dinner of chicken, pinto bean and green chile-filled burritos, squash soup sprinkled with roasted and ground squash seeds, followed by stewed apples for dessert, the women moved to the sitting room in front of the cozy fire. Maddie suddenly awoke and demanded her own dinner. Rachel picked her up and returned to her chair, nursing the baby into silence. The last of the sun's rays cast a golden glow through the windows facing west. The sun went down in a flash of auburn radiance. Dusk quickly settled over the village.

"What did you think of your day, Rachel?" Leah asked, as she tossed a few lavender sprigs on the fire. The sweet aroma of the gentle herb immediately filled the room.

Rachel smiled up at her. "You mean, besides being exhausted?"

Leah and the others beamed.

"What a schedule," Rachel added. "Is it like that every day?"

"Goodness no," Rebecca answered. "The villagers know that we will see them anytime. They know that our door is never closed and that we will always help them. But we are a small village; we don't have many patients. Today was unusual."

"And how do you get paid?"

Leah leaned forward. "The villagers take good care of us. They bring us produce, meat, breads, cheese, butter, any and everything they make themselves."

"And that is enough to live?" Rachel prodded further.

All the women nodded. "Our main source of income comes from some small crops we grow and sell," Rebecca answered. "We trade services with a couple of villagers to help us manage the planting and harvest. For healing, occasionally a villager gives us money if their family has done well and they do not have anything else to offer. If we need help with a broken wagon wheel or the horses, our neighbors help us just as we help them."

"What about those who can't afford to pay?"

"We care for them just the same," Rebecca answered. "No one is turned away."

Rachel looked around the room at each of them. "You are very generous women and this village is lucky to have you."

"We consider ourselves fortunate to live here," Rebecca responded. "Our ancestors were right to settle here. This has been a good place to live our lives."

The group barely settled into the peacefulness of the evening and let themselves relax when they heard a sharp rap on the door. Louisa got up and answered the door to find a young girl, panic on her face. A rush of a cool air swept into the room like a midnight wind. The girl reached out and grabbed Louisa's hand.

"Please Señorita Louisa, come quickly! The baby is coming! Mi Madre sent me to bring you back right away!" the little girl cried, pulling Louisa out the door.

"Momento, Josefina, I must get my bag," Louisa told her and rushed to the back of the house. She returned a minute later with a large woven bag and her shawl. Before exiting she looked over at Rachel who was still nursing Maddie. "I would offer to take you with me, but you appear to be needed in other ways," she said, a gleam in her eye.

Rachel shrugged her shoulders and nodded, grinning back.

"I will help you," Sarah piped up. She took down her shawl hanging on a hook by the door, wrapped it around her shoulders and left with Louisa and Josefina.

* * *

The next morning Louisa and Sarah loaded their guests' luggage into the back of the horse-drawn wagon in front of the house.

"I can't believe you are going to drive us to Chimayó. You didn't get back from the delivery until an hour ago," Rachel said to Louisa and Sarah.

"We are used to it," Louisa said, forcing a tired smile. Puffy bags and dark circles surrounded her eyes, casting a sallow pallor to her skin. "Sarah and I will rest when we come back. Thank you for your concern, but we will be fine."

"And the baby you delivered?"

Louisa and Sarah grinned broadly. "A big, beautiful boy with enormous lungs!" Sarah answered.

Rachel reached over and hugged the sisters, then Rebecca and Leah. "I cannot thank all of you enough," Rachel said. "This has been more than I ever expected."

"We are not sure what you expected, Rachel, but we are glad you came and very happy that you wish to learn our craft," Rebecca said as the others nodded.

"We will see you next month?" Leah asked.

"Of course, I will write you with the date of my arrival," Rachel responded.

Louisa and Sarah got up onto the wagon, followed by Emily and Catherine. Rachel handed Maddie to Catherine and pulled herself up onto the wagon. Sarah clucked the reins and the horses began the journey to Chimayó.

Rachel had been so busy in Moralito she had not particularly noticed the area's geography. She always liked to examine an area's natural features; it made her feel connected to the land and its people. She looked out across the landscape and for the first time saw how the chaparral-spotted hills met a flawless sky, a sky so clear it looked as though someone had painted it that morning.

An hour later they arrived in town and saw the stagecoach waiting in front of the line office. The women handed the bags to a lineman who loaded the bags onto the coach. Catherine, Rachel and Emily each hugged Louisa and Sarah tightly. Catherine whispered into each of her sister's ears, "mi corazon". Rachel overheard and instantly her eyes blurred with tears as she remembered her sister in the 21st century who she would never see again. Catherine turned, saw the tears and took Rachel's hands into her own. "They are now your sisters too, Rachel," Catherine said loud enough for all of them to hear. Louisa and Sarah nodded, the edges of their lips forming sympathetic smiles. That was all Rachel needed; the tears flowed down her cheeks as she whispered "thank you" and stepped up into the coach.

* * *

Before the coach stopped in Santa Fe, Rachel could see Matt and his brother James, Catherine's husband, waiting in front of the line office. The resemblance between the two men was magnified by their height and the subtle way they carried themselves upright, their broad shoulders squared. They could have passed for twins, but were in fact several years apart. Busy as Rachel had been in Moralito, she had missed Matt, missed him terribly. She had so much to tell him, but all she wanted was to feel his big arms around her. She didn't have to wait long. As soon as she descended the coach, Matt wrapped her in a hug and kissed her tenderly. When she opened her eyes and let go she saw Catherine whispering into James' ear; a smile creeping across his face. Emily started to hand Maddie to Rachel, but Matt interceded cradling his little daughter in his arms.

"I never thought I would miss her middle-of-the-night cries," Matt laughed looking down at her. "But I did, the house was too quiet."

The group parted and went their separate ways toward home. As soon as they arrived at the house Rachel prepared some porridge for Maddie, who ate it hungrily. Before she finished she was already yawning.

"She doesn't usually fall asleep during dinner," Matt remarked. "She must be tired."

"I'm sure she is," Rachel commented watching her daughter. "She's not used to traveling so far." Rachel reached over and ran her hand over Maddie's head. The little girl laid her head in her mother's hand and closed her eyes. Rachel looked over at Matt to share the sweetness of the moment. "Looks like she will go to sleep early."

Matt grinned. "I'll take her up while you get comfortable. Are you hungry or can dinner wait?"

A broad smile swept across Rachel's face. "Are you suggesting what I think you're suggesting?"

Matt's eyebrows shot up his forehead. A playful smirk on his face answered her question.

"Then I'll meet you in the bedroom after you put Maddie down."

The three of them ascended the stairs into the quiet of the house, as though it was waiting for their presence.

A few minutes later, Matt entered their bedroom to find Rachel as naked as a newborn lying across their bed, her arms outstretched toward Matt. But he merely stood in the doorway, not moving. Instead he looked her over as though reacquainting himself with every contour of her body. She beckoned him, locking his eyes with hers. Slowly he crossed the room, removing an article of clothing with each step. By the time he reached her he had on only his shirt, which Rachel quickly unbuttoned and tossed to the side. As he bent down over her, Rachel began kissing him, -- his mouth, his chin, around his jaw, and neck, moving down his chest. When she reached his muscled belly he pressed her down, covered her mouth with his own and lost himself in a rapture that surprised them both.

Chapter Four

The next morning Rachel gathered up dirty clothes and headed to the back yard. She built a fire and set two large kettles on top that she filled with rain water. She shaved a whole cake of lye soap into the water of one when it boiled.

She took the whites, tossed them in the lye kettle and let them boil for a few minutes before she used a broom stick handle to draw up a shirt in one hand and set her scrub board across the kettle. As quickly as she could, using a rag to prevent the hot shirt from burning her, she rubbed the shirt on the board to remove the stains and dirt, then tossed the shirt into the second kettle to rinse. Once again she used the broom stick handle to draw it out and place it in a big basket. She stood back and wiped her arm across her forehead to keep the sweat from running down into her eyes. "I can't wait for the 20th century and for washers and dryers to get invented!" she mumbled aloud. "Washing clothes in this century really sucks." She repeated the process for all the whites, then the colored items and finally the darks. When she finished she dumped the water and carried the basket over to a clothes line Matt had erected for her and hung the clothes to dry, clamping them on the line with wooden clothes pins. She trudged back into the house, glad to be done with her least favorite chore.

Awhile later, Rachel was in the kitchen when she heard a howl come from the garden. She rose up on her tiptoes to look out the window and saw Matt covering his forearm with his opposite hand, bending at the waist. On the ground lay a long knife he often used to prune tree branches. She picked up a cloth and ran out the back door.

"What did you do?"

"The knife slipped. Just cut myself a little is all," Matt grimaced, clenching his teeth.

"I'd say that you cut yourself more than a little," Rachel admonished him. "You're bleeding all over the place. Let me wrap it."

Matt started to shake his head from side to side when he caught the stern look on Rachel's face. "Okay," he acquiesced.

Rachel removed his hand and wrapped the cloth around his arm to halt the bleeding. "Hold your arm above your head," she instructed. He held his arm up, wincing as he did so. "Now come inside."

Matt followed her indoors and sat at the kitchen table. Rachel retrieved several clean cloths, got a bowl and filled it with water still warm from the tea kettle.

Gently she removed the blood-soaked cloth and cleaned the wound with a clean cloth dipped in the warm water.

"It's deep," she commented, inspecting it closely. "But it's so fresh I think it will close quickly."

Rachel proceeded to wash Matt's opposite hand.

"What are you doing that for?" he asked.

"I need for your hand to be as clean as possible because you have to pinch the wound together while I prepare an astringent wash and a poultice to stop the bleeding and initiate the healing."

"You already know how to do that?" he asked in amazement.

Rachel smiled. "Of course. I'm a fast learner."

She placed his clean fingers over the wound and showed him how to pinch the cut edges together without making it bleed much. Matt raised his eyebrows as though impressed.

Rachel went on, "Actually, a patient came to the clinic with a similar wound and I got to observe how to treat it. Catherine's sister Sarah taught me how to prepare the wash and poultice. She gave me a bag of herbs to practice at home. You are my lucky first patient!"

Matt nodded. "Seems to me, that I've been your patient before." He looked down at the scar on his chest from the bullet that nearly killed him three years earlier.

A bullet wound that Rachel treated with an antibiotic injection she had in her backpack from the 21st century.

"Yes, well that's all good, but if you don't keep still and keep pinching the wound together I can't make the poultice and save your life again. So be a good patient and stay still," Rachel admonished him teasingly.

He grinned. "Yes, ma'am."

Rachel reached into her bag of dried herbs, took out several jars and her journal. She began flipping through it looking for the remedy that she remembered writing down. "Oh, here it is," she mumbled.

Rachel removed a couple camphor weed leaves, placed them in a bowl, crushed them with the back of a spoon and poured hot water over the crushed leaves. She let the mixture steep for several minutes, then dipped a clean cloth in it, squeezed a bit of the moisture out, and applied it to the cut on Matt's arm. He watched her closely, but said nothing. She dabbed the cut until she removed most of the dried blood.

"Here." She took his opposite hand and pressed it against the cotton. "Apply as much pressure as you can stand." He nodded.

Rachel stepped back over to the counter, opened another jar and repeated the previous process. This time she used less water, adding only enough to make a paste. She turned back to Matt.

"What's that?" he asked.

"They called it alamo; its ground up cottonwood leaves. They have healing properties. Who knew, huh? In my time cottonwoods were sometimes nuisance trees planted in yards where they grew too big. Turns out they help reduce inflammation. Well, that's not exactly what they said, but it's what they meant."

Rachel unwrapped the cotton cloth, laid Matt's arm on the table. Using her fingers she gently applied the alamo paste onto the wound. Then she took the cloth soaked with camphor weed, redipped it into the camphor water, squeezed out much of the liquid and rewrapped it snugly around Matt's arm, tucking in the ends to prevent them from unraveling.

"Okay, patient, you're done," Rachel said proudly, her hands on her hips. "But no using that arm today."

"What?" Matt squawked. "I've got work to do."

"Not using that arm you don't," Rachel insisted. "If you injure it again or even stretch the skin it will start bleeding again. You really need to back off using it today."

"Back off? Another one of your strange phrases," Matt snickered.

"Yeah, well, you get my meaning. You have to relax today. Why don't you read a book or something? Maybe that book of English sonnets you like so much."

Matt got up, shaking his head. "I really do have work to do. Hope I don't regret sending you to medical school at Catherine's family home."

"Read!" Rachel stated emphatically.

Matt smiled, grabbed his hat and said, "Sure, I'll read down at the saloon," he grinned and headed out the door.

Rachel stood there shaking her head and began putting away her herbs. "Work? My ass!" she mumbled, smiling and feeling quite proud of herself.

Chapter Five

A month later Rachel heard a knock at the door and answered it to find Emily standing there wrapped in a thick shawl. The girl shivered in the crisp morning air.

"Come in, Em," she motioned, "it's cold out there." She ushered Emily in the door and closed it quickly behind her.

"Can you come home with me? Auntie Catherine needs you."

Rachel immediately grasped Emily's arm, concern in her voice. "What's wrong? Is she hurt?"

"No," Emily responded, "but she's real sick. She's been throwing up for days. She wants to know if you have some herbs that would calm down her stomach."

"Did she eat something bad?"

"I don't know," the girl answered.

"Okay, come with me. I have to dress Maddie for the cold, get my coat and my medicine bag."

A few minutes later Rachel, Emily and the baby were in route to the home of Catherine and James. As soon as they arrived, they found Catherine sitting in a chair in the kitchen, wearing her dressing gown, her dark hair pulled back into a pony tail hanging down her back. She looked up at Rachel. Catherine was pale, all color drained from her usually glowing skin. Rachel rushed over to her, bent down on one knee, and took Catherine's hands in her own.

"What's wrong, Catherine? You don't look well at all."

"I have been vomiting every morning for the last week," Catherine whispered. "At first I thought it was something I ate, but if that was the case it should have gone away in a day or so."

Rachel sat back on her heels and looked squarely at Catherine. "You say it's happening in the mornings. What about the rest of the day?"

"I seem to be fine, and then it starts all over again the next morning. I cannot imagine what is wrong. Did Sarah give you any herbs to settle a bad stomach?"

A wild laugh erupted out of Rachel's throat. She laughed hysterically, gutturally, it nearly choked her. Catherine and Emily both stared at her as though she was a crazy woman.

"Why are you laughing?" Catherine asked, a thread of irritation lacing through her voice.

"I'm sorry; I'm not laughing at you. I'm laughing with joy."

"Why" Catherine shook her head, confused.

"Did you miss your period?" Rachel asked.

"My what?" Catherine stared at Rachel, not understanding.

"You know, your monthly!"

Catherine looked down at her lap, a look of embarrassment sweeping her face. "Well, yes, but it is probably just late."

"When was it due?" Rachel prodded, still holding Catherine's hands.

"A couple of weeks ago," Catherine whispered, still not looking up.

"Have you and James, um, um, been doing, well you know…."

Catherine looked up quickly; the corner of her mouth arched into a small smile. "Yes, every night," she whispered to keep Emily from hearing.

"I can't believe your mother's repositioning of your womb and your sister's herbs worked that quickly. This is amazing!" Rachel squealed. "That's it! Don't you see? You're not sick, you're pregnant!"

Catherine stared at Rachel as the words penetrated. Suddenly, a flood of tears burst out of Catherine's eyes. "Do you think so? Truly do you believe that?"

"Hello? Of course I believe it. There is no other explanation. Have you been drinking that tea Sarah told you to make?"

Catherine nodded, a tiny smile gracing her lips. "Several times a day."

"Then that's it, Catherine. No doubt about it. You're going to have a baby!"

At that moment Emily, who had been standing silently in the corner holding Maddie, rushed to her aunt's side. "Auntie Catherine, I'm so happy for you!" Emily cried, tears also streaming down her face.

"Well, why don't we all just have a cry fest here?" Rachel asked, tears also seeping out the corners of her own eyes. Catherine and Emily looked at her curiously. "Hey, this is a party," Rachel responded to their looks. "A reason to celebrate!"

Catherine took a deep breath and leaned back in her chair. "If you are right, this is a milagro, a miracle. James and I have been trying to have a family since we married five years ago," Catherine wiped a tear off of her jawline. "Any idea how long this nausea will persist? It is terrible."

"Well, if it's anything like mine, it will go away in a few weeks. But you know, I recall Sarah giving me an herb called mariola. She said it was good for nausea and especially morning sickness nausea. Hold on a minute and let me look through my book for the remedy I wrote down. Let's see....." she said as she thumbed through the little journal. "Here it is, mariola. It requires a cold infusion."

"Meaning it will not be ready for awhile, correct?" Catherine asked.

"Correct, but I'll make it now so it will be ready in a few hours. If you're not getting sick in the afternoon it will be ready for your next bout tomorrow morning."

Catherine nodded her head and laid her hands over her stomach and looked down. "I can barely believe it. I cannot wait to tell James."

"Where is he?" Rachel asked.

"At the assay office. He should be back sometime this afternoon."

Rachel reached over and gave her a big hug. "I am so happy for you. And your family will be too. You will have wonderful news to share with them when we go back to Moralito next week."

Catherine looked back up at Rachel, a look of passive nausea on her face. "I am not sure I will be able to go. The mariola will probably help, but I doubt it will go away completely. I cannot travel vomiting as I have."

Rachel sat back on her heels again. "Yes, you're right," a serious look etching across her face. She chewed pensively on her lips, thinking. "And if you don't go Matt will have a knock-down, hissy fit if I try to go alone."

Catherine and Emily looked at Rachel as though she was speaking a foreign language. They both cocked their heads sideways trying to understand the meaning of Rachel's words.

"Auntie Rachel," Emily asked, "Do you mean Uncle Matt will be angry?"

Rachel grinned. "Yes, that's exactly what I mean," Rachel nodded. "I have to come up with a strategy."

"I have an idea," Catherine interjected.

Rachel looked up at her with curiosity.

"Dear Matt is worried about your safety, even though he has one of his men on the stagecoach, correct?" Catherine asked.

Rachel nodded.

"Why don't I teach you to shoot Lillian? You could take her on the coach with you. That might calm his fears."

Rachel looked off to the side, then began nodding her head. She looked back at her sister-in-law. "Yes, yes, that's a great idea. It might work."

"Of course it will. Now if you do not mind, would you make the mariola infusion while I go get dressed?"

"Consider it done," Rachel stood up. "You go on upstairs. Emily, can you stay down here and help me find what I need in the kitchen?"

"Yes, Auntie Rachel," the child grinned, clearly pleased to be asked to do something. She walked over to a wooden high chair they kept in the kitchen for Maddie's visits, set Maddie in it, secured the top and turned to Rachel, ready to help.

By the time Catherine returned to the kitchen, the mariola was infusing in a pot of cold water. She was dressed and her hair was up in her usual bun. Color had returned to her face.

"This will need to infuse for several hours, the longer the better," Rachel instructed, stirring the pot. "Later today, strain it and put the liquid in a glass jar and keep it cool. Anywhere away from heat will be fine. Then have a glassful each morning when you get up."

Catherine walked over to Rachel and put her arms around her shoulders. "Thank you. I knew you would be a great healer."

"Hey, I haven't done anything yet. Let's see if this works."

"I am confident that it will. My sister is a good teacher," Catherine smiled. "Now, for your lesson with Lillian."

"Are you sure you're up to it? Maybe you need to rest awhile?"

"I am fine now. Truly I am."

"Then I'll put Maddie down for her nap first." Rachel picked up her young daughter, walked her upstairs to the extra bedroom where Catherine and James kept a cradle for Maddie's visits, put her down and covered her with a small quilt. Rachel began singing Maddie's favorite lullaby.

"Rock-a-bye baby, in the tree top, when the wind blows, the cradle will rock. When the bough breaks, the cradle will fall, and down will come baby, cradle and all."

By the time Rachel had finished singing it a second time Maddie had already fallen asleep. She returned downstairs to find Catherine in her long coat, Lillian in her hand. She turned to Emily. "Emily, my dear, would you mind staying inside and watching over Maddie while I teach your aunt how to shoot?" Catherine asked, leaning over toward Emily, who nodded with great enthusiasm.

Rachel put on her shawl and followed Catherine out the back of the house. "Are you sure you feel well enough to do this right now?" Rachel asked as they descended the stairs.

"Yes, you have given me renewed strength and abundant happiness that seems to have calmed the nausea for now," Catherine beamed. She walked to the middle of the yard, raised the rifle and pulled the lever down, which opened a chamber where Catherine inserted several bullets. When she pulled the lever back up, the action advanced the bullet into the chamber. She held the gun up, focused the bead on a target and pulled. A shot rang out. The two women walked over to a scarecrow at the opposite end of the yard. They inspected the face where Catherine's shot had blown apart the right cheek.

"I'm impressed!" Rachel cooed. "Nice shooting."

Catherine handed the rifle to Rachel. "Now it's your turn."

Rachel took the rifle, turned it over in her hands and inspected each side. They walked back to the front of the yard and positioned themselves in the same place.

"Hold it up here," Catherine instructed, raising the rifle up so that the butt rested on Rachel's shoulder.

Rachel curled her hands around the rifle, one on each side, and placed her index finger on the trigger. "Like this?" she asked, pointing the gun toward the target.

"Exactly," Catherine nodded. "Focus the bead on your target, that is this here," she said, tapping her finger on a small piece of metal at the end of the barrel. "Now see this metal piece here that looks like a V?" Catherine asked.

Rachel nodded.

"Line up the bead to sit right at the bottom of that V. When you are ready, pull the trigger."

Rachel held the bead on the scarecrow's face, shifted slightly to make sure the bead lined up inside the V, narrowed her eyes and pulled the trigger. The rifle jumped in her hands as the crack of gunfire reverberated across the yard. "Whoa!" she yelped. "Didn't expect that!"

"Sorry, I should have warned you. Try it again, and this time, hold tight to keep it from jerking."

Rachel raised the rifle and repeated her actions, this time holding on very tight. When she pulled the trigger, the gun did not move as much.

"This is going to take a lot of practice, I can tell that right now," Rachel let out a long breath.

Catherine nodded. "Yes, but you will get it. You seem to handle the rifle easily. Let us go see how you did."

They walked over to the scarecrow. They found one bullet in the arm but didn't see the second one. "Oh, there it is," Catherine pointed to a branch on a tree.

"Oh great, I killed your tree branch," Rachel moaned.

"Rachel, have you ever shot a gun before?"

"No."

"Then I would say you did fine. You maimed the target by hitting the arm. If this was a real person you would have stunned the person enough to stop him and take you seriously. Sometimes that is all you need to do."

Rachel rolled her lips inward, a habit when she was thinking. "Catherine?"

"Yes?' Catherine turned toward Rachel.

"Have you ever killed anyone?

"Killed? No. Shot, yes."

Rachel's eyes flew wide open. She studied Catherine's face, but saw no fear or sadness. "What happened? When did it happen?

"A long time ago, when I was around 15. My father was away and a man came into our house and tried to rape mother."

Rachel jaw fell open. She was too stunned to speak.

Catherine's voice fell to a whisper. "I got out my rifle and shot him in the back."

"Did he, did he manage to, um, hurt your mother?" Rachel stammered. She laid her hand on Catherine's arm for support.

"He was about to, but the bullet stopped him." Catherine looked away. Rachel could see that talking about it troubled her. But Rachel couldn't help wanting to know more.

"What did he do then? Weren't you afraid he would come after you?"

"No. I got him in the lower back. Severed something. He could not move. He screamed like a burro."

"You paralyzed him?!"

Catherine nodded.

"And what did the authorities do? Were you arrested?"

Catherine drew her eyebrows together in confusion. "Why would they do that? I stopped him from raping our mother."

"In my time, you would have been arrested, even if you were in the right. You might have been acquitted in a court of law, but you would still have been arrested and charged for shooting him."

Catherine shook her head from side to side. "That does not make sense. I do not think I would like living in your time. The Sheriff congratulated me; he told me I was a good shot and rid the town of a ne'er-do-well they had been trying to catch for a long time."

"I'm not disagreeing with you. Whatever happened to the guy?"

"Well, we called on our neighbor, a kindly man, who put him in the back of his wagon and hauled him to the Sheriff in Chimayó. He was taken to Santa Fe to stand trial. We had to testify. He was found guilty and sent to prison. Last I heard, he is still there. But even if he gets out he will not cause trouble again."

"How do you know? Aren't you afraid he will come after you?"

"Remember? My shot paralyzed him," Catherine reassured her. "He will never walk again. You see, you do not have to necessarily kill someone. You can maim a man enough that he not only cannot harm you, but he will not be able to harm others either."

Rachel nodded. "Guess I never considered that."

"You should practice some more. Try again, all right?"

"Don't we need to reload?"

Catherine shook her head. "Lillian holds 15 bullets per load. We have enough to finish our lesson."

"Okay," Rachel agreed and walked back to the starting point with Catherine, where her second volley resulted in more accurate hits.

"I think I'm getting this," Rachel commented when she found she had managed to hit the scarecrow both times.

"Yes and this one will both do the most damage and make the man incredibly angry," Catherine chuckled pointing to the scarecrow's crotch which the bullet shredded. "You just destroyed my scarecrow's manhood!"

The women laughed hysterically and headed into the house as a fierce wind began blowing dust all around the yard.

"I think I'd better get Maddie and go," Rachel said as they stepped inside. "I can't thank you enough for the lesson."

"You will return tomorrow? The best way to get good, fast, is to practice every day. That is how I learned from my father."

"I don't want to use all your ammunition," Rachel hesitated.

Catherine waved her hand in front of Rachel's face. "That is what ammunition is for and we have plenty. See you late morning?"

"Okay," Rachel agreed, "but what about your morning sickness?"

Catherine grinned. "I am sure your infusion will take care of it. I will be fine."

Rachel reached over, gave her a hug and headed upstairs to retrieve Maddie. She bundled the baby and headed out with her medicine bag, waving as she went down the path.

* * *

That evening, Matt hunched over his dinner plate, toying with a biscuit, swirling it in chicken gravy before he popped it in his mouth. "You know what I love about you the most?" Matt asked as he finished the last bite of biscuit. Rachel shook her head. "You never stop surprising me." Matt grinned, reached over and ran his hand around Rachel's neck, pulled her close and kissed her lightly.

"How so?" Rachel asked, a look of surprise on her face.

Matt ran the back of his fingers across her face. "I had no doubt that you could be a healer, but no idea you would take it on so quickly. I am proud of you that you figured out Catherine is with child. I know that my brother is a happy man this evening."

"Matt, it really wasn't that big of a deal. When I found out when she was vomiting and the nature of it, truly, it wasn't rocket science figuring out that she was pregnant."

Matt stared at her. "Rocket science?"

Rachel shook her head. "Sorry. Never mind. I just meant that it wasn't hard to figure it out."

"Nevertheless, I'm proud of you."

Rachel smiled shyly and looked down at her lap. "And what do you think about Catherine teaching me to shoot with Lillian?"

Matt chuckled. "I've always thought you should learn to shoot, but you never expressed an interest. I think it's a good idea. Just be careful you don't go shooting anyone's balls off. That is a surefire way to make enemies," he chuckled.

"So you're okay with my going to Moralito next week without Catherine?"

Matt nodded. "Sure. I've got one of my men on the stage; you'll be all right. Maybe Catherine will loan you Lillian and, if not, and we can probably find a rifle for you to take on the trip."

"Really?" Rachel squealed, excitement riddling her voice.

"Why not? You'll be armed and I'll feel better about your being on the stage without Catherine. Is Emily going with you?"

"Not this time. She's staying behind to help Catherine. Besides, she can't take any more time off from school. Her teacher said the first trip was fine, but would not allow any more absences, except for emergencies."

"Who will help you care for Maddie while you are in Moralito?"

"Are you kidding? Catherine's family practically fell over themselves trying to care for her. I barely got to hold her when I was up there last month. If it hadn't been for nursing her, I doubt I would have gotten to hold her at all!"

"All right. Sounds like a good plan." Matt looked down at his now empty plate. He had eaten every morsel of the hefty portion of chicken and dumplings Rachel had served him. "This was very good. Did you make this?"

Rachel's eyes bolted wide as she thrust out her chin. "Matt! You know I did! My cooking is getting a lot better."

Matt chuckled. "Yes, sweetheart, I know. Any more in the pan?"

"Yes!" Rachel sung with joy. She grabbed his plate, reloaded it with another helping and proudly set it down in front of Matt who cut into it like a starving man.

Chapter Six

The next trip to Chimayó was not nearly so interesting without Catherine to keep her company and Emily to play with Maddie. In fact, Rachel was downright bored. She spent most of the trip listening to the wheels sing on the road and the moan of the wind. Looking across one of the valleys she watched cloud shadows stippling upon the hillside, bits of sunlight pointing down like daggers on the rolling grasses. Maddie tried to get her attention several times and finally gave up, falling into sweet, baby slumber.

As soon as they descended the stage in Chimayó she saw Sarah and Louisa standing to the side waving to her. They ran to the coach and picked up her bags. Sarah poked her head into the coach.

"Where is Catherine?" she asked, turning back to Rachel.

Rachel grinned. "Well, you did such a valiant job during our last visit that she's with child and couldn't make the trip."

Both sisters broke out in glorious smiles accompanied by tears.

"Madre will be so happy!" Louisa cried. "We have prayed for this. You could not have brought us happier news."

"Let us go home and tell Abuela and Madre. They will be so pleased," Sarah chimed in as she placed Rachel's bags in the back of the wagon. "Come," she beckoned to Rachel, motioning her up into the wagon. "Sit next to me," Sarah patted the hard wooden panel. "I want to hear about all your remedios on the way home. Did you use the herbs I gave you?"

* * *

As soon as the group finished their dinner of green chile enchiladas and sweet tamales stuffed with dried apricot paste and wildflower honey, Rebecca walked over to a cabinet and removed a tall bottle. She held it close, turned around and smiled proudly at the group.

"Rachel, your wonderful news calls for a very special celebration. This is wine we made from our own grapes. I can think of no better reason to drink it than to celebrate Catherine's good fortune."

"You don't have to talk me into drinking wine, Rebecca. Filler her up!" Rachel said holding up her glass.

"You do use strange expressions, Rachel," Louisa chided her. "But they are sweet in a funny way."

Rebecca filled everyone's glass. She sat as Leah stood, folding her hands in prayer and bowing her head. The others followed suit as did Rachel when she saw what everyone else was doing.

"With this glass we thank our Lord for bringing new life to our dear Catherine. We pray that she will have a tranquil expectancy and that the Lord will look after them both. Amen."

Rachel tipped her glass to take a sip when she spotted everyone drinking their entire glass of wine. She followed suit and let the semi-sweet wine trickle down her throat, tickling her tongue.

"Wow! Did you say you made that?" Rachel asked looking at her empty glass. They all nodded. "Forget about being healers, you should open a winery!"

* * *

The next morning the group gathered in the clinic room in the back of the house. They had no sooner set up when residents began filing in with their illnesses and injuries. The day sped by as the women treated one person after another. Broken limbs, stomach aches, wounds, bites, stings, colds, arthritic pain and every imaginable ailment. The day's end did not come soon enough. Rachel could feel her lower back screaming at her for standing too long in her boots on the hard floor.

Just as they finished putting everything away they heard a very loud knock on the door, then the sound of something falling against the portal. Louisa walked over and opened the door to find a man slumped over. Rebecca and Sarah rushed to her side to help pull the man into the room. They lifted him up onto the bed and laid him out flat on his back. The man emitted a distinctive sour odor. His wild black eyes flashed, his head shook violently and his arms flailed. Black, greasy hair lay plastered on his forehead while several days of dark beard growth gave his face a raw, grizzled look. Rachel stood to the side, frozen in place, unable to move.

"Rachel, will you help me remove his boots?" Sarah called to her, not turning around.

Rachel didn't move. Sarah turned around and saw a look of sheer terror on Rachel's face, every drop of color gone from her skin. She looked as though she had seen a demon.

"What is wrong?" Sarah asked. "He is simply having a seizure of some kind, he will calm down soon."

Rachel stood there wide-eyed and immobile. A hot rush of tears pressed behind her eyes. She blinked furiously to keep them at bay and swallowed the fear rising in her throat. She shook her head. "No, that's not it."

"Then what is wrong, Rachel?" Rebecca asked going to Rachel's side, a note of concern scoring her motherly brow.

Rachel's mouth hung open as she stared at the man; her breaths shortened to quick, labored pants, a vein pulsed madly along the side of her face. "I, I, I know this man," she stuttered, her voice quivering. "He shot my husband in the middle of a street and was convicted for attempted murder."

"Then what is he doing here?" Louisa asked looking down at the man as she held down his arms.

"I don't know," Rachel said barely above a whisper, her eyes never leaving the stranger's face. "He was sentenced to 15 years in prison. He must have escaped." Even though spoken softly, her words echoed throughout the small room.

"Are you sure this is the man?" Rebecca asked, looking from the man to Rachel.

"I will never forget that face, ever. He's evil, vile. Mean as a two-tailed snake," Rachel turned to Rebecca and hung onto her arm. "Rebecca, we can't help him, we shouldn't help him. We must get the Sheriff and get him out of here. We're in serious danger."

"My dear Rachel," Rebecca said calmly, taking Rachel's hand and patting the top reassuringly. "We do not turn away anyone in need and clearly he needs our help."

"But you don't understand; this man will kill us!"

Sarah and Louisa watched Rachel carefully, and then looked at each other.

"Madre, Rachel may be right," Louisa suggested. "Maybe this time we do not help, if he is as bad as Rachel says."

"Oh he's bad all right," Rachel repeated. "Unbelievably bad. He shot Matt in cold blood. I'm telling you that, given the opportunity, this man will harm us and he will definitely kill me. Emily and I were his original targets on the stagecoach ride out of Oak Valley three years ago."

Rebecca stood back and assessed the man; she looked over at Leah who silently nodded her head, glanced at Rachel, and back at Rebecca.

"Get the straps," Leah instructed.

Rebecca went to a cabinet, took out rope and leather straps. She handed them to Louisa and Sarah who used them to tie the man down so that when the seizure stopped he couldn't move. Louisa grabbed some muslin, and stuffed it in the man's mouth. Rachel stepped to the corner of the room where she had leaned Catherine's Winchester against a cabinet, picked it up, and carried it over to where the man lay. She held it up at her chest level, pointing it at the man's face.

"This feels so wrong," Sarah lamented looking up at the others. "We heal, not hurt."

"Trust me, he will hurt you, given the chance," Rachel cautioned her. "I tell you I know this man. He does not have an ounce of decent blood in his body."

Rebecca looked sternly at her daughters. "Please go next door and ask Mr. Chavez to come help us. We will send him to the Sheriff in Chimayó." Rebecca turned back to Rachel, her lips held taut in a stern, thin line. "You are sure about this? Absolutely sure?"

"I have never been more sure of anything in my life," Rachel stated, her voice trembling. "His name is Hank Goddard, but it might as well be Lucifer." A tremor raced up Rachel's back causing her to shiver. She ignored it and held the rifle's bead steady on Goddard's face. "When he stops shaking, you will see for yourself. Look into his black eyes. They are the epitome of malevolence. You will see no evidence of a soul."

Louisa and Sarah returned shortly followed by a man of dark hair and light amber eyes. He removed his hat and nodded respectfully to Leah and Rebecca. "Buenos dias," he murmured.

Rebecca introduced him as their neighbor Noah Sanchez. Their families had lived by one another for generations.

By the time the introductions finished Goddard's seizure had stopped. He swept his dark-hooded eyes, focusing on each member of the group. When he saw Rachel, he narrowed his eyes into slits, his nostrils flared. He opened his mouth as best he could around the cotton, only enough to sneer at her, revealing his rotting teeth.

"See?" Rachel said, looking at the others. "The man smiles like a scorpion!"

"We did not doubt you, Rachel; we just needed to be sure. Let us take him to the law," Leah instructed.

The group stood Goddard up; weakened by the seizure, he seemed too exhausted to fight them. They tied his hands behind his back and his ankles together. Chavez, a short, solid man with arms thick with muscle, picked him up and threw him over his shoulder, and carried him outside. Chavez loaded Goddard into the back of his wagon, and secured his hands and legs to hooks on the wagon sides. He jumped up on top into the driver's seat. Rachel handed Maddie over to Leah.

"I'm going with him," Rachel declared.

"That is not necessary, Rachel," Rebecca declared, her deep brown eyes glancing from Goddard to Rachel.

"Oh yes, it is," Rachel raised her chin authoritatively. "I know who he is and I can give the Sheriff the specifics on his crime. Plus," Rachel held out Catherine's Winchester, "I've got Lillian and I know how to use her if necessary."

Rebecca took off her heavy knitted shawl, laid it around Rachel's shoulders, gave Rachel a motherly embrace and nodded. She placed her hands on each side of Rachel's face and looked her in the eyes. "Then go quickly and do not stop for any reason. Deliver him and return right away. We will pray for your safety."

Rachel chuckled. "I don't think it's my safety you should be worried about – it's his," she said pointing with her thumb to the back of the wagon where the man was now wiggling and grunting to get free. "He makes one wrong move and I'm going to put the barrel of this rifle where the sun don't shine and let him have it."

Rachel hoisted herself up on the seat next to Noah Chavez as Goddard looked up at her, his face contorted with a mixture of hate and disgust. Chavez and the Medina women were all looking at one another in confusion trying to understand the meaning of Rachel's statement. Suddenly Chavez got it and let out a loud belly laugh, his shoulders shaking in hysterics.

With a broad smile carved across his face he slapped the reins on the horse's rump and steered the horse toward Chimayó.

* * *

After hearing the bare details of Rachel's story Sheriff Evans locked Goddard in a cell. He walked back to his desk, took down a wanted poster on his wall and handed it to Rachel. "The law throughout the region has been looking out for Goddard. How did you find him again?" he asked Rachel.

"He knocked on the door at the home of my sister-in-law's family, the Medinas of Moralito. I suspect he found his way to their home because he was sick and they are healers; someone must have directed him to the home. In fact, he was having a seizure when one of the daughters opened the door," Rachel recalled.

The old Sheriff scratched his face, prickled with a day's beard growth and stretched out his jaw. "Well, I'll be," he said shaking his head from side to side. "We got a telegram months ago that he had escaped. Wonder what he was doing up this way? Probably trying to get as far away from Yuma as possible I imagine."

"Yuma?" Rachel asked.

"Yeah, Yuma, the territorial prison," he answered dryly, pointing to the narrative on the wanted poster where it said he escaped from the prison. He turned around and eyed Goddard like a specimen he had never seen before.

Rachel's eyes widened. "I had no idea he was incarcerated in Yuma. My husband said he was put in prison far away and that he would never cause us harm again."

"Obviously he wasn't far enough," the grizzly Sheriff said.

Rachel lowered her voice to almost a whisper. "I don't think he came looking for me, he couldn't have known I was at their home."

The Sheriff nodded in agreement. "You go on back now; we'll telegraph Yuma to come pick him up." The Sheriff escorted Rachel and Noah Chavez out the door and to the wagon.

Rachel looked back at the door. "He can't escape from here, can he?" she asked nervously.

The Sheriff looked at the Winchester in Rachel's hand. "You know how to shoot that rifle?"

Rachel nodded.

"I've never had an escape," he said reassuringly. "Most prisoners who break out have some kind of help.

124

I'm guessing that no one knows he's here so the odds of someone helping him are pretty slim. I can't promise you that he won't escape but, we will do our best to keep him here. Meanwhile little lady, you keep that rifle loaded and close by, ya hear?"

A lump formed in Rachel's throat. She managed a nod and a quiet "thank you" before she pulled herself up onto the wagon seat next to Noah. She turned to him. "Let's go," she said quietly, saying a prayer under her breath that Goddard would stay put until he was taken back to Yuma, where she hoped he'd rot in prison.

As the wagon began moving she looked over at Noah.

"I can't thank you enough, Mr. Chavez."

"I did no more or less than any neighbor," he spoke haltingly; he continued to look straight ahead, his brown leather hat hung low to shade his eyes. "We are all family in our small village. Mrs. Leah saved my wife during a hard childbirth many years ago. I will always be indebted to her."

They pulled out of town and a slight breeze picked up, whistling past them, singing the high pitch of a gust looking for its mate. Rachel pulled the shawl tightly around her shoulders, buffering herself from the dropping temperature. Suddenly she heard a low resonate voice and looked around, then at Noah.

"Did you say something?" she asked.

He shook his head. She could have sworn she heard someone talking to her. A few minutes later she heard the soft voice again. This time it was diffused, as though the person was speaking through a wall. She couldn't quite understand the words and looked over at Noah. He was silent, still looking forward. She shook her head, and then heard it a third time. Again she looked at the driver.

"You hearing voices?" he asked, without turning toward her.

"Yes," she answered, a little alarmed.

"Do not be frightened. It is only the whisperwind. If you listen carefully you will hear clearly. They talk only to people who can hear them and only when they have something important to say."

"Who?"

"The spirits."

"What kind of spirits?" she asked, looking all around, a shiver running up her spine.

"Good spirits. They mean no harm and only speak when someone needs comfort. You have been through a scare; they are probably telling you that they are looking after you. That is what the whisperwind does."

Rachel listened for the rest of the trip, but heard no more, only the creaking of the wooden wheels on the grooved, hard dirt road and the clopping of the horse's hooves.

By the time they reached the Medina home, the day's final events had taken a steep toll on Rachel. The adrenaline that had given her the ability to cope with Goddard's presence and take him to Chimayó had suddenly drained from her body. She climbed down from the wagon; her legs felt as though they were melting and would not support her weight. Rachel turned toward the house as the door opened and all the women stepped out. As Rachel started towards them, her legs buckled under her. Louisa and Sarah ran to her side and caught her before she completely collapsed. In a moment Rebecca and Leah were also at her side.

"What is wrong? Are you ill?" Leah asked, placing a hand to Rachel's forehead.

Rachel shook her head. "No, I think I'm just exhausted. It's been a long day."

"Let us get her inside," Rebecca instructed as Sarah and Louisa helped Rachel through the door. Leah waved goodbye to Noah and thanked him for his help.

Once inside, they sat Rachel down on one of the large comfortable chairs in the sitting room and placed Maddie in her arms.

"Your daughter is hungry," Louisa told her. "She has been very fussy for the last hour."

Rachel bent down and kissed her daughter on the head, unhooked the front of her dress and set Maddie to nursing. As her baby suckled, Rachel laid her head back, closing her eyes. After she finished nursing, both mother and child fell into a deep sleep. Sarah removed Maddie and placed her in the bassinette, covering her with a small quilt. She walked over to a cabinet, took out another quilt and draped it over Rachel. Sarah looked up at the others who nodded and beckoned Sarah to join them in the kitchen.

A couple of hours later Rachel awoke to a grumbling stomach. She inhaled the aroma of beef and potatoes, opened her eyes and found Leah looking down at her.

"Have I been asleep long?"

Leah shook her head from side to side; tendrils of dark hair laced with gray tumbled forward. "A while. Come and eat. It will renew your strength."

Rachel fastened the front of her dress, stood up and slowly walked over to the dining table where Rebecca placed a plate of warm tortillas and a steaming bowl of soup in front of her. The aroma of shredded beef, potatoes and chiles rose up and filled Rachel's senses. She realized the others had eaten while she slept, and lost no time in devouring the soup and tortillas. When she finished she told the group what she learned from the Sheriff.

"Do you think there is a chance he will escape and come back here?" Louisa asked cautiously.

"No, I don't, but I am a bit nervous about it. How could I not be?" she looked around the table at the concerned faces. "The man tried to murder my husband. I think it was simply a coincidence that he came here. I'm hoping he goes back to Yuma and never sees the light of freedom again."

Louisa reached over and laid a hand over Rachel's. "Will the prison increase his sentence?"

"I'm not sure if they will tack on more time because of the escape. But from what I've heard, a lot of people don't survive long 19th century prison sentences. They aren't the same as prisons in my time where some people commit crimes to get into prison."

Horror spread across the women's faces. Each of their jaws opened in surprise.

"Why would anyone want to get into prison?" Sarah asked excitedly, her voice a notch higher than normal.

"In my time, prisoners in the United States get free healthcare, three hot meals a day, job training and lots of other benefits. If they are married or get married in prison they are allowed conjugal visits."

The women's jaws dropped open even further; they looked at one another, hunching their shoulders.

"But what is the incentive to deter crime if they are treated so well?" Leah asked.

"Go figure," Rachel responded sarcastically. "Personally I don't think there is a lot of incentive; other people feel differently."

"But the whole point of going to prison is to be punished, to pay repentance for doing harm. In your time this is not so?" Rebecca asked.

Rachel shook her head. "People in my time seem to think that being incarcerated is enough; however the laws require it to be humane incarceration. I must admit, it isn't effective. Many people go right back into crime as soon as they complete their sentences. There is a phrase that crime doesn't pay."

"Yes, we are familiar with it," Louisa interjected.

"Well, in my world, it does," Rachel responded.

"You lived in a strange world, Rachel," Leah stated, adding a "tsk, tsk".

"When I first got here I would have disagreed; however after spending three years in your time, I must say that now I agree with you," Rachel smiled at all of them. "My world is a bit dysfunctional."

"As you are fond of saying, Rachel, that is an understatement," Sarah chimed in.

* * *

Two mornings later, Rachel embraced Rebecca and Leah while Sarah and Louisa put her bags in the back of the wagon.

"Rachel, we discussed it last night after you went to bed," Rebecca began, looking over at Leah, "and we feel that next month, if you don't mind, we would like to send Sarah to you for a few days to continue your study of herbs. Would that be acceptable?"

Rachel looked from Rebecca to Leah and back to Rebecca again. "Of course, but why?"

Rebecca looked over at Leah who spoke. "This has been a difficult visit for you with what happened with the man who tried to kill your husband. You need time away from Moralito, to settle any demons that may be bothering you."

"Demons? I have no demons," Rachel responded, startled, looking back and forth at the two women. "What do you mean?"

131

Leah reached over and took Rachel's hands into her own, her arthritic fingers curling around Rachel's. "That man frightened you, Rachel; we could all see it. You will associate him with our home; you need time away from us to distance those feelings. That does not mean you should stop your learning. That is why we wish to send Sarah to you next month. And then if you are content once more and able to the following month, you may return to us. Do you understand?" Leah asked.

Rachel started to speak; Leah placed a finger on Rachel's lips to quiet her. "Allow the good spirits to surround you, listen to them," Leah reassured her.

Rachel gently removed Leah's finger from her lips. "Do you mean the whisperwind?" Rachel asked.

"Yes," Leah and Rebecca answered together.

"Consider it your angel," Rebecca told her, placing a hand on Rachel's shoulder. "The whisperwind will watch over you, guide you, protect you, if you open your heart and mind and let it."

Rachel began to cry silent tears, even though she wasn't sure why. She kissed both Leah and Rebecca on their cheeks, turned to the wagon, handed Maddie up to Louisa and hoisted herself up. Sarah clucked at the horse and started the journey toward Chimayó.

* * *

As soon as Rachel disembarked from the stage in Santa Fe, Matt saw the look of worry and wear on her face. She seemed to have aged 10 years in a few days. Her skin was not its usual porcelain clear with rosy cheeks, but was markedly sallow, and lines marked her face, especially at the edges of her eyes. He pulled her to the side, placed his thumb and forefinger on Rachel's chin and gently tilted her face upward.

"What's wrong? You look terrible."

"Gee, thanks, honey."

"I'm serious, Rachel. I've never seen you look so pale. Are you sick?"

Rachel shook her head from side to side. "No, just incredibly tired and a little freaked out is all."

Matt looked at her with a confused expression she had come to realize meant he did not understand one of her 21st century expressions.

"Sorry, Matt," she said apologetically. "Something happened in Moralito. I'll tell you about it at home after we settle Maddie."

Matt reached over and took her in his arms, holding long and tight, until Maddie began to scream at being sandwiched between them. He eased up on his embrace and they both looked down at their daughter, who was clearly put out at being squished. For the first time in days Rachel smiled. Matt picked up their luggage and they headed home.

After Rachel fed Maddie and put her to bed, she returned downstairs to find Matt putting the final touches on dinner – a baked ham, roasted blue potatoes and a glass of wine. Rachel headed straight for the wine glass, took a hearty mouthful and sat down while Matt served the dinner. He too sat down, looked over at her and raised his eyebrows in curiosity. She told him what happened with the visit from Goddard.

"That's it, you're done going up there," he announced emphatically.

"Matt, please don't make such statements. I must continue my training; I've come so far and I have more to learn."

"At what risk? That Goddard will find you and finish the job he started, of hurting my family? Absolutely not."

"That doesn't make sense. He knows where we live here in Santa Fe. He could just as easily come here. I truly believe that it was coincidence that he stumbled upon the Medina home and found me there."

"But should he escape again what is to keep him from going back there to look for you?"

"Hon, he would be stupid to go back there, especially if he has to travel clandestinely from Yuma,"

Rachel sighed, trying to make Matt understand. "The Chimayó Sheriff seems to think that Yuma will put him under stricter confinement knowing that he is a flight risk."

Matt leaned his chin on his knuckles, staring down at his untouched plate of food. "I don't want to lose you; I can't lose you."

Rachel reached over and took both of his hands. "Look at me."

Matt slowly turned his gaze to Rachel. In his eyes she saw pain and worry and a wisp of anger.

"He's gone, Matt, he won't harm me and he won't harm Maddie. We're okay," she emphasized, as though she had to prove it to him.

"I'm buying you your own gun tomorrow, to have here at the house," Matt stated. "I'm not taking any chances."

"That's fine. It's probably a good idea for me to have a gun in the house that I'm comfortable using. Tomorrow I need to return Catherine's rifle. All I can say is thank goodness I had it."

She reached over and ran her hand over Matt's cheek, brushing the waves of chestnut hair away from his face. "You should know that Catherine's family also felt it best that I not go up there next month."

"Oh?" Matt looked at her, his eyebrows arched.

"Not permanently, just a break. They will send Sarah down here next month for me to continue my training. Then we will see the following month. Okay?"

Matt nodded, but he didn't look convinced. For now, that was enough for Rachel. In a couple of months when she was ready to go back to Moralito she would deal with Matt's mind-set then. They spent the rest of the meal in silence, concentrating on their dinner. As soon as they finished eating and cleaned the dishes together, a rare occurrence, Matt picked up Rachel. Taking two stairs at a time, he carried her upstairs and into their bedroom.

* * *

The next afternoon, Rachel and Matt returned Lillian to Catherine, and showed her Rachel's new gun, a .45 caliber 1875 Smith & Wesson Schofield revolver, that Rachel proudly named "Zoe".

"May I see it?" Catherine asked her eyes bright with interest.

Rachel handed it over. Catherine turned the revolver over and ran her long fingers around the latch on the frame and down the 7" barrel.

"It's quite nice," she cooed as though it were a fine piece of lace. "How do you feel about shooting a revolver opposed to a rifle?"

Rachel shrugged "I wanted a rifle, but Matt convinced me that a revolver would be more practical; easier to hide in a purse or my skirts." Rachel looked over at Matt who nodded. "I need some target practice. It will take a little getting used to, but I expect I should be able to shoot it as well as Lillian."

Catherine let out a note of approval and nodded, impressed.

Matt laughed. Both women turned and looked at him with curiosity.

"What's so funny?" Rachel asked.

Matt grinned with amusement, "Just the two of you. Most women would be more interested in discussing the latest fashions from New York or childrearing practices, but you two derive your pleasure from examining a gun. You have to admit, firearms are usually the domain of men."

The two women stared silently at Matt.

"Don't get me wrong; I'm not criticizing," Matt protested in defense, holding up his hands, "It's kind of charming."

"Hmpf!" Rachel snorted. "As I recall you wanted me to have my own gun."

"I did and I do," Matt smiled. "And I'm proud of you that you're taking self-defense seriously. Still, you have to admit it is funny."

Rachel rolled her eyes and turned back to Catherine to show her where the gun stored the .45 caliber rounds. She demonstrated how, when she released the latch, the barrel could be pulled down and the revolver would eject the spent cartridges.

"It loads really fast. See how I can operate the latch with my thumb?" Rachel showed Catherine. "I can easily open the gun for loading with one hand. At the shop the man told me that with practice I should be able to quickly reload all the chambers, without looking, in 10 seconds or less. I don't know about that, but it's nice to know it has the capability."

"I hope you never have to use Zoe except for target practice," Catherine stated after thoroughly examining the revolver. "But if you do, I believe that Zoe will serve you well."

Rachel beamed, obviously happy that Catherine approved. She couldn't wait to begin target practice. The wear and worry Matt had observed on her face when she disembarked the stagecoach the day before was gone, replaced by a look of determination and renewed energy. He breathed a sigh of relief.

"Would you like to go home now and practice?" Matt asked Rachel.

"Yes!" she responded, the edges of her lips curving upward. She turned toward the door, revolver in hand. "Oh, I almost forgot," she turned back around. "Catherine, how are you feeling?"

Catherine smiled demurely, just as her husband James entered the room and sauntered to his wife's side. It never ceased to amaze Rachel how much James looked like Matt yet they both retained a distinct individuality about themselves. While both were tall and lean, James sported a beard and his hair was darker and straight, so different from Matt's wavy locks. He too had the Bradshaw blue eyes, but unlike Matt's, which were the color of the sea, James' eyes were a light crystalline color, nearly powder blue.

"She's doing remarkably well, I'd say," James said, running his arm around his wife's shoulder. "Whatever you gave her has settled her stomach. She keeps her food down and doesn't have to heave first thing every morning."

Catherine and Rachel giggled, remembering that Rachel's pregnancy was marked by retching every morning for weeks.

"That reminds me," Rachel reached into her bag. "Louisa gave me more mariola for you."

Catherine nodded, taking the small jar. "She wrote me that she was sending more. Thank you. I was nearly out."

As soon as Matt, Rachel and Maddie got home, Rachel fed Maddie and put her down for her afternoon nap. She fell asleep before Rachel finished singing the first lullaby. She tiptoed out of the room, partially closed the door and walked downstairs. Matt was standing in the kitchen holding Rachel's new Smith & Wesson.

"You ready?"

"Of course!" Rachel replied, taking the gun and heading toward the back door.

Matt set up a target at the back of the yard, came back to Rachel and started to guide her closer to the target.

"No," she pulled back. "I don't need to be so close. I can hit from a distance now."

"But this isn't the same type of firearm. You learned on a rifle. A revolver shoots a little differently; the recoil is not the same," he cautioned.

"Let me try," she urged.

Matt looked at her and raised his eyebrows. "Okay, show me," he grinned, stepped to the side and placed his hands on his hips.

Rachel loaded the revolver, turned a quarter way to the left, turned her head back toward the target, raised her arm, held the gun up to eye level and pulled the trigger. Matt let out a whistle and Rachel grinned without looking at him. She continued to shoot until she ran out of bullets. They both walked over to the target. Matt leaned over slightly, inspected where the bullets hit and whistled again.

"Where did you learn to shoot like this?"

Rachel smiled demurely. "Catherine."

"Well, I don't think you need any more practice," he said seriously. "Most people need to relearn a bit when they switch from one type of firearm to another, but I think you are as good as it gets."

"Really?"

"Look for yourself," Matt pointed to where her bullets hit.

Rachel bent over and looked where Matt had placed his fingers. "Wow!" she said proudly.

"Rachel, you're a natural. This is quite extraordinary, not just because you haven't been shooting for very long, but because you've never shot a revolver before."

Rachel bowed her head and smiled modestly. Matt reached over and laid one hand on her shoulder, lifted her chin with the other hand and gazed into her emerald eyes.

"I don't know why I should be surprised. Nothing you do is surprising."

Rachel grinned, rose up on her tiptoes and gave him a kiss that nearly knocked him backward.

* * *

The next morning Matt told Rachel he had an appointment to see a new architect who had opened an office in Santa Fe. He checked his references; he would be a good choice for the Oak Valley house.

"Do you want to come along?"

"Hello!" Rachel responded, a high pitch in her voice. Matt had come to understand her unusual use of the greeting, but it still struck him as odd.

"Can you leave in 30 minutes?"

"Sure," she answered. "Maddie is fed and dressed. I just need to put on our coats and bonnets."

Thirty minutes later, with Matt carrying Maddie, the little family walked to the plaza area of town, into a two story brick building and up the stairs to the second floor. They entered an office marked "Brown and West, Architectural Services" on the glass door. They no sooner sat down than a tall, blonde, smartly dressed man came out, shook hands with Matt and introduced himself to Rachel as Harold West. He showed them into his office where he laid out preliminary sketches of the Oak Valley house on his desk. Rachel's face lit up seeing drafts of the home where they would live, back in the charming town where they met.

"Before I go into more detail, I have a number of questions about what you want in the house," Mr. West began, looking at Rachel. "Your husband said it would be wise to get your input. He wants the house to suit your wishes and needs."

Rachel looked over at Matt and whispered "thank you." She looked back at Harold West and responded, "Ask away."

For the next hour they discussed how many bedrooms Rachel wanted, the size and amenities of the kitchen, the parlor, and other features that surprised the architect. Rachel explained that she wanted large closets in every bedroom, a request that confounded both the architect and Matt.

"What for?" Matt asked.

Rachel looked at him as though now he was the one from Mars. "For clothes, of course."

"But that is why we have armoires."

"They're not big enough, certainly not for my dresses."

"Of course," Matt smiled. "Is this something common where you, where you, um, lived?" he asked, trying not to reveal Rachel's origins to the architect.

Rachel nodded. "Yes, every bedroom had a closet."

The architect interceded. "I have never heard of this and I read all the architectural journals."

Matt quickly said, "In her town they did things a little differently. If she wants closets let's put a closet in every bedroom," he looked over at Rachel who nodded in agreement.

"And I'd like a large pantry in the kitchen," Rachel added.

The men looked at her, knitting their brows together, clueless. "It's more orderly," she responded figuring that was the source of their puzzlement. She was thinking that how in less than 20 years, after the turn of the century, there would be kitchen appliances that she would want. It would be good to have a place to store them, as well as dry goods. She also knew that washing machines and dryers would become available; she convinced Matt and the architect to include a washing room with a large sink.

"I'd like wrap-around porches that circle the house and enough room in the garden for roses, fruit and nut trees, a gazebo and a swing for Maddie."

The architect nodded as he wrote down her requests. Then she rolled her lips inward, creased her brows together and searched her brain trying to remember when indoor plumbing became available. She was pretty sure plumbing began being installed in the 19th century, although probably not commonly.

"Oh, and I'd like indoor plumbing in the kitchen, and private washrooms on each floor with a bathtub, sink and a privy."

The two men looked at Rachel, stunned. Matt started to ask if this was common in her town, but didn't get the chance before Rachel nodded her head at him.

"This is quite a request, Mrs. Bradshaw," Harold West commented, a stern look in his gray eyes. "While these amenities are starting to be built into homes in other parts of the country, it is not yet standard practice for our area, much less in a town as rural as Oak Valley."

"Are you saying you can't do it?" Rachel asked, meeting him eye to eye, challenging his expertise.

"No, not exactly," the man answered rubbing his short, dark blonde beard. "I will have to investigate how to design plumbing in the house, a water and waste system and how to get the materials to the territory."

"Okay," Rachel relaxed and smiled sweetly. "We can be patient."

The architect leaned back in his chair, and tapped the fingers of his right hand on the wooden arm of the chair. He looked at both of them, then directly at Matt. "You do realize that the house your wife is requesting is not what you originally described to me, correct?"

Matt nodded and looked over at Rachel. "You're sure this is what you want?"

"Absolutely," she nodded, thinking how divine it would be to have indoor plumbing and not have to use a chamber pot or an outhouse. Just the idea of using an indoor toilet made Rachel feel giddy.

Matt sucked in a large breath of air and looked back at the architect. "Whatever she wants," he consented. "But before you start building I would like to see an accurate estimate. I don't want it to cost more than my company is worth."

"Of course, sir. As soon as I have some figures worked up I will let you know and if the sum is agreeable I will draw up a contract with you, order what we need and start building. Will that be acceptable?"

Matt nodded. Rachel reached over and squeezed Matt's hand. She couldn't remember the last time she felt so elated. Suddenly Maddie let out a hunger scream. All three of them looked at her with alarm. She had been so quiet they all but forgot she was there.

"If we're done for now, we should leave, I don't think Maddie will wait much longer for her feeding," Rachel said.

As soon as they had departed the building Matt stopped and turned Rachel toward him. "You know that I would do anything for you, give you the world if I could, but an indoor toilet? Is it really that important to spend a small fortune on installing indoor plumbing?"

Rachel tip-toed up, stretched her neck and lightly kissed his lips. "My darling, you have no idea how much you will love having an indoor privy. It is the one feature of the American home that I miss the most, more than central heat, more than air conditioning, more than modern kitchen appliances."

Matt slowly nodded his head. "Whatever those are……if it is that important to you and it is how homes are built in the future, then perhaps this makes sense. I want you to be happy. Plus," and he rubbed the back of his head, "this may increase our home's value. But you do realize that this will significantly delay the building and completion of construction?"

Rachel nodded and squealed with happiness, ran her arm around Matt's neck and kissed him again. He reciprocated by circling her with his strong arms and pulling her toward himself. But before he could pull any tighter Maddie let out a howl, seemingly anticipating

147

that her parents were once again going to make her the ingredients of a sandwich. At Maddie's insistence they turned toward home.

Chapter Seven

The following month, Rachel and Catherine met the Chimayó stage. Sarah stepped down, holding up her full skirts. A small velvet hat covered the top of her head, a chignon of her thick brown hair knotted at the back of her head. She wore a heavy coat and knitted gloves that guarded her from the early winter temperatures. She grasped onto a large leather bag, its straps worn with use. Sarah first hugged Catherine, then Rachel. She then stepped back to take a full look at her sister.

"My, you're showing already, Catherine!"

Catherine looked down and smiled humbly. "Yes, I know. I think I'm only a couple of months along; seems a bit early to be so large, does it not?"

Sarah broke out in laughter. "Not if you are carrying twins, dear sister!"

Catherine's eyes flew wide open. "You cannot be serious!"

"Oh yes, that or you are carrying an elephant!" Sarah laughed.

Rachel picked up Sarah's second bag, which the station master had taken down off the top of the stage, and they walked back to Catherine's home. When they arrived, Rachel retrieved Maddie from upstairs, where Emily had been babysitting the little one.

"Sarah, I'll come back tomorrow morning and bring you over to my house, okay?" Rachel said. "We can continue my herbal studies there." Rachel let Maddie give each of them a wet baby kiss goodbye and headed home.

That evening a winter storm blew across town, screaming winds slipping through wall crevices and howling around doors, sounding like weeping coyotes. The house creaked with mournful sighs until the winds stopped blowing, settling into a tranquil calm. The next morning Santa Fe awoke to snow blanketing the town turning it an angelic white.

Rachel stepped outside the front door and drew in a sharp breath of crisp air. She pulled her long coat tight, gathered her skirts about her, and headed to James and Catherine's home to retrieve Sarah. At that early hour the town was largely deserted and that suited Rachel fine. She loved the blissful quiet of a first snowfall, how snowflakes sparkled like crystals, and icicles hung off the adobe eaves, gleaming in the early light. Even though she was cold she walked slowly, taking in the snow-laden sights and breathing in the intoxicating, earthy aroma of cedar and piñon wood burning in home kiva fireplaces. It brought back vivid childhood memories of her sister Lauren and how they would attempt to build a snowman after the first snowfall. There was never enough snow to build much of a snowman, but that never stopped them from trying. The memory of her sister brought a lump to her throat as it did every time she reminisced about Lauren in the 21st century, and how she would never see her again. She shook her head to clear her mind and rushed the rest of the way to her in-laws' home. Sarah was waiting for her and together they hurried back to Rachel's house before the clouding skies decided to open again.

Once they settled in the house and Sarah met Matt, the two women sat down at the kitchen table to renew Rachel's training. Sarah removed several bottles and packets of herbs from her large bag. None of them were labeled.

"I had hoped," Sarah began, "to take you out to the back area and show you how to identify plants you will want to harvest, but with the snow, that will not be possible," she sighed, her mouth downturned.

Rachel reached over and laid a hand on her shoulder. "Not to worry, Sarah, you can still train me. Why don't we start with the herbs you brought? Are these herbs that I already know?"

A smile crossed Sarah's face and her eyes brightened immediately. "Why yes, they are, most of them. I could hand you each one and you can smell and feel them if you need to, and you tell me what they are and what they are used for. Would that be all right?"

Rachel beamed. "More than all right. Let's get started!"

For the next two hours Sarah removed one packet of herbs at a time and handed them gingerly to Rachel, who would open each packet, take a whiff, inspect the herb with her fingers and pronounce the herb's name as well as its healing properties, what it was used for, and the proper method of preparation.

"I am very impressed, Rachel. You remember all the herbs and their properties," Sarah stated, her chocolate-brown eyes radiant, pleased to see her pupil doing so well. "Have you always had a good memory?"

Rachel nodded, tranquility in her voice. "Usually I need to hear or see something only once and it sticks. There are a lot of things I'd like to forget frankly, but I can't. It's just how my mind works I guess."

"Not only do you have an extraordinary memory, but a blessed mind. Now let us try something more challenging. Is your journal nearby? You will need it."

Rachel got up, opened a drawer, took out a large bound book and brought it back to the table, along with a pen and small jar of ink. Sarah looked at the book.

"What is this?" she asked.

Rachel smiled affectionately. "Matt bought me this larger journal. I had nearly filled the one your family gave me. I've rewritten all the remedies in here," she said pointing to the new larger journal. "I've organized it by type of healing, whether for illness or injury."

"That must have been a lot of work," Sarah commented, opening the book and browsing through it.

"Yes, but excellent practice," Rachel responded. "Rewriting the remedies reinforced them in my memory."

"Then it was time well spent," Sarah uttered.

Before they proceeded Rachel got up and made the two of them anis tea, the flavor of licorice.

"Why anis?" Sarah asked.

Rachel rubbed her chest. "I may be getting a chest cold; I've been coughing a little. I figure it doesn't hurt as a preventative."

"Right you are," Sarah agreed, nodding at her student. "Now I will go through the book and test you."

"Or we could use my flash cards," Rachel suggested.

"What are flash cards?" Sarah blinked, as though unsure she had heard correctly.

"Oooh, just wait, you'll love 'em," Rachel said, a sweet lilt in her voice. She got up and walked back over to the drawer, where she got the journal and pulled out a stack of 4 x 6 inch pieces of paper. She laid them in front of Sarah. "We use them in my time to study," Rachel explained showing her how on one side she had written the name of the herb and on the other was the definition, usage and preparation.

Sarah looked through several of the cards, a slow grin spreading across her face. "How very smart," she exclaimed. She reached up and tucked a loose curl behind her ear. "You can study and test yourself."

"Exactly, I used flash cards all the way through school, mostly for math and chemistry exams."

"What is math?"

Rachel chuckled. "Sorry, that's what we call it in my time. You know it as arithmetic. I would write the multiplication tables on them. They saved me. I doubt I would have passed my exams without them."

"I think they are quite clever and will certainly be easier to use than the journal. Are you ready?" Sarah asked in school marm fashion, as though bringing class to order. She picked up the first card, "Barba de Maiz."

"Pick a harder one," Rachel sighed.

Sarah cocked her head slightly to the side. "How do I know that you know it unless you define it?" she said smiling, a playful whimsy in her voice.

"Oh, all right. Corn silk in English. It has multiple uses, but is primarily made into a tea used to treat bladder inflammation and arthritis, and can be made into a wash that soothes spider bites."

"Excellent! Verbena?"

Rachel nodded. "Called vervain in English. The flowers and leaves are made into a tea to treat colds and winter flu. It has sedative properties to make a person sleepy and it also induces perspiration to make the person sweat off the cold."

For the next hour Sarah tested Rachel, who answered every card correctly. Finally Maddie bellowed from upstairs, ready for lunch. They set the cards aside and went upstairs to bring Maddie down and make lunch.

* * *

"How is the student doing?" Matt asked Sarah over a mid-day meal of pea soup, slices of cold roast beef, and hearty bread wedges slathered in fresh butter.

"Extremely well," Sarah answered. "She has learned quickly and knows all the remedios. Next, I need to show her how to identify the plants for harvesting and I cannot show her that until the spring, when the snow melts." Sarah looked over at Rachel, pride showing in her glance of affection.

"Does that mean she doesn't have to return to Moralito until the spring?" Matt asked innocently.

Rachel stared at him. "Matt!"

"What?" he responded, placing his hand over his mouth, trying to hide a grin. "Okay, okay, if you need to keep going to Moralito, then go. But what can you do up there in winter when you can't learn to recognize and harvest the plants?"

"Matt, there is still much she can learn from helping us treat the many patients that come to our door," Sarah responded softly. "But if it is interfering with your home and family----"

"It is not interfering," Rachel interrupted, darting a stern glance at Matt, then back to Sarah. "I will travel to Moralito next month as I did before. If Catherine wants to come with me I will bring her. If she is not able to travel, and I suspect she might not, then I will come alone." She looked back at her husband. "Right, Matt? You agreed."

Matt nodded his head. "Fine, if the road is passable."

Rachel grinned triumphantly, "I'm sure it will be, even if I have to plow it myself."

Matt shook his head. "Yes, I'm sure you would, I'm sure you would," he said repeating himself, smiling as he finished his lunch.

Chapter Eight

The following month Catherine felt well enough to join Rachel on the trip. It was an uneventful visit except for Catherine's family marveling at her pregnancy. They determined she would likely give birth in late spring and decided that Louisa and Sarah would come to Santa Fe in April and stay with Catherine to await the twins' birth.

"Rachel, would you be able to assist us in the delivery?" Louisa asked. "Although there will be two of us, with two babies we will need another set of hands."

"Of course! I wouldn't miss it," Rachel squealed with happiness looking from Louisa to Catherine.

"While we wait for the babies to arrive I can show you how to identify the plants you will need to harvest for your botanica," Sarah suggested.

"Perfect!" Rachel replied.

Rebecca got up, stepped forward and placed her hands on Rachel's shoulders. She gave them a light squeeze as she looked into Rachel's eyes, then stepped back. "For now, we have taught you all we know; you have been an excellent student," Rebecca began. "You are certainly welcome to continue to come to us, but we believe you are ready to heal on your own."

"Go solo? Already?" Rachel asked, an instant flutter in her belly. She abruptly sat up straight in her chair, quickly raising her hands to her face and nearly dumped Maddie, who had been lying in her lap, on the floor. She caught her before she fell. When she looked up, Rachel's face was shining with unabashed joy; she gently bit her lip and looked from Rebecca to Leah to all the sisters. "Really?"

The women grinned at yet another of Rachel's strange expressions. Leah coughed slightly to get Rachel's attention. She leaned slightly forward in her chair and let out a deep, satisfying breath. She laced her knobby fingers together in her lap.

"You have learned beyond our expectations, Rachel," Leah began, slightly raising her normally composed voice. "Truly, you have become more than we ever anticipated of you. We all feel that you are prepared to work alone, to heal. Now you must collect into your soul, into your heart, all your knowledge and your memories, and make them your destiny."

Rachel felt warm tears pooling in her eyes and begin to flow down her face.

"Why the tears?" Rebecca asked.

"I cannot not tell you how much I have missed my family in the 21st century. I finally feel like I've found an extended family here," she responded through

159

her tears, wiping her fingers across her face. She looked to her sister-in-law. "Catherine, thank you for bringing me here and making me a part of all your lives."

Each woman got up, walked over and kissed Rachel lightly on the cheek. As though on cue, Maddie gave out a howl letting everyone know she was hungry. Together they gathered in the kitchen and prepared a celebratory meal of chile rellenos, tamales, posole and tortillas, washed down with a bottle of the Medinas' sweet homemade wine. When Rachel lay her head down on the pillow that night, she fell asleep quickly, content that all was good in her world.

* * *

Matt and James stood waiting for Rachel and Catherine's stagecoach at the line office, bundled in their leather coats. As soon as they saw the coach arrive, they stepped outside into the snow flurries whirling all around them, layering flakes on their broad-rimmed, leather hats. The two women descended into their husbands' arms. James stepped back and took a full look at Catherine, a proud grin forming across his lips.

"What is it?" Catherine asked, not understanding the source of his amusement.

160

"Just you," James answered, a glimmer flickering in his eyes. "You've been gone only a few days, yet you look more with child than you did a week ago."

"Are you sure there isn't a third one in there?" Matt chimed in, laughter spiking his voice.

"Matthew!" Rachel chided him, lightly slapping him on the arm. "What a thing to say."

The two brothers shot side glances at one another. Catherine stood there looking at the two men, shaking her head. "You both are incorrigible. Now if you are done making jokes at my expense can we please go home? It is freezing out here."

The men picked up all the bags and the two families went their separate ways towards home.

After feeding and putting Maddie to bed, Matt brought out a bottle of a dark liquid and poured a glass for each of them. He handed Rachel her glass and guided her into the sitting room where a cozy fire burned in the adobe kiva fireplace, hissing at the droplets of tree resin sparking in the blaze. Flames licked at the logs, curling around them like a courting dance.

She sat down in her favorite overstuffed chair and took a sip. "This is nice," she said looking over at him. "I don't remember having whisky in the house. Where did you get it?"

"I had drinks last night with some men from the railroad who are interested in contracting with me for train security. They brought it with them; said it was something special."

Rachel took another sip. "That's an understatement, this is excellent." Her green eyes took on a dusty tinge, a look that Matt had come to know as her seductive side. "My, is it hot in here or what?" she grinned sweetly, fluttering her lashes at him and fanning her face. She drank down the rest of the bourbon in one gulp and set the glass down on a table. She got up and stepped around in front of Matt and began to slowly remove her clothing.

"What the---?" Matt began, startled. Rachel leaned over and placed a finger on his lips.

She stood back up and slowly continued removing every item of clothing as Matt watched her with hungry eyes. He quickly finished the bourbon in his glass and stared, watching Rachel dance around the sitting room, with each turn another piece of clothing falling on the floor. In a few minutes she was completely naked and sauntered over to Matt. She sat down on his lap, straddling her legs around his. Matt could hold back no longer and took her in his arms kissing her passionately on the mouth, the shoulders, the neck and finally down to her breasts. Within moments they fell onto the floor, frantically removing Matt's clothes and making love with a fervor they hadn't experienced since before Maddie was born.

Afterwards as they lay on the floor in each other's arms, Matt leaned over and kissed Rachel on the forehead. Her chin lay comfortably in the valley between the muscles of his chest.

"What inspired that little display?" he asked.

She looked up at him, the corners of her mouth forming a slight smile. "Nothing really. I just missed you. And it was sort of a gift for your patience with all my trips to Moralito."

Matt reached over and embraced Rachel tightly again, holding her as though she would disappear if he loosened his grip. She lay her head back down on his chest, his chin cupped over the top of her head.

"I won't be going back up to Moralito anytime soon," Rachel stated. Matt looked down at her, his eyebrows raised. "They said they have taught me all I need to know and that I'm ready to do this on my own. Now I only need to stock my supply of herbs," she said quietly. Matt finger combed her hair and kissed her tenderly on the head. "They gave me a good amount of their own collection, and when Sarah and Louisa come for Catherine's birthing Sarah will take me out and show me how to identify the plants and harvest on my own."

Matt continued stroking her hair. "Do you know how proud I am of you?"

She looked up at him. "Are you? I know it's been a burden on you." She reached up and ran her fingers across his cheek. It felt smooth as butter under her fingertips.

"It's been worth it, especially since you have a job offer."

"What?" Rachel yelped, jerking her head up higher and looking him in the eye.

He smiled reassuringly. "A woman came to see you while you were gone. A Dr. Henrietta Nash."

Rachel blinked and nodded, "Go on. What did she want?"

Matt smiled teasingly, dimples creasing his lower cheeks. "She wanted to talk to you."

Rachel waited for him to continue, but he didn't, he only smiled like a teenage boy with a secret, waiting for a good enough deal in exchange for the information.

"Matthew Bradshaw, you cut that out!!" she pouted. "What did she say? What about a job offer?"

Matt took in a long breath, then another. "Oh nothing much," he drawled on, taking his time, "just that she had heard that you trained in herbal healing and wondered if you might be interested in helping her at a new clinic she's starting here in town."

Rachel leapt out of his arms into a kneeling position over him. She placed a firm hand on his chest. "Oh my gosh, oh my gosh, this is incredible! Oh, I'm so excited!"

"Yeah, I can see that," Matt grinned broadly, staring straight at her chest.

"I don't mean that kind of excited," she admonished him. "When did she come by? Why didn't you tell me before?"

"I was going to tell you as we were drinking the bourbon, but you obviously had something else on your mind," he grinned devilishly, reaching up with one hand and smoothing his moustache with his thumb and forefinger. "I certainly didn't want to get in the way of your priorities."

Rachel grunted in exasperation. "If you'd told me, I would have stopped."

Matt belted out a deep belly laugh. "And miss that performance? No ma'am!"

"Well, how do I find her?"

"You don't," Matt responded reaching over and taking one of her curls between his fingers. "I told her when you would return. She will stop by tomorrow."

Rachel collapsed back down on the floor and stared straight up at the ceiling, a huge grin plastered on her face. Matt reached over and folded his arms around her, pulling her close into his embrace. She laid her head back on his chest.

"I missed you," he said, lightly kissing her head again.

Rachel listened to Matt's heartbeat. It had a melodic effect on her, as her breathing had on him. In moments they fell asleep enveloped in blissful slumber until the fire burned out, and chilled air filled the room and woke them. They smiled at one another, picked up Rachel's clothing and retreated upstairs where they promptly returned to a deep sleep wrapped in each other's arms.

* * *

The next day Rachel anxiously paced the floors, waiting for her visitor. Mid-morning she saw a woman she did not know coming up the walk. She was a tall, attractive woman with a stately air about her. She wore her blonde hair tied in a bun at the back of her neck, a small hat perched on her head. The woman walked with a decided gait, her head held high. She no sooner knocked on the door than Rachel opened it.

"Mrs. Bradshaw?" she asked.

Rachel nodded. "Dr. Nash? Dr. Henrietta Nash?"

166

The woman nodded.

"How do you do?" Rachel extended her hand to the woman who took it and shook it vigorously. "Please come in." Rachel opened the door wide. The woman's high cheeks were flushed and the tip of her nose glistened red.

"May I offer you some tea?" Rachel asked as she took the doctor's hat, coat and scarf and hung them on a coat rack in the hallway.

"Would it be one of your herbal teas?" Dr. Nash asked, a gleam in her eye.

Rachel smiled. "It's pretty cold out, why don't I brew us a pot of manzanilla, anis and yerba buena? That will warm you up."

The woman widened her hazel eyes. "Why those herbs?" She extended her long neck as she looked at Rachel.

"It's simply a tea I like when I'm cold and need to warm up quickly. Manzanilla is chamomile which can calm the nerves, anis you know as anise and is traditionally used for chest colds. Yerba buena is spearmint which works wonders on upset stomachs. But like I said, in combination the herbs make a very nice drinking tea."

Rachel brewed the tea and brought out a teapot, cups and saucers on a large tray she set on the sitting room table. She suddenly noticed one of her stockings from the night before peeking out from the front of the settee. She quickly sat down and kicked the stocking further back under the furniture and spread her skirts to hide it. Rachel poured them both tea and handed the woman a cup of tea on a saucer. The woman held the saucer in her lap and wrapped her fine-boned hands around the teacup. She lifted the cup, took a sip and smiled sweetly.

"It's very pleasant."

She took another sip and set the cup back in the saucer on her lap.

"Did your husband tell you why I stopped by to see you while you were away?"

Rachel nodded.

"Then you know I am opening a clinic here in Santa Fe," she began, a confidence in her voice that calmed the excitement in Rachel's stomach. "The population of Santa Fe and the surrounding area is growing. The town could use another doctor and I could use help. I looked around for a nurse, however did not find anyone. Then I heard about your skill with herbs," Dr. Nash said.

"Are you working with Dr. Horgan?" Rachel asked.

The woman let out what sounded like grunt. "Charles Horgan? Hrumphf! Absolutely not!" she responded in a high pitch, clearly annoyed at the mention of his name. "You know him?"

Rachel let out a laugh, "Oh yes! He's a real chauvinist."

The woman's eyes widened. "What do you mean?"

Rachel heaved a sigh at being misunderstood once again for using 21st century language. "He is a bigot, Dr. Nash. He does not believe that women belong in medicine other than as meek assistants," Rachel snorted derisively.

"Yes, very, very true," Dr. Nash nodded, little crow's feet creasing at the corners of her eyes as she smiled. "You sound like you have had an encounter with him."

"Actually he is our doctor. When I approached him about training with him he told me to go home and be a good wife and mother."

This time it was Dr. Nash who laughed. "I am sorry, Mrs. Bradshaw; I am not laughing at your expense. It's just that you described him precisely."

Rachel grinned. "Tell me, where did you go to medical school? The Woman's Medical College of Pennsylvania?"

169

"Very good, yes," Dr. Nash responded. "You have heard of it, obviously."

Rachel nodded. "In fact I attempted to point out to Dr. Horgan that the college was training good female doctors; he brushed it off as insignificant."

"Unfortunately Mrs. Bradshaw, there are more men like him than not." She picked up her cup of tea and began sipping it again. Rachel noticed that her long, delicate fingers were devoid of all jewelry. She looked down at her own hands and fingers, which were not what anyone would call delicate. They weren't thick, "man" hands as she had seen on some women, but were of a regular size and shape.

"Rachel, when will you finish your training? I believe you are receiving instruction with curanderas in the mountains, correct?"

"Yes," Rachel acknowledged, looking up quickly. "I've been training with a family of curanderas in the small town of Moralito in the hills outside of Chimayó. Actually, when I was there on my last visit they told me I am ready to work alone, although I have a somewhat limited stock of herbs. In the spring my sister-in-law's sister will be in town and will show me where to collect herbs that grow locally. I already know how to dry and store them for medicinal use."

Dr. Nash listened attentively, nodding her head in satisfaction. "And how do you record your remedies?"

Rachel got up, went into the kitchen, and returned with her leather-bound remedies book that Matt gave her to record her treatments. She handed the book to the doctor, who set her teacup and saucer on the table, took the book, and opened it in her lap. She looked at every page and finally raised her head.

"You know how to render all of these remedies?" Rachel nodded. "How much have you worked with respiratory ailments?"

Rachel took back the book and flipped to the section on respiratory conditions. She handed the book back to the doctor and pointed to the pages. "That's actually the most common complaint. I've treated several people with common colds, the flu, fever, coughs and sore throats."

Dr. Nash carefully read the respiratory treatments, ignoring Rachel who was not sure if she was impressed or disappointed in her book. Finally the doctor looked up, sweeping her long blonde lashes nearly to her brows.

"If you are interested I would like to have you join me at the clinic. I will have conventional medicines and will perform surgery when necessary, but it will be advantageous to have someone trained in local folk medicine for those patients who prefer the area's traditional ways."

Rachel's eyes widened.

"It's hard to say how many or what type of patients we will see," the doctor continued. "As such you will need to be ready to treat any kind of ailment. Are you prepared to do that??"

Rachel felt elation seeping out of every pore; she nearly burst out 'Hell, yes!' but restrained herself and instead nodded and demurely said, "I would be very pleased to work with you. When would you like to get started?"

Over the next hour the doctor told Rachel about her facility on the southern end of town, when she expected to begin seeing patients, how much she would pay Rachel, and other details.

"Initially I will need you only a few hours a week," Dr. Nash continued. "Later as my practice grows I may be able to afford to have you come more often. Would that be suitable?" she asked.

Rachel had been thinking about how to combine full time work within 19th century limitations with her home life. It wasn't like she could stop at the grocery store at the end of a long day and pick up a roasted chicken and cole slaw to serve for dinner. She was relieved to hear that initially the doctor would need her only a few hours a week.

"That would be fine," Rachel agreed. "My daughter is still young and I need to nurse her several times a day so a limited schedule would work best in the beginning."

"Then we are agreed. Why don't you begin after the New Year? That will give me time to set up a work space for you."

The two women shook on their arrangement with Rachel promising to report to the clinic in January. As Dr. Nash made her way out the front door and down the front path Rachel could not hold in her excitement any longer. She closed the door, turned and screamed "Yes!!!" simultaneously leaping into the air and reaching for the sky like the cheerleaders she used to watch at her old high school.

* * *

On her first day of work, Matt accompanied her, first to James and Catherine's home to drop off Maddie, then to the clinic. Dr. Nash greeted them when they arrived, and shook hands with both of them. She gestured for them to follow her, wherein she conducted a tour of the clinic, showing off treatment rooms, common

173

areas, the laboratory, and Rachel's therapy room where the doctor had installed numerous shelves for the many jars of herbs Rachel would store. There was also a table for mixing her herbs, a stove, kettle, several sizes of cooking pots, various utensils, a desk, office chair and several sitting chairs.

"I will leave you to examine your room. There is paper, pen and ink in the top drawer of the desk. Make a list of anything you anticipate needing. Join me in my office when you are ready. Mr. Bradshaw, it was a pleasure to see you again." Dr. Nash nodded to them both, turned and left Rachel and Matt alone.

As soon as she had left, Rachel threw her arms around Matt who gave her a bear hug, then stepped back to look at her.

"You ready for this?" he asked sincerely, looking deep into that place where he knew her insecurities lie.

"You bet I am!" Rachel responded, a grin spread across her face. "Never more ready."

Matt bent over and kissed her lightly. Rachel escorted Matt to the front door, bid him goodbye and made her way back to her room where she inventoried everything Dr. Nash had stocked in the room, and made a list of what more she would need. She made her way to Dr. Nash's office, where she found her perusing a copy of the New England Journal of Medicine. Dr. Nash looked up when Rachel walked into her office. Rachel handed her the list of items she would need in her treatment room.

"Is this all?" Dr. Nash asked.

"For now, yes, however my stock of herbs is limited until the spring when I can harvest and dry new cuttings."

Dr. Nash smiled slightly. "I'm sure it will suffice for now as we don't have people crowding the waiting room to be seen. If you want to stay around you are welcome to, however, you may wish to come back on Friday. My sign will be installed by then and we may start seeing patients come in for care."

Rachel nodded, went to the treatment room to get her belongings, and left to walk home. She had to stop herself from skipping; joy resonated through every bone in her body. By the time she reached the house her face was tired from grinning.

Chapter Nine

Spring 1884

Just as they planned, Louisa and Sarah journeyed to Santa Fe to await the birth of Catherine's twins. Rachel took Emily and Maddie with her to meet their stagecoach. As soon as the stagecoach came around the corner they saw Sarah waving out the window. The sisters disembarked the coach into Rachel and Emily's arms. Each sister bent down and gave Maddie an affectionate kiss on the head; she cooed with baby joy.

"Look how big you are!" Louisa marveled at Maddie.

"She's 15 months old and eating all sorts of food now," Rachel volunteered. "And she's walking, which is both a blessing and a curse. She gets into everything! Some days all I do is chase her from room to room."

"Yes, babies do that," Sarah said looking around, then at Louisa. They both looked back at Rachel.

"Where is Catherine?" the two sisters asked simultaneously, a slight mark of worry across their brows, their dark eyes glowing with concern.

Rachel and Emily looked at one another and grinned. "Your sister is too big to walk around very much," Rachel answered. "She's huge."

The two sisters smiled at one another.

"Yes, I would imagine she would be by now," Louisa conceded. "She is healthy otherwise?"

"Oh yes," Rachel answered immediately. "She's fine, just uncomfortable."

"To be expected," Louisa acknowledged, nodding her head.

"Uncle James offered to make a sling that would wrap around her belly and go around her neck," Emily volunteered, trying to be helpful.

The two sisters' eyes grew large as their brows shot up their faces.

"Don't worry," Rachel interceded. "Your sister turned down his offer. She said that the weight of the babies would break her neck."

Sarah and Louisa broke out in chuckles. "That is our Catherine," Sarah said between laughs. "Always the practical one."

"Let's get you to the house. No one likes for her to be left alone long just in case the babies decide to leave the oven," Rachel said, picking up one of the suitcases with her free hand.

"The oven?" Emily, Louisa and Sarah asked together, leaning forward.

Rachel hung her head low and tossed it from side to side. "There I go again," she moaned. She lifted her head. "It's just a funny term from my time. Means the babies are fully baked and ready to be taken out of the oven."

Rachel looked at the three of them and saw no comprehension on their faces.

"Her womb is the oven," she tried again. "In other words the babies are ready to be born."

"What an odd expression!" Sarah remarked.

"It sounds a bit morbid to me," Louisa added.

"Sorry. But you get my meaning. Let's go, all right?" Rachel suggested.

The women picked up the rest of the bags and walked to Catherine and James' house. They no sooner stepped through the front door than Catherine waddled out from the back of the house holding one hand against her lower back for support. Sarah and Louisa set their bags down and ran to their sister, each giving her a sideways embrace. Catherine kissed each of her sisters on the cheek.

Catherine turned to her niece. "Emily my dear, would you please make a large pot of tea and bring the little cakes you made this morning? I'm sure that Louisa and Sarah would love to sample your fine baking skills," Catherine asked.

Emily grinned shyly and darted off to the kitchen without hesitation. The four women retreated to the sitting room where they chatted for several hours.

When the sun began to wane, Rachel excused herself to take Maddie home, promising to return the next day.

* * *

Rachel arrived back at her in-laws' house mid-morning. She relinquished Maddie to Louisa and left with Sarah in search of herbs growing on the outskirts of town. They didn't have far to go before they found their first specimen, a small manzanilla bush. Sarah showed Rachel how to distinguish the chamomile bush from similar looking plants and how to harvest only the tiny flowers. Next they found salvia, ablaze with tube-shaped red flowers. They harvested several branches of sage for using the leaves and stems in poultices for wounds and skin abrasions, and teas for stomach aches. When their baskets were full, they retreated back to Rachel's home to clean and hang the herbs for drying. Every day the two women journeyed out into the countryside collecting as many cuttings as they could carry. By week's end they had collected as much as Rachel would need for a year. And just in time too, because the day after they finished collecting Emily burst into Rachel's kitchen.

"Come quickly Auntie Rachel! Water came out of Auntie Catherine!"

"Hold on, Em, I just have to get a few things and I'll be ready." Rachel ran into Matt's office and told him Maddie was his responsibility for the day then asked him to find James at the assay office, and tell him it was Catherine's time. She didn't wait for him to agree. She grabbed the bag she had packed with herbs and cloths she would need to assist, and ran with Emily. By the time they arrived, the sisters had Catherine in bed and began talking her through what she would begin feeling and what she needed to do.

"I am so fortunate to have you," Catherine said with admiration to her sisters. "And both of you, Rachel and Emily," she added, looking at the two newcomers. "My babies will be the luckiest children in the world to have all of you as aunts and cousin-----arghhh!" She screamed suddenly and grabbed her stomach.

"And so it begins," Louisa remarked pulling off the covers and placing her hands on Catherine's stomach. Gingerly she felt around her abdomen and very carefully pushed and prodded.

Catherine looked down as Louisa massaged her. "What are you doing, sister?"

"Aligning the babies. They are ready to be born but are fighting over space and who goes first," Louisa smiled. "I think they must be boys."

"As long as they come out healthy, I don't care-- --rrrrrrr!" She shrieked with another contraction.

Hour upon hour passed as the contractions grew closer and closer together. Every half hour or so, the women sent Emily to James and Matthew waiting downstairs, to give them an update. The women traded off wiping Catherine's damp brow, holding and massaging her hands. When the contractions were barely a few minutes apart, Louisa propped herself at the end of the bed and began watching between Catherine's raised legs for the crowning of the first head. Sarah and Rachel stood at each side of Catherine's head and urged her to push. On her final trip downstairs Emily told the men that Louisa said the babies would emerge soon, within a half –hour, but it wasn't that long. As soon as Emily re-entered the room Catherine let out a window-shattering scream, pushing as hard as she could. Louisa was positioned close with a clean cloth in her hands and caught the first small baby that slipped out of Catherine's womb. Louisa deftly cut the cord, wrapped the baby in a clean cloth and handed the baby off to Rachel.

"Keep pushing, Catherine!" Louisa called to the head of the bed. "One more good push and the other one will come out."

181

Catherine grunted and pushed as hard as whatever strength she had left in her would allow. A minute later a second baby emerged. Swiftly Louisa cut the second cord, wrapped the baby in a cloth and handed the child to Sarah. Both Sarah and Rachel busily cleaned up the babies and grinned at one another when they noted the babies' genders. Meanwhile Louisa cared for Catherine's afterbirth and cleaned up the mess. Emily affectionately wiped down Catherine's face and brushed back her damp hair. Emily and Louisa changed Catherine into a clean nightgown and put clean sheets on the bed. As soon as they settled her back in the bed, Rachel and Sarah placed a baby on each side of Catherine to snuggle in her arms. Louisa arranged each baby on a breast and showed them how to nurse. They caught on immediately. Catherine looked at her sons. A wayward tear escaped one eye; joy glowed from her face giving her the look of an angel. And indeed in her white gown, with her shiny locks pulled back, and a rosy complexion she embodied every artist's personification of a winged seraph.

Rachel couldn't hold back. "Louisa should be a fortune teller! She nailed it!" Rachel said cheerfully expecting her meaning would be understood, but quickly realized they did not understand her meaning at all. The group looked at her with blank expressions on their faces. "Boys. Louisa said they were behaving like boys in the womb and she was right," Rachel explained.

Catherine smiled and kissed each boy on the head. After a few minutes the boys stopped nursing. Catherine covered herself and settled one boy in each arm. She looked up at all of them. "Please ask James to come in."

Emily ran downstairs and in moments returned with both James and Matt. James immediately went to his wife's side while Matt stood back with Rachel.

"Allow me to introduce your sons, Samuel and Benjamin Bradshaw," Catherine said proudly, just above an exhausted whisper.

James leaned over his wife, gave her a gentle kiss on the cheek and kissed each of his sons on the head. He knelt down on the floor beside the bed. Neither of them noticed or heard everyone leave the room to give them time to enjoy the moment of their new family together.

Chapter Ten

Summer 1884

Rachel was mixing a tincture for wounds when she heard someone enter the front office of the clinic, followed by Henrietta's footsteps and then a loud voice. Alarmed, she put down the tincture and went to the waiting room where she found Henrietta in a heated exchange with Dr. Charles Horgan. She stopped abruptly as soon as she saw them and they saw her.

"I should have known you would be in on this with her," Horgan spat out, looking at Rachel, his face as red as his halo of tomato-colored hair.

"What?" Rachel asked, confused. "In on what?"

Ignoring her, Horgan looked back at Henrietta. "I told you not to come anywhere near Santa Fe. In fact, I specifically told you to stay out of New Mexico!" he hollered at Henrietta who stood in stoic resistance, glaring at him with fierce, hardened eyes.

"I don't take orders from you or anyone else," Henrietta said calmly. "I can open a practice wherever I choose. I am just as qualified as you, Doctor."

"Qualified as me? Not at all! You're a woman and are not capable of the intellectual capacity it takes to be a doctor," he seethed back at her.

"Oh, please!" Rachel interrupted. "You're not going to start with all that again, are you?"

Horgan turned around and glared at Rachel with chilling cold eyes. She held herself up taller and straighter in defiance.

"Seriously," Rachel continued. "Get over it! Women can be healers just as well as men. It is nearly the 20th century. Get with times!"

Horgan squinted his eyes into snake-like slits and started to move toward Rachel, when Henrietta put up an arm to block him.

"Intellectual capacity is not what is angering you, Charles. Get on with it. What is the real problem? Is it your patients that have come to me for care?" Henrietta asked as congenially as she could, holding her head high, but unable to control the erratically pulsing vein on the side of her face, or the flush across her cheeks.

"As long as you bring it up, yes," Horgan responded turning back to her, anger still seething through his voice. "You have no right to take away my patients."

Henrietta's eyebrows arched and an ever-so-slight smile crept across her thin lips. She crossed her arms over her chest and leaned on one leg. "I don't believe I 'took' anyone, Charles. Patients have the right to go to whomever they choose for their medical care. If your patients came to me, perhaps it was because you did not treat them well, and they sought assistance elsewhere."

"That's a lie. I treat all my patients well!" Horgan fumed back at her.

Henrietta stood her ground, raising her height as tall she could stand. She lifted her chin to look down her nose at him. "Apparently not, or they would not have abandoned you," she said snidely. "You should try to be nicer to people. You will find it will work miracles for even a curmudgeon like you."

Horgan let out almost a growl-like sound. "You have no right to be here! I told you not to come to Santa Fe!"

"Spilled milk," Henrietta brushed him off, flitting her hand as though waving off a fly. "I'm here and I'm staying."

Horgan stood still, clenching his fists at his sides, his crimson face raging with anger. He looked on the verge of a massive heart attack.

"Not if I can help it," he seethed back at Henrietta, turned and left the clinic, slamming the door behind him.

Rachel and Henrietta stood there staring at the door and finally turned back to one another.

"That was certainly unpleasant," Rachel said, a slight quiver in her voice.

"He is always unpleasant!" Henrietta responded, disgust threading her words. "He has always been imperious and always will be."

"It sounds like you've had dealings with him before," Rachel began tentatively, hoping to learn how she knew him.

"Yes, I have," Henrietta answered matter-of-factly, offering no further detail. From the irate look on her face Rachel decided she would not press further.

"Okay then!" Rachel pointed back toward her treatment room and began stepping in that direction. "I'm going to go back and finish the tinctures. I've got several to make this afternoon."

Henrietta nodded, took a deep breath and headed toward her own office without another word. The altercation with Horgan had clearly bothered Henrietta, even if she did not let on to Horgan that he had gotten under her skin.

* * *

A week later Matt walked into the house with a newspaper under his arm, calling for Rachel. He found her upstairs with Maddie.

187

"You might want to read this," he said as he handed the paper to Rachel and pointed to a letter to the editor on the front page.

Rachel looked down and saw the headline: 'Esteemed Santa Fe Physician Dr. Charles Horgan Declares New Doctor in Town a Charlatan.' She looked up at Matt with alarm. "Oh no!" and dropped down into a chair to read the letter.

Dear Editor:

For many years, I have valiantly served as Santa Fe's only physician. I have skillfully delivered babies, set broken legs, removed bullets from various body parts, treated respiratory ailments, and every other form of sickness to the health and benefit of the citizens of our fair city. Therefore, it is with a heavy heart that I inform you that a charlatan has come to Santa Fe, posing as a doctor and treating our citizens for the sole reason of personal gain. The woman, Henrietta Nash, is neither a legitimate doctor nor properly medically trained and qualified to treat our citizenry. She purports to be a graduate of a 'woman's' college of medicine which as all good men know is a ridiculous notion. It is a well-accepted fact that women lack the cerebral capacity to understand the scientific foundations upon which scholarly medicine is based. Just because she has graduated from a so called 'woman's' college does not make her qualified to practice as a legitimate physician.

I call upon the leaders of Santa Fe to stop this woman before she harms one of our hard-working residents. If she does harm someone, I will do my best to rectify the injury. But I cannot be held responsible, as I have given the city due warning of the danger this woman poses. I cannot perform miracles in the face of her ineptitude and incompetence. The city will only have itself to blame if this woman is allowed to continue to illegitimately carry out the honorable practice of medicine and causes harm as a result.

I am sincerely yours,
Dr. Charles Horgan

"Oh my God!!!" Rachel exclaimed looking up at Matt. "I can't believe he did this!"

"Is there any truth to what he says, that she is not a legitimate doctor?"

Rachel scrunched her face in exasperation. "Of course not! I've seen her diploma from the Woman's Medical College of Pennsylvania. She's a legitimate doctor. The man is a bigot – that's all this is about. He's highly intimidated by women with a brain. Remember I found that out myself when I asked him to train me?"

Matt nodded, reached up and rubbed his chin with his forefinger. "Is that what this is? Nothing more?"

Rachel looked at the floor, thinking, and then looked back up at Matt. "There could be more; I'm not sure."

"How so?"

"Last week when Horgan came to clinic and he and Henrietta got into their argument, it sounded like there was some past history, like they knew each other. I tried to find out more from her after he left, but she wouldn't say and I didn't ask. She clammed up and never spoke of him again."

Matt crossed his arms and nodded, as though gauging a theory. "So you think something happened in the past between them?"

"I'm sure of it. They both made references to the past, though not enough that I could figure out the connection." She let out a sigh. "This is bad, really bad. It's so unfair. She hasn't done anything wrong."

"Are you going into the clinic today?" Matt asked.

"I hadn't planned to, but I am now. I have to see her."

"Then I'm going with you."

"Why?"

"Just a feeling. It's probably nothing, but I'd feel better going with you in case some idiot decides to do something to the clinic."

Rachel looked closely at Matt; she saw worry on his face. "Ok, I'll be only a few minutes."

Rachel got Maddie ready to go and in short order the threesome left. They dropped Maddie off with Emily and hurried to the clinic. Matt's instincts proved right. A group of people were gathered around the entrance shouting "Charlatan! Leave Santa Fe! Don't Harm Our Families!" Rachel was appalled by the display of misguided anger. She led Matt around the back and in through the rear door. They found Henrietta in her office, her face ashen and her eyes puffy. Clearly she had been crying. The newspaper lay on her desk. She stood up when they entered the office.

"Oh Rachel, this is not what I envisioned when I opened this clinic," she cried. "Not at all."

Rachel walked over and embraced her employer. It felt awkward. Henrietta was always so composed and straightforward. She had never seen Henrietta express any emotion; this display was completely out of her character. She was sure it was as painful for Henrietta as it was for her to watch her employer's exterior crack.

191

"This will pass Henrietta, it will," Rachel assured her.

"I don't see how," Henrietta wept. "Did you hear what those people out there are calling me?"

Rachel nodded. "Don't let him get away with this. He's jealous and trying to run you out of town. You have to fight back."

Henrietta cleared her throat and wiped at her eyes. "How do you expect me to do that?"

"Write your own letter," Rachel declared, her voice now strong and spirited. "If the editor of the paper and leaders of this town truly believe in due diligence and democracy they have to give you a chance for rebuttal, just like in a court of law. They can't deny you that right."

Henrietta took in a large breath of air, then another. Her chin dropped to her chest and with it a long curl fell out of her well-manicured chignon. She looked back up at Rachel and wiped away an errant tear.

"That is all well and good, Rachel, but we all know that women are not treated the same as men. In the eyes of the law, while it is supposed to be due diligence for all, when it comes to practicing the law particularly here in the west, it primarily applies to men." Henrietta looked over at Matt standing near the door. "Is that not correct, Mr. Bradshaw?"

192

Matt nodded.

"I refuse to believe that and I refuse to accept it!" Rachel declared. "You write that letter and I will go with you to personally deliver it. If the editor won't run it I will elicit the support of every woman in this town to protest the paper until they run it."

Henrietta's eyebrows shot upward in surprise. "And how would you do that?"

Rachel looked over at Matt then at Henrietta. "Use the economic tool. Get the women to convince their husbands to cancel their advertising in the paper until the paper runs your letter."

"Why would the husbands do that?" Matt asked.

"Seriously, Matt? You have to ask me? Isn't it obvious?"

"No," he answered giving her that familiar look of not comprehending her modern uses of language.

"I don't understand either," Henrietta added.

Rachel knew this wasn't about language but about using a strategy women had been using for millennia to get what they want. Rachel rolled her eyes and shook her head. "It's so obvious, you two. Withhold relations!"

Again Matt and Henrietta looked at Rachel, blank stares on their faces.

"Geez, do I have to spell it out? Sex! Withhold sex!"

Henrietta gasped and covered her mouth in shock as Matt burst out laughing. "I have to say Rachel, you do think of the craziest ideas, but this one might work," he said.

"Of course it would work!" Rachel stated. "If I pulled it on you, wouldn't it work?"

Matt turned a shade of pink, grinned and looked down at the floor, suddenly interested in the grain of the wood.

"Rachel, I am grateful for your assistance but I cannot let you do this on my behalf," Henrietta said.

"And why not? This is as much about my livelihood as yours. If you close down your clinic I'm out of a job."

"Well, true..." Henrietta started to say.

"Of course it's true. Listen, you write that letter. I'll be back tomorrow and we will deliver it together to the paper. They have no idea what they will be in for if they refuse to run it."

"I could give them a pretty good idea," Matt chuckled. Rachel whipped around and glared at him, eyes wide and hands on her hips. "I'm kidding, I'm kidding," he protested, grinning wildly and holding up his hands.

Rachel reached over, patted Henrietta on the shoulder and said, "You might want to lock your doors for the rest of the day. No point in giving those morons outside a reason to misbehave."

Henrietta followed them to the back door and locked it after they left, then went to the front door to double check that the door was locked. It was. She retreated to her office, sat down and began to compose the letter.

* * *

The next morning Matt accompanied Rachel back to the clinic. Since not a protester was in sight, he kissed her goodbye and headed to a meeting in the town's center. Rachel went inside and straight to Henrietta's office. Henrietta appeared vexed when she looked up from her desk. Her pinched face reflected the worry in her eyes.

"Well?" Rachel asked, walking up to the desk.

Henrietta slid a piece of paper across the desk. Rachel picked it up and read it.

"I think this is a good rebuttal," she said agreeably. "Are you ready to go to the newspaper's office?"

A reluctant half-smile replaced Henrietta's frown. "Yes," she nodded. "Let's get this over with as soon as possible."

The two women headed out for the newspaper office and reached it in a few minutes. They stepped inside and were met by a friendly clerk at the front desk. He was young and obviously industrious.

"What can I do for you two fine ladies this morning?" he asked leaning over the desk.

Rachel stepped forward. "We would like to see the editor, please," she said in her most confident voice, her head held high.

"Is there something that I can do for you? He is in a meeting right now."

"No, we will wait until he can see us," Rachel answered politely.

"I'll let him know you're here," he said.

The two women sat down in chairs while the young man went into the back. A few minutes after he returned an older man who was nearly bald walked up to the counter. His paunch revealed a penchant for good food and drink, and his rumpled attire suggested he was not married and didn't have a woman to look after his clothing. His chubby face accentuated his small bulbous eyes.

"I am the editor, how may I help you?"

Rachel and Henrietta stood up and walked to the counter that separated them from the man. Henrietta held out her envelope.

"Good day. I am Dr. Henrietta Nash," she began slowly, carefully choosing her words. "Yesterday you ran a letter from Dr. Charles Horgan that grossly defamed me. I have written a letter in response and ask you to run it as soon as possible."

"And why would I do that?" the man said with a mocking tone to his voice and a grin on his heavily jowled face.

"Because, it is the right thing to do!" Rachel interjected.

"And who are you?" the man asked gruffly, taken aback by Rachel's interruption.

"Rachel Bradshaw. I am a resident of Santa Fe, the wife of Matthew Bradshaw and the sister-in-law of James and Catherine Bradshaw, all upstanding citizens of this town." She held her head high and her back erect, signaling she meant business.

"Hmmm," the man responded glancing down at the letter. "I'll think about it."

"That isn't good enough," Rachel responded. "Promise us you will run it immediately."

The man drew back and grimaced. "With that kind of attitude, young lady, I won't promise anything."

"Why not?" Rachel persisted.

The man stared at her with empty bewilderment. His already ruddy face began to grow crimson. "First, because it is my paper and I can do as I please, but most importantly," he turned to Henrietta, "she is a fraud and it is not my practice to give a voice to frauds."

"How do you know I am a fraud?" Henrietta asked, her face stern, her lips tight. "Because Charles Horgan says so?"

"Yes," the man answered. "He is a trustworthy citizen whereas you are not."

"How do you know that?" Rachel pressed. "What proof do you have that what Charles Horgan says is the truth?"

"Listen ladies, I have known Dr. Horgan for many years. If he says something I believe him."

"Even if he's lying?" Rachel asked, trying to modulate her voice instead of screaming at the man.

"That is a terrible accusation!" the man snapped.

"Just as the accusations he made against me were equally terrible!" Henrietta responded.

"It is the American way to give due justice in a dispute and clearly this is a dispute. You owe it to Dr. Nash to give her a chance to respond publicly and defend her good name and reputation," Rachel told the man, her voice rising.

"Pshaw!" the man spit out. "I don't owe you anything!" he said directly to Henrietta then turned to Rachel. "Besides, New Mexico is a territory of the United States, not a state; therefore I don't have to follow federal law."

"Actually if you look at the laws, you do, but it's very clear that you have no intention of running Dr. Nash's letter," Rachel retorted.

The man pursed his lips together and took several moments to size up the women. "No, I don't. Nor do I have to. Like I said, it's my paper and I run what I deem news. What you are offering is not news. And ladies, that is my final decision." He handed the letter back to Henrietta.

Rachel looked at Henrietta, her lips curling up at the edges, her eyes dancing devilishly. "Ok then, now we execute Plan B."

The editor and the clerk watched as Rachel led Henrietta out of the office onto the front wooden boardwalk. Rachel looked at Henrietta, who had an expression of defeat written all over her face. She was looking at the ground, and when she glanced up at Rachel, tears filled her eyes to the brim.

"No time for tears, Henrietta. Now is the time for action," she said trying to cheer up the doctor.

"I don't think I have that kind of fight in me, Rachel," she said quietly.

"No? Well, I do! That pompous editor is not going to get away with denying you your right to a rebuttal. Nor is Horgan going to kick you out of town."

Henrietta continued to look crestfallen, reaching up and wiping away the tears that were falling down her porcelain cheeks. Rachel reached over, gave her hands a squeeze and took the letter from her.

"You go on back to the clinic; I have work to do. I may not be in today depending on how long my visits take. If I don't see you this afternoon I'll see you tomorrow." Rachel gave Henrietta a quick hug and scurried away, headed uptown.

As soon as Rachel got home, she laid the newspaper out on her kitchen table and took note of all the advertisers. She was delighted to see that she knew the wives of all the advertisers. In fact, some of them she considered good friends. She left the house to start paying calls to the ones she knew best. The first woman she visited was the wife of the hotel keeper, a curvy woman with light brown hair who was as jovial as she was smart. Rachel had never heard her say an unkind word about anyone. She wasn't sure how she would react, but her husband ran a significant size ad in every issue so she needed her support. When Rachel showed her both Horgan's front page letter and Henrietta's response, and explained the editor's reaction, she could see the woman's blue eyes clouding with anger. A reddening blushed across her face and her nostrils flared.

"Are you sure Dr. Nash is legitimate?" the woman asked, carefully choosing her words.

"Absolutely!" Rachel responded, detailing Henrietta's training and background, adding that this appeared to be a blatant case of bigotry against a woman. Rachel was surprised when the woman piped up and suggested that the best way to get the editor to run Henrietta's response would be to pull their advertising from the paper. Rachel silently squealed inside, happy that she didn't have to make the suggestion that the woman refrain from marital relations until her husband agreed to cease his advertising. She smiled tentatively as the woman's surprise announcement sunk in.

"That's a brilliant idea, Cora. Will your husband agree?" Rachel asked innocently.

"I don't care if he agrees or not. The hotel is mine. My father willed it to me and I handle the finances."

Rachel gasped with giddiness and blinked her eyes. "I didn't know that."

"Most people don't, just as most people don't know that I place the advertising, not my husband," Cora stated matter-of-factly. "I'll write a letter and deliver it today, canceling my advertising," the woman said proudly, holding her head up high. "Rachel, I would suggest you also visit wives of other advertisers."

Inwardly Rachel felt another silent squeal, realizing she didn't need to completely do this on her own.

"This is not an insurmountable problem, my dear," Cora said. "In fact, if you will give me a minute to put on my shawl and hat, I'll go with you."

A few minutes later, the two women headed out to make visits to as many of the wives as they could find at home. They found and met with the wives of all the major advertisers and several of the minor ones too. Although Rachel was well prepared to tell the women what they could do – or rather, not do – in the bedroom to induce their husbands to go along with the pulling their ads, she found it was not necessary. All the women were infuriated. Several had experienced the chauvinistic side of Horgan and found his letter an insult not just to Henrietta, but to them as well. Every one of the women promised they would have their husbands cancel their ads in writing and would make sure their cancellation specified the reason why. By the end of the day Cora and Rachel had promises from nine women. With Cora's letter the canceled ads would comprise nearly all the advertisers. Once the canceled ads started hitting the paper's pocketbook Rachel was sure that the editor would come calling on Henrietta.

A week later that is precisely what happened. Rachel was giving a patient an herbal gargle for a sore throat when she heard someone enter the waiting room. She finished up with the patient and walked to Henrietta's office where she found the door closed. She quickly stepped into the room next door where she knew the walls were so thin she could clearly hear a conversation. She put her ear to the wall.

"Dr. Nash, do you remember me from the newspaper office?"

"Of course. It was only a week ago."

"I have reconsidered your request and am now prepared to run your response letter."

"That is a very honorable decision," she heard Henrietta say. Rachel was sorry she wasn't in the room to see the expression on Henrietta's face. "But I am curious, why did you change your mind? You seemed pretty adamant last week that you would never run the letter."

"Dr. Nash, let us be honest with one another. I know what you did, contacting all my advertisers. In short order your actions will put me out of business. I have no choice but to run your letter."

"Mr. Carter, I am aware of what has transpired, but I assure you I had nothing to do with the businesses cancelling their advertising with you. That occurred because enough people of Santa Fe, including your advertisers, heard about your unfair treatment of me and decided to handle the injustice as they best saw fit."

"Dr. Nash, may I have the letter now please?"

"That depends; do you assure me that you will run it exactly as I have written it, without any editing?"

Rachel heard a heavy moan and assumed it came from the editor.

"Yes, I promise. Now will you or whoever you had contact my advertisers tell them to reinstate their advertising?"

"Of course, after the letter runs," Henrietta said in a strong, confident voice.

"No, that is not acceptable. I don't have another issue coming out until next week, which means it will be a week after that before the advertisements would run again. That will sorely damage my financials."

"Perhaps you should have thought of that when you turned me away last week." Rachel felt her insides leap with joy; she was incredibly proud of Henrietta. "No," Henrietta continued. "Your advertisers won't be contacted until after the letter runs."

"You don't understand; this could break me. I need the accounts reinstated now."

"Well then I suppose the only other option available to you is to run a special edition, before next week."

"That would cost a fortune!" the man barked.

"Like I said before, you took this upon yourself. It is not my problem."

Silence ensued. Rachel wished she could see through the wall and assumed they were probably having a stare-down. '*What would Henrietta do?*' She hoped that Henrietta wouldn't cave.

"Is that all, Mr. Carter?" Silence. "Good, then if you would leave I have work to do."

Heavy footsteps plodded out of the room, through the waiting room and out the front door. Rachel ran out of the room and into Henrietta's office. She couldn't suppress the glee on her face.

"I heard the whole thing. You were phenomenal!" Rachel declared rushing over to Henrietta and giving her a big hug.

"How did you hear it? Where were you?"

Rachel grinned and looked down at the floor. "I'm sorry; I eavesdropped. I had my ear plastered against the wall," she said pointing to the adjoining wall. "I'm so proud of you, especially for sticking up for yourself, forcing him to run it before we call off the wives."

Henrietta looked affectionately at Rachel. "I cannot thank you enough, Rachel. I could never have done this on my own."

Rachel smirked and waved her hand. "It was nothing. Actually it was fun. I think the ladies enjoyed using their influence."

"I hope you heard that he did not realize it was you who orchestrated this endeavor."

"I heard it. But believe me – if he doesn't know already that it was me, he will soon. I don't care one way or the other; he can't hurt me."

"Let's hope not, my dear," Henrietta said, a sigh of relief leaving her lips.

Chapter Eleven

The following week Matt walked into the house and found Rachel in the kitchen attempting to make an apricot pie. He grinned when he saw what she was doing.

"Here, take a break and read this," he said handing her the paper. "Little troublemaker," he added, his eyes flashing.

Rachel rubbed her hands on her apron, took the newspaper and sat down to read it.

Dear Editor:

You recently ran a letter from Dr. Charles Horgan defaming me as a charlatan and fraud, purporting that I am not a legitimate physician. Nothing could be further from the truth. I graduated from the Woman's Medical College of Pennsylvania, a well-regarded medical school that educates and trains women to be lawful physicians. Anyone who doubts my training is welcome to visit my office and see my diploma. I am proud of my position and my ability to help others. Unfortunately, not all men believe that women have the intellectual capabilities to comprehend and grasp the field of medicine. Dr. Charles Horgan is one of those men and that is regrettable because his small-mindedness and vindictiveness has done a grave disservice to Santa Fe's fine citizens. I am as educated and capable as he to practice medicine. Dr. Horgan is clearly behind the times. In his recent letter published in this newspaper he wrote that he fears I may harm the populace. The purpose of his statement was to instill fear in the citizenry. Dr. Horgan is a bigot and simply jealous of my abilities, nothing more. I call upon Santa Fe's citizens to ignore Dr. Horgan's vicious comments and seek their medical care with the practitioner with whom they feel most confident. I welcome any of those citizens to my clinic and will do my best to deserve their trust and treat them with honor and esteem.

Respectfully yours,
Dr. Henrietta Nash

Rachel looked up at Matt, her eyes shimmered. "It worked, I can't believe it worked!" She leapt up, bounced on her toes and hugged Matt.

"You doubted that it would?" Matt asked incredulously looking down at her. "You told me yourself that the editor showed up at the clinic asking for the letter."

"Yeah, but until it actually ran I couldn't be sure," she said, a trill in her voice. "I have to finish this pie then run over to Cora's and the clinic. Can you keep an eye on Maddie and watch the pie for me and take it out when it's ready?"

Matt nodded. "I think I can manage that," he said giving her a gentle kiss on the forehead.

Rachel turned back around to her pie, finished the top crust and put it in the hot oven. Within minutes she was on her way out the door.

After rejoicing with Cora, who promised to notify all the other wives, Rachel headed for the clinic. The city's air seemed to be particularly saturated with the sweet fragrance of summer's blossoms. It felt like a reward for all the recent tension and put a smile on Rachel's face. She found Henrietta in her office reading the paper. She looked up when Rachel entered, a mixture of delight and satisfaction displayed on her face.

"Oh Rachel, I am so grateful, truly I am!" she exclaimed. "Perhaps now patients will return."

"I have no doubt that they will," Rachel reassured her. "And I am hopeful that this is the end of all this. It's draining!"

Henrietta agreed, but it wasn't the end of it by any means. At week's end Henrietta received a letter from Charles Horgan inviting her to his office the next afternoon to reconcile and forge a truce. She walked into Rachel's treatment room and showed her the letter.

"I'm going with you," Rachel announced. "This could be a trick."

"What kind of trick?"

"I have no idea, but I don't trust the man."

The next day they went to Horgan's office. He appeared surprised to see Rachel, but said nothing. He ushered them past his receptionist, who eyed both women warily, and down the hallway into his office. He offered them both chairs opposite his desk. They waited for him to begin.

"I want to call a truce." He stared at them down his long nose, a tone of arrogance lilting through his voice.

"What kind of truce?" Henrietta asked, a note of caution in her tone.

"A simple truce. You have maligned me in the press. It is damaging my practice. If you will write a letter of apology to the paper we can put this behind us," he stated condescendingly, as though instructing a small child.

"Me?" Henrietta nearly shrieked. "I did not write the first letter, you did! You maligned me! I was only defending myself."

"Inconsequential details," he muttered, slightly shaking his head. "Just write the letter."

"I will not!" Henrietta announced harshly.

"Why should she? You're not offering a truce." Rachel interjected, her tone raised. She was miffed that he would even make the suggestion, though not surprised given the man's self-importance.

"This is not your affair!" Horgan snapped at Rachel.

"Of course it's my affair," Rachel shot back. "I work with Henrietta and your actions affect us both."

Horgan ignored Rachel and turned back to Henrietta. "Are you going to write the letter or not?"

"Absolutely not!" Henrietta answered.

Horgan's lower lip began trembling. They observed his face redden and his eyes grow large, then narrow into slits.

"You harlot!" he seethed at her. "You are no better than a common prostitute." His words slapped them as though he had struck them with his hand.

"How dare you!" Henrietta bit back. "How dare you!"

Rachel was hot. She knew she should keep her mouth shut but she could no more easily stay quiet than a raging river could stop from overrunning a bank.

"You've got a lot of nerve," Rachel began, her voice rising with each syllable. "You are so intimidated by Henrietta that you can't see that this situation does not require your outrageous response. If anything you owe her an apology, not the reverse."

"Like hell!" he spat out, his own voice meeting the same high pitch as Rachel's.

For the next few minutes the three of them shouted at one another and over one another, their voices reaching a horrific timbre. No one could hear what anyone else was saying as they screamed insults back and forth. Finally all three stopped shouting and merely glared at one another. The women got up and left the office without saying one more word. As they walked down the hallway they saw patients and the receptionist peering down the hallway, staring at them with their mouths agape. They brushed past everyone and exited as quickly as possible. Once they were outside Henrietta slumped against the building's front wall; she was breathing heavily.

"Are you okay?" Rachel asked placing her hand on Henrietta's arm to steady her.

"I will be in a moment. I just need to gather myself. He always has this effect on me," she whispered.

"How exactly do you know him?" Rachel asked.

Henrietta shook her head. "It doesn't matter. Let's go. I have to get away from this building before I do something I regret."

"Like what?" Rachel asked, feeling worried, about what she was not sure.

"It's nothing," Henrietta shook her head looking at the ground, evading Rachel's eyes. "Please, let's leave."

Rachel held Henrietta's arm and the two walked silently back to the clinic where they found several patients waiting in front of the door. Though shaken by the exchange with Horgan, as soon as they began seeing patients the uneasiness subsided. By the time they left at day's end they had all but forgotten the uncomfortable argument.

* * *

The next morning news flew through the dusty streets of Santa Fe like the October winds. When the receptionist let herself into the office, she found Charles Horgan dead of a gunshot wound to the head. She screamed, which brought other building tenants dashing to her aid. Someone ran and got the Sheriff, who arrived quickly.

213

Rachel and Maddie were visiting Catherine and the babies when James burst in the door and found them in the nursery.

"Dr. Horgan has been murdered!" James shouted, his usual calm demeanor absent from his voice and manner.

"What?!" Rachel cried. Her smile disappeared and her face suddenly lost all color as did Catherine's. Catherine fell back in her chair and clutched her chest in shock.

"Dr. Horgan's receptionist found him shot this morning. The Sheriff has wired Denver to get a doctor down here to dig out what kind of bullet killed him," James answered as cohesively as he could.

"Why is he doing that? Henrietta could remove the bullet," Rachel responded.

James looked at her with grave concern. "Word around town is that she may be a suspect, and you may be as well."

"What?!" Rachel and Catherine shrieked at the same time.

James nodded. "Yes, apparently a lot of people heard the argument you and Dr. Nash had with Dr. Horgan yesterday in his office. The two of you are the prime suspects."

Rachel's eyes bulged. "That's ridiculous! Yes, we had an argument, but we didn't kill him!"

Catherine reached over and drew Rachel into her arms. "Don't worry my sister; there has obviously been some terrible, terrible mistake. We will weather this together, as a family."

Rachel's shoulders began to shake. She could feel a penetrating dread burrowing under her skin. She looked up at James. "Does Matt know?"

"I couldn't find him," James shook his head helplessly. "I'll go back out and keep looking. Meanwhile you stay here. Don't go home." With that he turned and rushed out of the house.

Rachel and Catherine looked at one another with horror. "Oh my God, my dear God," Rachel murmured. Her eyes took on the frightened look of a mother's concern for her young. She had not felt this scared since she landed in the 19th century and realized she had no feasible way of getting home. She began to shake with biting fear.

An hour later James returned with Matt, who leapt up the stairs two at a time. As soon as he entered the nursery, Rachel stood up and ran to him. He embraced her so hard it hurt, but she didn't care. She pulled back and looked up at him. Her eyes were puffy and blood shot from crying.

"We're going to get to the bottom of this," he said reassuringly, stroking her head and wiping away the tears beginning to stream down her face.

Rachel nodded and tried to speak. She couldn't, the tears blocked her voice. She looked up into Matt's eyes and saw what looked like storm clouds gathering. Rachel knew that look well; he was on the cusp of rage. She dabbed at her eyes and finally she regained her bearings. "Where is Henrietta? Have you seen her?"

Matt shook his head. "I went to the clinic; she's not there. No one has seen her."

"My dear God, what am I going to do?" Rachel asked feebly.

"The question is what are WE going to do," Matt responded a little sharply. "I'm the one who got you into this mess and I know as well as you do that you didn't murder Horgan. We have to approach this sensibly."

Rachel nodded and bravely she held back the tears that were trying to fall again. As she did, Maddie began to cry reaching upward for her mother. Rachel bent down and picked up her daughter, who seemed to sense her mother's anguish.

"James, can you keep them here? I'm going to go find Thomas Singletarry."

"The lawyer?" James asked. Matt nodded.
"Good idea. Go!" Matt kissed Rachel and Maddie, ran
down the stairs two at a time and out the front door, his
shoulder length locks flying behind him.

Rachel collapsed into a chair, hugging Maddie
so tight that the little girl yelped.

A short while later Matt returned with a man in a
suit, carrying a satchel. He removed his hat and slightly
bowed to Rachel. He was a small, tidy man with an
orderliness about him. His hair was dark and neatly
combed; it set off his prominent nose and the sharp eyes
behind his wire-rimmed glasses. Matt introduced
Thomas Singletarry to the group; the man took special
interest in Rachel.

"I am truly sorry that you find yourself in this
position, Mrs. Bradshaw," the lawyer began. "In a
situation like this it is never too early to avail yourself of
legal counsel. If you are agreeable I would be happy to
represent you should it be necessary."

Rachel nodded, keeping at bay the fear that
sought to consume her.

"If we can go downstairs for a few minutes I
have some legal papers to go over with both you and Mr.
Bradshaw."

"Of course," Rachel responded, handing Maddie
off to Catherine, rising and exiting the room. She felt her

217

heart aching as she heard Maddie whimper at her leaving.

An hour later the lawyer left and although Rachel did not feel cheerful, she felt better knowing that if the Sheriff did come calling, at least she had a resource lined up ready to defend her.

"Matt, what do we do now?" Rachel looked at Matt for guidance. She still felt like an outsider in the 19th century, and when it came to the laws, she was a neophyte and knew it.

Matt reached over, cupped his hand around her neck and lightly brushed her lips with his. "We will do what the lawyer suggested; we will wait and see what happens."

Rachel's face tightened. "Where? Where do we wait?"

"Wherever you want. Here? Home?"

Rachel nodded. "Home. Let's get Maddie into her own environment, where she is at ease. Besides, if the Sheriff does come arrest me, I don't want a scene here at James and Catherine's house. It will be bad enough that Maddie will be affected; I don't want to put James, Catherine and Emily through that."

"Are you sure?" Matt asked. "Maybe it would be a comfort for you to have Catherine nearby."

"I understand what you're saying, but I think I want to go home, for Maddie's sake. And if they do come get me, you can bring Maddie here or care for her at home." Rachel looked down at her hands then remembered something and her head bolted upright. "Oh my gosh, I just remembered! You're going to Oak Valley tomorrow."

"Not anymore I'm not, not now. I'm staying here until this blows over. I'll wire the architect and we can discuss whatever needs to be settled via telegram."

Matt stood up and guided Rachel up the stairs, found the rest of the family and told them their plans. In a few minutes Rachel and Matt carried Maddie home. They barely spoke a word, each deep in thought. When they arrived home they attempted to behave as though everything was normal. They knew that Maddie was at an age where she perceived even small changes in behavior. The slightest change would alarm her, so to keep her relaxed they went about the rest of their day as though nothing was wrong. But there was much wrong. A heavy suffocating quiet settled on the house, not quite paralyzing them, but their usual noisy activity had all but disappeared. It was the kind of consuming quiet that invades a home when there has been a death.

That evening Rachel made Matt's favorite dinner, a roasted chicken with boiled potatoes tossed in melted butter and flan for dessert. She was proud of herself that she had finally mastered making custard; it wasn't easy. After dinner they put Maddie down and retired themselves, making love like it was the first time – both sensing that if things went badly, it could be their last.

The next morning they awoke early and began their day like any other. They were just finishing breakfast when they heard a knock on the front door. Rachel looked at Matt with alarm. He reached over and squeezed her arm.

"It's okay, I'll get the door. You take Maddie upstairs," he said calmly.

Rachel picked up Maddie and ran upstairs, not looking toward the door. As she entered the nursery she heard male voices downstairs, voices other than Matt's. A few minutes passed and Matt entered the room.

"It's as we thought, Rachel, they're here to take you in."

Rachel bowed her head, shut her eyes and rolled her lips inward, biting them in an attempt to stem the onslaught of tears she could feel welling in her eyes. As soon as she felt she could function, she opened her eyes and looked at Matt.

"Okay, then let's proceed as we planned. I'll get my shawl."

Rachel bent down and hugged Maddie for several minutes, giving her a kiss and telling her to mind Papa while she went on an errand. The little girl cooed and smiled which was just the way Rachel wanted her to be. She walked into their bedroom, put her shawl around her shoulders and went downstairs, Matt following. She could feel the eyes of the two men at the base of the stairs boring through her. Of the two men, one appeared older, perhaps around 50, his umber colored face weathered by life on the frontier. His dark, hollow eyes and a shadow of a black beard made him look formidable.

"Mrs. Bradshaw?" the older man asked. Rachel nodded. "I am Sheriff Garcia. I have a warrant for your arrest." Rachel pursed her lips, glanced to Matt and back to the lawman. "Then let us be civil about this. If you promise not to run or make a scene we can calmly walk to my office and not bring you any more attention than has already occurred."

"You mean the jail, don't you?" Rachel asked politely, trying her best not get short with the Sheriff.

"Yes," he answered.

"I promise." Rachel looked at Matt who bent down and kissed her on the forehead. "Take care of Maddie for me. She will be hungry in about three hours. Please take her to Catherine."

"I plan to have you out by then," Matt responded, his voice strong and redolent of authority.

"I wouldn't count on that Mr. Bradshaw," the Sheriff said. "I'll be holding her until I take her before the judge who will decide whether or not to charge her. I'm pretty darn sure she will be charged with murder. We don't usually let murderers out on bail, even if they are young mothers."

"And have you ever had a young mother in your jail?" Rachel asked as congenially as she could muster, trying hard to mask the disdain she was sure was evident in her voice.

"Well, no; you are the first. But that's not my point. Murderers don't get out on bail."

Rachel could feel her blood beginning to seethe. *'Murderer? I'm already a murderer?'*

"I beg your pardon, Sheriff, but am I not considered innocent until proven guilty in a court of law?"

"Technically yes," the Sheriff replied. "But not in a clear-cut case like this."

Rachel felt her knees go weak as though they would buckle; she stood straight and refused to let her body fail her now. "And what clear-cut case would that be?" Rachel asked, her voice rising in timbre. She felt Matt's hand grasp onto her arm.

222

"My wife is correct, Sheriff, she has not yet been found guilty of a crime. By law she is innocent until a jury of her peers convicts her."

"Yes, yes, yes, can we stop the stalling now?" the Sheriff asked sarcastically, impatience threading his voice. "Are you going to cooperate or do I have to cuff you?"

Rachel nodded as politely as she could, given that her head was about to explode with fury, and headed to the front door. The Deputy opened the door, took Rachel by the arm and escorted her outside. Rachel looked up at the Deputy who stood about a foot taller than her. He was young, so young that he still bore acne on his face under his sparse blondish red moustache. He was thin, too thin. His body hadn't quite filled out yet, making him look more like the scarecrow in the Wizard of Oz than a rough and tough lawman of the Wild West.

"What is your name?" Rachel asked him.

"Deputy Herbert Alford," the young man responded, a slow drawl in his voice.

"Well, Deputy Alford, I don't think it's necessary to hold onto me as we walk down the street. I promised that I wouldn't run away and even if I did," Rachel stopped, picked up the edge of her dress and showed him her heeled shoes. "I'm pretty sure you could outrun me."

She grinned at him to make her point. The Deputy hunched his shoulders, let go of Rachel and walked beside her, the Sheriff on their tail. As the threesome walked toward the jail, dry lightning cracked across the distant sky. Rachel felt a shiver run up her spine. She hoped it wasn't a dire omen of the unfolding legal drama swallowing her in its snarled pit. Suddenly, she heard the same whispering sound she heard in the wagon with Noah Chavez. She looked at the Deputy who stared straight ahead. She realized it was the whisperwind.

"Trust," the wind sang into her ear. "Trust your heart." Then it was gone, but it was enough for Rachel. She knew that she had an angel on her side and for now that was sufficient. She took in a large breath of air, confronting the fear head-on; it was the only way she knew how to face the unknown.

As soon as Matt saw Rachel, the Deputy and the Sheriff turn the corner Matt ran upstairs, picked up Maddie and ran back downstairs and out the front door. He ran the whole way to James and Catherine's house, Maddie giggling at what she thought was a game. He didn't even bother knocking, but burst in calling for them. He found them with Emily in the kitchen.

"Did they…" James began to ask but Matt cut him off.

"Yes, they just picked her up. Can you take care of Maddie while I go get the lawyer? That damn Sheriff is already referring to Rachel as a murderer!" Matt said darkly.

Catherine gasped. "Oh, this is bad," she whispered, her eyes widening with worry. She reached over and took Maddie out of Matt's arms. "Don't worry about Maddie; we will care for her until all of this is over."

Matt bent over and first kissed Maddie, then his sister-in-law on the cheek. "Thanks." He turned to go then spun back around. "Maddie will need to feed again in three hours."

"Of course," Catherine said. "You go; your daughter is fine here."

Matt ran out of the house, down the porch stairs and toward the center of town. He arrived at the lawyer's office in minutes, breathless from the run. The lawyer looked up with alarm when Matt bolted into his office. Singletarry's eyes narrowed.

"Has the Sheriff arrested her?" he asked. Matt nodded. The man picked up his coat and satchel, jutted his chin toward the door and said, "Let's go; I have work to do."

* * *

Rachel stepped inside the jailhouse and immediately caught the scent of something strange. Not the usual expected bodily smells of people incarcerated too long without bathing, but the acrid smell of misery. It was thick as humidity, hanging in the air. She no sooner crossed the threshold than the Deputy led her to a cell and locked her inside. She saw another woman in the cell, seated on a bench and bent over so low she couldn't see the woman's face which she covered with her hands. But Rachel could tell from the dress and blonde hair flowing out of a disheveled bun that it was Henrietta Nash.

"Henrietta?" Rachel said gently.

The woman raised her head and indeed it was Henrietta Nash. Her eyes were swollen and her face puffy from crying.

"Oh Rachel, I am so, so sorry to have dragged you into all this. Truly I am," her voice broke as she tried to continue, but sobs overwhelmed her.

Rachel sat down and put her arm around Henrietta's trembling shoulders. Although the day before, Rachel herself had nearly split apart with fear and grief, now her emotional Novocain took over. The terror was gone replaced by a glorious fury that stoked her courage. Her adrenalin kicked in like the rush of a mountain lion whose lair had been violated.

226

"Now listen to me," Rachel began, "you have to pull yourself together. I know how you feel because I too am scared to death and have to do the same. We know we didn't do this and truth will prevail. Matt hired a lawyer yesterday and he's on his way there now. Everything is going to be all right."

Henrietta looked up at Rachel, tears staining her cheeks. "I am not as hopeful as you," Henrietta said softly. "Charles may be dead but he will bring me down from the grave. I just know it."

"That's silly talk, Henrietta. Think positive. For now that's all we have going for us." Rachel tried to reassure the woman she had come to think of as her friend, even though she was having trouble feeling positive herself. It wasn't long before she heard the front door open and saw Matt and the lawyer enter.

"Sheriff," the lawyer tipped his hat to the head lawman sitting in a chair in the front area.

"I expect that you are representing Mrs. Bradshaw?" the Sheriff asked, not bothering to rise from his chair.

The lawyer nodded. Singletarry pulled himself up straight and tall as he could muster, which wasn't much. "Let me see the warrant. On what charges are you holding her?"

The Sheriff handed him the warrant. "The willful murder of Dr. Charles Horgan. She and Dr. Nash shot him in cold blood."

"And how do you know that?" Singletarry challenged him, raising one eyebrow skeptically.

"There was a big argument at Dr. Horgan's office. Mrs. Bradshaw and Dr. Nash got into a loud quarrel with Dr. Horgan. Several patients and the receptionist heard it. And everyone knows about the pissing match the two doctors have been having in the paper," the Sheriff answered as though his response obviously addressed the lawyer's question.

The lawyer leaned his hands on the edge of the Sheriff's desk and focused his eyes firmly on the man, not bothering to mask his annoyance. "So? What does that have to do with Mrs. Bradshaw? She's guilty of willful murder because of an argument? Is that all the proof you gave the judge for issuing the warrant?"

Sheriff Garcia leaned back in his chair and laid his hands on his copious belly. "It's proof enough for me to hold both women until they are arraigned in court. Besides that, it's well known that Mr. Bradshaw here," the Sheriff gestured to Matt, "bought his wife a gun and it's well known that she knows how to use it. As soon as the doctor from Denver arrives and dislodges the bullet out of Dr. Horgan's head, we'll know the size of the bullet. If it's the same as what Mrs. Bradshaw uses she's as good as ready for the noose," the Sheriff smiled.

"You're enjoying this, aren't you?" Singletarry asked, his thick brows rising up his forehead, his mouth set in a hard line.

"Lots to enjoy here, Mr. Singletarry. Can't say I've ever had two ladies as lovely as this in my jail." The Sheriff grinned and casually leaned his chair backwards.

Singletarry took in a long slow breath. "When is the arraignment scheduled?"

"Whenever I mosey over to the courthouse and inform the judge that the prisoners are in my custody." The Sheriff kept grinning and started picking at a piece of food lodged between his front teeth. "I'll try to get over there sometime today when I have time. I'm kinda busy right now."

Singletarry quickly turned around, and glanced at Matt, waving him to the door, "Let's go."

Outside the closed door, Matt pulled on the lawyer's arm. "What now?"

"The courthouse," Singletarry barked. "If that moron thinks he's going to get my goat, he's dead wrong."

"What can you do?" Matt asked, trying to keep the worry out of his voice and the rage building in his gut from surfacing.

"What can I do? What can I do? Go see my brother, that's what I can do!"

"Who's your brother?"

Singletarry looked at Matt as though he were a child. "Don't you know that my brother is the judge? I thought that's why you hired me. Everyone knows I am the judge's brother; that's why I get a lot of clients."

For the first time in two days Matt laughed, his characteristic dimples appearing down the sides of his face. He shook his head. "No, I didn't know. I hired you because I heard you were a good lawyer."

"Well I am, but don't get excited, Matt," the lawyer cautioned. "All I can do is tell my brother what has transpired. He will schedule the arraignment as soon as possible."

Matt furrowed his brow and looked down at the diminutive man who, while short, clearly was not a man to mess around with or make angry. "Doesn't the Sheriff have to do that?"

"Huh! That's what Sheriff Garcia would have you believe. Tell you what; you go on home, while I go see my brother."

"No, I need to go with you."

"For what reason? You can't do anything, but I can. And I will be able to have a much more frank discussion with my brother if you are not standing there. Do you get my meaning?"

Matt nodded. "Yeah, yeah, I get it." Matt turned, walked a few steps, then stopped and turned back around. "I'm going back in to see Rachel then I'll go to my brother's. Will you come to my brother's house and let me know what happens at the courthouse?"

"Or course," the lawyer answered, slightly bowing his head. He then turned and with a deliberate step headed to the courthouse.

Matt walked into the jail and straight for Rachel's cell.

"You can't just walk in here like that!" the Sheriff barked at Matt, who snapped his head around and glared at him with such loathing that the man backed off. "All right; you can see her for a few minutes."

"I'll see her for as long as I damn well please!" Matt seethed back at him, not losing his stride as he continued toward the cell. Rachel was waiting at the bars. Matt bent as close to her as he could. She raised her hand and threaded it through the bars to his lips. He kissed the tips of her fingers. They spoke in hurried whispers.

"Stay strong, Rachie," he murmured. "Thomas's brother is the judge. He's on his way there now to see him and schedule the arraignment."

Rachel nodded and managed to keep back the tears burning behind her eyes. "Thank you," she whispered back.

"You okay here if I go back to James and Catherine's? I left Maddie with them. Thomas will meet me there after he sees his brother."

She let out a quiet sigh. "Other than it being colder in here than a witch's boob, I'm fine."

Matt grinned. She still had her sense of humor and that was good. Matt laced his fingers through Rachel's; they stood there holding their hands in as close an embrace as they could manage, watching one another for several minutes until Rachel pressed her face against the bars, as did Matt, allowing them a brief kiss before the Sheriff yelled at them to stop. Matt gave her one more kiss, turned and glared at the Sheriff as he walked out of the jail. But before he stepped out the door he turned back to the Sheriff. "Your job does not require you to be an asshole. You take yourself too seriously." The Sheriff jumped up out of his seat; Matt was long gone by the time he got to the door.

Two hours later Thomas Singletarry knocked on the door of James and Catherine's home. James answered the door and led the lawyer into the sitting room where he invited him to sit; the lawyer declined.

"I won't stay long. My brother has scheduled the arraignment for both women at 4 o'clock this afternoon. A prosecuting attorney will be there if my brother deems that a case should proceed. I will be there and you are welcome to attend. Because it is so quick I doubt many people will attend. Dr. Nash has engaged a lawyer who will represent her."

"We'll be there," Matt and James said in unison.

The arraignment took only a few minutes. Rachel and Henrietta were charged as co-conspirators in the first-degree murder of Dr. Charles Horgan. Bail was denied due to the severity of the crime. The Sheriff grinned as though he had won a victory. Matt leaned over and whispered into the attorney's ear.

"Will the court agree to allow the prisoner, Mrs. Bradshaw, visiting rights with her husband and infant daughter who he will bring to the jailhouse?"

Judge Singletarry, who looked like the twin of his lawyer brother nodded and said, "Agreed, for as much time as the family wants to spend together."

Sheriff Garcia stood up immediately. "Your honor, I must object."

"Object if you want, Sheriff, but that is my final decision. Furthermore, find a place for the family to spend time together privately, other than the jail cell."

"The only private place in the whole jailhouse is my office!" the Sheriff protested.

The judge leaned forward and stared down at the Sheriff. "Then give them your office, for as long as they want it, Sheriff. If I hear that you have been uncooperative in this manner I will have you locked up in one of your own jail cells. Understood?"

The Sheriff, whose face turned a blotchy red, bowed his head and nodded. The moment that the arraignment was adjourned, the Sheriff and his Deputy handcuffed Rachel and Henrietta and led them out of the courtroom.

"Was it really necessary to handcuff them?" Matt asked Thomas when they departed.

"No, but obviously the Sheriff is none too happy with my brother's last statement. He can't do anything about it, but he can make things uncomfortable for your wife and Dr. Nash. In fact, if you can manage it, I urge you to bring the women any female toiletries they require and some soft blankets and pillows. Oh, and one other thing, the jail has never been known for its excellent cuisine, but given the Sheriff's state of mind, he might try to feed them roasted rats and stale bread. If you can I encourage you to bring them all their meals."

Matt's eyes bulged at the word 'rats'. "I'll head over to the jail now and let the women and the Sheriff

234

know that we will provide the meals and the other items. I can't wait to see the look on that Sheriff's face when he sees the meals we bring to the women." Matt and James grinned like young boys devising an adventurous escapade.

James headed home to tell Catherine the plan and Matt walked over to the jail. After seeing Rachel and telling her what they intended to do, Matt returned home, packed several items for Rachel and walked to his brother's, where Catherine and Emily were already making dinner. As soon as Matt walked into the kitchen Emily ran to him and threw her arms around his waist.

"Oh, Uncle Matt, I am so scared for Auntie Rachel. Will she get out of jail?" Tears brimmed on the edge of her Bradshaw-blue eyes.

Matt reached down and stroked his niece's head. He pried her arms off and kneeled down to eye level where he placed his large hands on her small shoulders.

"Em, I need you to be strong for your Aunt Rachel. She is innocent. You know that, right?"

Emily nodded as little tears began to seep out of the edges of her eyes. Matt reached up and wiped them away.

"Don't be frightened, Emily. We need you to be tough as you can be, just like you were on that long wagon trip from Oak Valley three years ago. We all have to work together as a family. Right now the best thing we can do is cook her wonderful meals and overwhelm her with love. Can you do that?"

"Yes, Uncle Matt, I can do that," the girl agreed, nodding her head enthusiastically. "I have an idea," she said suddenly. Matt nodded indicating she should continue. "Let's take her that quilt she brought with her on the balloon ride. She would like that and it would keep her warm."

Matt leaned over and kissed her on the forehead. "I'm one step ahead of you, Em. I already packed it in the basket that we'll take to the jail."

Emily smiled and hugged him then turned back to the counter to continue helping with dinner. When she and Catherine finished, they spooned shredded beef enchiladas, beans and rice onto plates that they covered tightly and placed in baskets. They added another container of cake slices, and a bottle of wine. Last they added glasses and eating utensils and covered the basket with clean cloths. James picked up the basket and walked to the front door while Matt put a coat on Maddie and picked her up. The two brothers walked to the jail, Matt carrying Maddie and James carrying the baskets. As soon as they entered the jail, the Sheriff walked out of his office.

"What's all this?" the Sheriff asked, a note of irritation in his voice.

"Exactly what I told you I would bring, Sheriff," Matt said, trying as hard as he could to remain pleasant. "Dinner and toiletries for the women."

"Well, I don't know. Let me see what you have in there. Can't just let you give them anything. Who knows, you might be smuggling in a knife or gun."

Rachel was standing at the jail cell bars watching the interaction and rolled her eyes upward. "Jerk!" she whispered to herself.

James held out the baskets as the Sheriff rifled through the contents.

"Looks like these women are going to eat better than I am," the Sheriff said after taking a long time to look at every item.

James glanced at Matt and gave him a look that only the brothers understood.

"Well, Sheriff, if you'd like we have more at home and could bring in a plate for you and your Deputy," James offered.

"That is mighty kind of you," the Sheriff grinned. "But I wouldn't want you to go to any trouble...."

"No trouble at all," James responded. "I'll head back now while you let the ladies and Matt into your office where they can eat their dinner." He stepped over to the door and opened it when the Sheriff spoke.

"Now, now, there. The judge didn't say anything about Dr. Nash getting to use my office, just Mrs. Bradshaw with her husband and child," the Sheriff protested. James stepped back inside, closed the door and stood next to Matt, his arms across his chest. The two brothers stared hard at the Sheriff who realized he wasn't going to get his enchilada dinner if he wasn't more cooperative. "Oh, all right," he conceded. "They can both eat in my office. But as soon as Dr. Nash is done eating she goes back in the cell."

The brothers nodded and James left while Matt went into the office to set up dinner. The Sheriff let the two women out of the cell and guided them to his office where Matt had laid out a lace tablecloth, china dishes, silverware, napkins and glasses on the large wooden desk. Holding Maddie in one arm he was dishing up their dinner when the women walked in. Rachel ran to him and threw her arms around the two of them. Maddie squealed and didn't seem to mind a bit being inside their human sandwich as Rachel and Matt embraced. Rachel kissed both of them over and over.

"Ladies, your dinner is served," Matt declared as soon as Rachel stopped kissing him. She took Maddie from his arms and sat down with Maddie in her lap. The little girl cooed as the two women ate quickly, testament to their hunger. Earlier Matt had quietly told them not to eat anything the Sheriff gave them. When they finished, they sat back in their chairs and took their time sipping on their wine.

"Mr. Bradshaw, I cannot thank you enough," Henrietta said gesturing to their empty plates. "This was better than I eat on a normal day."

Matt smiled. "I'll tell my sister-in-law that you appreciate her cooking. That will please her."

"And she can bake too. She is quite accomplished," Henrietta added.

Rachel looked over at Matt. "Is this Catherine's doing? I didn't think she baked much."

Matt shook his head. "Emily made the cake. She wanted to do something special for you. She's very upset."

Rachel furrowed her brow and her eyes lost what little luster they had regained. "Poor girl, I'm sure she doesn't understand what is happening."

"Actually she does, that's why she's frightened. But we reassured her that all will turn out well."

"Let's hope so," Rachel responded. "Dear God, let's hope so."

Henrietta stood up and turned to Deputy Alford who was standing at the door. "If you will, please take me back to the cell. I would like to give them some privacy."

The Deputy escorted her out of the office just as James returned with dinner for both the Sheriff and the Deputy. As soon as Henrietta was secured behind bars, the two men dug into their dinners.

After Henrietta departed the office, Matt embraced Rachel once again. After what seemed like an hour, but was only minutes, Rachel pulled back and looked squarely at Matt. She didn't like what she saw.

"Why are you looking at me like that?" she asked.

"Like what?"

"Like I'm already a memory. I won't lose you, Matthew Bradshaw, and I won't lose our daughter. Terrified as I am, I know I will get through this; we will get through this."

Matt grinned his characteristic dimpled smile. He ran his hands through Rachel's hair. "Rach, that's the best thing I've heard all day." He bent down and kissed her passionately, sweetly, to leave her with good remembrances for the long night to come.

Chapter Twelve

Over the next two days, time slowed to the pace of a light desert breeze. With nothing to do in the jail but wait, hours dragged on like days. Mealtime provided their only distraction. The scene repeated itself at each meal with the brothers bringing meals for the women, as well as for the Sheriff and his Deputy. James and Matt's plan of showering the Sheriff with food worked. It didn't take long for the Sheriff to begin treating the women with more civility and allowing Rachel to spend as much time with Matt and Maddie in his office as they wanted. On day three, just after everyone finished lunch and Henrietta returned to her cell, Thomas Singletarry walked in.

"You asked to see me, Sheriff?"

The Sheriff nodded and gestured for him to join him in the office. Matt and Rachel looked up when they walked in; the Sheriff closed the door behind him.

"I have some news," the Sheriff began. "The doctor from Denver has been delayed and Dr. Horgan's body is starting to get ripe. We asked Dr. Norton if he could remove the bullet."

"Dr. Norton? The dentist?" Matt asked.

The Sheriff nodded. "We need to bury Dr. Horgan as soon as possible. Well, he was able to remove the bullet."

"And?" Thomas Singletarry urged him to continue.

The Sheriff reached up and ran his hand around his neck rubbing it. "The bullet was a .44 gauge."

Rachel and Matt looked at one another then back at the Sheriff.

"Rachel's gun uses .45 caliber," Matt stated.

"Yes, I know. I confirmed that when you brought in her gun the other day and with the store owner where you said you bought it."

"Then it wasn't Rachel's gun that killed Dr. Horgan?" Thomas stated the obvious.

"No, it wasn't," the Sheriff acknowledged. "And we think we found the gun that did kill him."

Rachel, Matt and Thomas all leaned forward waiting for him to spill it out. "We searched Dr. Nash's clinic and her home. We found a Remington Derringer in her bedroom bureau drawer. It uses .44 bullets. There was one bullet missing in the barrel."

Rachel let out a gasp; her hand went up and nearly covered her mouth. "What are you saying?"

"Ma'am, what I'm saying is that it doesn't look like you shot Dr. Horgan. It appears that Dr. Nash killed him," the Sheriff said using a tone much kinder than the way he spoke to her on the first day. "I'm real sorry I jumped to the conclusion that you murdered him."

Rachel looked at Matt and her attorney, confusion creeping across her face.

"We are delighted that you no longer consider Mrs. Bradshaw to be the killer," Thomas interceded, "but there are many guns in this town that use .44s and it's not uncommon for a woman to have a gun for protection."

"True," the Sheriff continued, scratching his throat which sported a couple of days beard growth. "But we also found some incriminating evidence showing a long history of a thorny relationship between the two doctors. They used to be married."

"What?!" Rachel shouted, her jaw dropping. "That can't be true. She would have told me."

"Apparently, Mrs. Bradshaw, there is much that she did not tell you," the Sheriff handed her several pieces of paper.

Rachel looked at each one. The first was the marriage license of Henrietta Nash and Charles Horgan, followed by divorce papers and several letters threatening to kill each other if one or the other got in each other's professional way. The final letter, from Charles Horgan to Henrietta, explicitly warned her not to settle in Santa Fe or there would be dire repercussions. Rachel looked up at the men, stunned into silence. Thomas took the papers from her and read them himself.

"This is damning evidence," Thomas concurred after reading everything. "Sheriff, what do you plan to do?"

"I've already spoken with your brother and the prosecuting attorney. They agree that Mrs. Bradshaw should be released. He is dropping the charges against her. Next, we need to see if we can get Dr. Nash to admit her guilt," the Sheriff stated. "It would sure save a lot of time and money if she would fess up." He looked straight at Rachel. "Seems to me, young lady, that the good doctor did not have your best interests in mind. She was going to bring you down with her."

"I-I-I can't believe this," Rachel stammered, hugging Maddie extra tight.

"You should believe it, Rachel," Matt intoned, his voice on the edge of anger. "She was leading you on, all the way to the gallows if necessary."

Rachel looked from Matt to the attorney and the Sheriff, then back at Matt. They all nodded. "Sheriff, please take me back to the cell and allow me some privacy. I need to speak with her. If in fact she did this, I won't leave this jail house until she admits her responsibility. I have to find out the truth. I have to hear it from her."

"With all due respect ma'am, you don't have to do that, we have our ways of getting criminals to admit their guilt," the Sheriff offered.

"I'm sure you do," Rachel responded a little more sternly. "But that won't be necessary. If she did it, I will get her to confess. Now if you'll let me into the cell, I want to do this before I change my mind."

Matt reached out to take Maddie, but Rachel wouldn't turn her over. "No Matt. She stays with me. I want Henrietta to look this innocent child in the face and take responsibility for nearly taking away her mother."

"All right, but stay calm. I can see you're getting angry, and if you're angry you won't get her to admit her guilt," Matt said, reaching over and tucking a stray curl behind her ear.

Rachel nodded. "I'm okay." She turned to the Sheriff. "I'm ready for this."

The Sheriff led Rachel out of the office toward the cell, leaving the office door open for the others to hear the conversation. He let her into the cell and locked the cell door behind her, returning to his office with the Deputy in tow.

Henrietta looked up when Rachel entered with Maddie. Rachel sat down next to her on the bench and turned Maddie so that Henrietta had to look the child in the face.

"How could you do this?" Rachel asked, steadying her voice, looking Henrietta in the eye.

"What do you mean?" Henrietta answered, a jittery, nervous tone in her voice. The woman's lips were pressed tightly together in a hard line, as though parting them a little would allow the truth to escape.

"You know exactly what I mean, Henrietta. The dentist removed the bullet in Horgan's head. It was a .44 and the Sheriff found your Remington Derringer in your bedroom bureau drawer. It uses .44 bullets. There was one bullet missing, the one in Horgan's head. "

"I'm surprised at you, Rachel! That doesn't mean I did it," the doctor responded haughtily, smugness seeping into her voice.

"No, but they also found your marriage license and divorce papers from Horgan along with several letters where you threatened to kill one another."

What little color was left in Henrietta's face drained, leaving her a pale shade of soured cream. She said nothing, defiantly looking Rachel in the eye.

"Why Henrietta? Why did you pull me into your war with him? I get that the two of you had a bitter divorce and that you hated him. I know how he treated women, but that was no reason to kill him."

"You didn't know him the way I did," Henrietta whispered looking down at the floor, strands of her blonde hair falling across her face. "He hit me every chance he got. He was jealous of me and wanted me to cook and clean for him instead of practicing medicine. When I left him he swore he would destroy me and now, he has."

"Why didn't you tell me the truth?"

"I never lied to you."

"Yes, you did. You lied by not telling me the whole story when I asked about how you knew him. You lied by omission."

Henrietta sat stone-faced for several minutes then looked up at Rachel.

"At one point I planned to tell you but, but, but…."

"But what?" Rachel asked.

"All was going so well, I didn't want to ruin it. If you knew about my past with Charles, you might not have wanted to work in the clinic, and I did not want you to leave. You don't realize what a fine healer you are."

"So better to suck me and my family into your web of deceit rather than be honest?"

"I never intended to harm you, Rachel."

"But you did. How could you? Look this precious child in the face." Henrietta would not look at

Maddie. "I mean it, Henrietta. Look her in the face. Look at her innocence."

Henrietta looked up at Maddie who grinned her baby smile causing tears to fall down Henrietta's face.

"I get that Horgan abused you. He was awful. But you were prepared to deprive this child of her mother, me, to get even with him instead of admitting to your guilt. How can you call yourself a doctor whose purpose is to heal when you were prepared to harm, to harm me, who has done everything I could to help you?"

Henrietta burst out into hard, loud sobs that shook her whole body. The sobbing scared Maddie who began to cry. Rachel turned the child around and hugged her tightly, rubbing her little head and back to soothe her.

"It's all right, sweetie. We're going home soon." Rachel got up and walked to the front of the cell, then turned back. "Do the right thing, Henrietta. Admit your guilt and save this town the indignity of a trial. I don't want to testify against you, but rest assured, I will if you plead innocent. Because clearly, you are not."

Henrietta's sobs grew louder even though she held her face in her hands, looking down at the floor. Her body shook with the cascade of tears. Even so, Rachel heard her distinctly say, "Yes, yes, I will. I'm so sorry."

248

"Sheriff?" Rachel called out the cell door. In moments the Deputy arrived at the door, unlocked it and let Rachel out. The Deputy stepped inside the cell and gathered up Rachel's belongings. The others walked out of the Sheriff's office where the Deputy handed Rachel's belongings to Matt. "I think she is ready to confess," Rachel said quietly. She rubbed her eyes with a thumb and forefinger; they felt hot and weary.

The Sheriff nodded and turned to Thomas Singletarry. "Counsel, I need a witness to the confession. Will you accompany me into the cell of the accused?"

"Gladly," Thomas answered. Once again the Deputy unlocked the cell door, letting the two men inside.

As Rachel, Matt and Maddie headed to the front door they heard a piercing cackle of laughter, not unlike the Wicked Witch of the West in the Wizard of Oz. They turned back and saw Henrietta standing defiantly in the middle of the cell, her fists planted on her hips. Her eyes glittered like a snake right before it strikes. She screamed, "Yes, I did it! I killed the son of a bitch and he deserved it!" Rachel and Matt turned and rushed out the door, the echo of Henrietta's shrill laughter echoing in their ears. They no sooner stepped outside than Rachel felt her knees go weak. She handed Maddie to Matt right before she passed out and fell to the ground.

Chapter Thirteen

Rachel awoke in her own bed, Maddie sleeping between her and Matt. When she opened her eyes she saw Matt watching her.

"What time is it?" she whispered.

"Friday, probably around 8 a.m."

"How could that be? Didn't we leave the jail on Wednesday?"

Matt nodded. "Do you remember fainting outside the jail?"

She shook her head. "I fainted? How embarrassing."

"Joe from the blacksmith's was walking by when it happened; he ran back to the shop to bring a wagon and horse. We loaded you in and brought you home. I put you to bed and you've been sleeping ever since. Did you get any sleep in jail?"

Rachel shook her head. "Not that I remember." Rachel closed her eyes and smiled. "It's good to be home," she murmured before she fell back to sleep.

Matt got up, dressed and left Rachel and Maddie to share their dreams. He no sooner started making coffee than James knocked at the door.

"How is she doing?" James asked when he stepped inside.

"She's exhausted, but all right. Coffee?" Matt asked holding up a coffee cup.

"No, I gotta get back. The whole Medina clan is at the house waiting to visit Rachel as soon as she is up to it."

"She would like that, but I'm not sure when she's gonna wake up again. She said she doesn't remember getting much sleep in jail. I'm guessing that she didn't get any. Why don't you ask Emily to come over and she can let you know when Rachel wakes up for good."

James nodded, patted his brother on the shoulder and headed out the front door.

* * *

Around noon Matt heard another knock on the door. He opened it to find that James had brought Emily, Catherine and the twins, along with Leah, Rebecca, Sarah and Louisa – all looking very anxious. Cornelius August stood in back. They stepped inside and Catherine introduced Matt to Leah and Rebecca. Matt introduced everyone to Cornelius, identifying him as the person who brought Rachel to 19th century New Mexico.

"How is Rachel?" Leah asked.

"We have been so worried about her," Sarah chimed in before Matt could answer.

"She's very tired but otherwise fine. Would you like to see her?" Matt asked the group. Everyone nodded. "Then I'll have her come down. She woke up an hour ago and is taking a bath. I'll go up and see if she's presentable."

"I'm perfectly presentable!" Rachel called out as she descended the stairs in her robe, her damp hair falling down her back.

The group ran to the base of the stairs. As soon as Rachel reached the floor, the group threw themselves around her, each giving her a tight hug. She looked around at the women from Moralito.

"What are you all doing here?" she asked.

"We came as soon as we heard you were arrested," Louisa responded.

Rachel shook her head in confusion. "Why?"

Rebecca stepped forward. "Because Rachel, you are like a sister and daughter to us now. We came as soon as Catherine wired us."

Rachel looked over at Catherine who held one baby while James held the other. Catherine smiled and Rachel knew not to ask why she contacted her family. Though she thought it unnecessary for them to come to

Santa Fe, nevertheless, she was happy to see them. She looked around and saw Cornelius.

"Oh my goodness, Cornelius, you're here too!"

"Yes, Rachel, I'm here. I am sorry I was not able to help you with your latest predicament. Magic can do only so much," he responded.

James turned to him. "You mean you can fly a woman between centuries, but you can't help her get out of a wrongful murder charge?"

August nodded sadly. "I'm afraid so."

"Oh, Cornelius," Rachel reached out and laid her hand on his forearm. "Please don't fault yourself. You couldn't have prevented what happened or helped for that matter."

The jeweler nodded and tried to smile. Rachel felt a tug on her sleeve. She looked down to see Emily standing there with tears running down her face.

"Oh, Emily, you sweet girl. I'm okay," Rachel wiped her tears. "No need to cry."

Emily ran her arms around Rachel and hugged her tightly. "I was worried about you." Rachel grinned and placed her hands on the girl's head.

"Well I was a little worried too, but everything is fine now."

Emily looked up and scanned Rachel's face to make sure it was the truth.

"Honestly, Em, I'm fine. You know, if it hadn't been for all those cakes and cookies you baked I might still be in jail. You made a great impression on the Sheriff and his Deputy. They said you are the best baker in Santa Fe and I have to agree with them."

Emily beamed and released her aunt as the group chuckled.

"Speaking of goodies, we brought some of our wine," Rebecca offered. "Why don't we have a toast to Rachel?" She handed the bottle to Matt.

"Good idea!" Matt said. "All of you go sit in the parlor while James and I play butler."

"I'll help you," Rachel started toward the kitchen.

"Oh no, you don't," Matt turned her around toward the parlor. "You sit. James and I can do this."

The two men took the bottle into the kitchen. A few minutes later they emerged carrying trays of glasses filled with wine, a glass of juice for Emily, and sweets. Everyone lifted their glasses and toasted Rachel. Just as Rachel finished her glass, Maddie hollered from upstairs. Rachel grinned.

"Guess somebody woke up. I'll be back in a minute." Rachel went upstairs and brought a fussy Maddie down. As soon as she saw everyone she brightened and giggled.

"Look how she has grown!" Leah remarked. The Moralito women cooed over Maddie, each taking a turn holding her.

Rachel looked around the group and suddenly remembered the whisperwind's message from a few days earlier. *'Trust.'* Hard as it was she did trust and in the end it worked. Words could not describe the elation she felt being back with her family, her *whole* family.

* * *

The next day Rachel was feeling much like her old self and told Matt she was going over to the clinic to pack up her herbs, bottles and belongings at the clinic.

"No need," Matt responded. "Look on the back porch. James and I packed everything while you were sleeping like a bear hibernating in winter."

Rachel grinned. "Thanks," and headed to the back porch.

On the porch Rachel found everything she had stored at the clinic, including her cherished book of remedies. She stood back, placed her hands on her hips and wondered if she would do any healing again. A few minutes later Matt walked onto the porch with an older man Rachel did not know. She looked up at Matt with a question on her face, lifting her shoulders.

"Rachel, this is Señor Morales. He is sick and needs your help," Matt said. "I'll bring out a couple of chairs."

Rachel started to protest; she wasn't set up to do any remedies. But Matt was gone before she opened her mouth and the man looked at her with genuine desperation. As soon as Matt returned with chairs she sat the man down and sat down herself, opposite him.

"Señor Morales, what is the problem?" she asked gently.

"I think a bruja has cursed me. I feel bad," he said quietly, rubbing his throat. His voice was weak and hoarse, sounding like it hurt to talk.

"Why do you think it was a bruja?"

"Because I have never been sick and now I am. Do you believe in witches?" he asked, searching her face.

Rachel didn't answer immediately. One thing she learned from the Medina healers was that if a patient believed he had been the victim of a bruja or the evil eye, the healer must believe too, in order to help the patient get well.

"Yes, Señor Morales, if you believe you have been cursed by a bruja, then I believe you have."

The man let out a sigh; his lips curved up into a slight smile as he nodded, seemingly satisfied with her answer.

"Now tell me what is bothering you."

The man reached up and rubbed his throat. "It hurts here, and here," he said moving his fingers over to the sides of his neck. "It hurts real bad."

Rachel nodded as she listened. She leaned over to him. "May I touch your neck?" He nodded and Rachel placed her fingers along his throat area, pressing lightly where he indicated it hurt. She could feel swelling.

"Give me a few minutes to unpack my supplies and I'll give you something that will help you recover." The man nodded and sat back in the chair.

Rachel dug into her baskets and the cases that Matt and James packed. Finally she found a jar of alferillo, also called fillery. She spooned out a good portion, placed it in a small muslin bag, and tied it shut with string. She turned back to the man.

"This is alferillo," she began, showing him the ingredients of the jar and handing him the little muslin bag. "Go home and boil a pot of water, and add the alferillo to the water. Let it steep for at least ten minutes and then strain it through a cloth. You can drink it as a warm tea sweetened with a little honey if you wish, or let it cool and use it to gargle. Do that four to five times a day. Keep it in a cool place and use all the liquid until it is gone. You will start to feel better in two or three days."

The man looked down at the bag and back up at Rachel. "This will get rid of the bruja? The witch will leave me alone?"

Rachel nodded confidently. "Yes, it should. If it doesn't, please come back and see me."

"I have no money to pay you."

"That's all right, Señor, helping you feel better will be payment enough."

The man nodded and got up. Rachel led him out the front of the house. As she was closing the front door, Matt appeared at her side.

"Do you plan to set up a clinic here at the house?"

"Good question," she turned and looked up at him. "I hadn't planned to, in fact, after the debacle with Henrietta I wasn't even sure I wanted to do this anymore. But now Santa Fe is without a physician. I can hardly turn anyone away."

"You're right," he said watching her and rubbing his chin, something he did whenever he was thinking. "You can't keep seeing people and making your remedies on the back porch. What if I build you some shelves along the back wall of the kitchen? You can put your jars there and see people in the kitchen."

"Would you do that for me?" Rachel asked, excitement lacing her voice.

Matt bent over and kissed her on the head. "I would do anything for you. Don't you know that by now?"

Rachel raised her head and kissed him tenderly. "Thank you, sweetie. It would mean the world to me."

"So how are you going to get patients? Advertise in the newspaper?"

"Hah!" she laughed. "I doubt the newspaper would take my ad given what I did to them. I'd like to be low-key about this. Señor Morales didn't say how he found me, but if he was able to, I imagine others will as well. Let's just wait and see what happens, okay?"

"Good plan," Matt responded. "Meanwhile I'll find some boards to build you shelving." He kissed her and headed out the front door.

A short time later Rachel heard a knock on the front door. She answered, thinking Matt needed her to open the door for him to haul in wood, or that it was possibly another person with an illness. She was surprised to see Cora Sandoval, her friend the hotel owner, standing there. Rachel noticed that her friend did not look happy. Her lips were pursed tightly in a sour expression.

"Cora, hello! Please come in," Rachel opened the door wide and stepped aside to allow her friend to enter.

"Rachel, I am not here on a social call," Cora stately sharply, refusing to step inside. "I am here to tell you how disappointed I and all the ladies of Santa Fe are in you. We believed you and you scorned our faith." Cora held her head high and looked down her nose at Rachel.

Rachel slightly shook her head thinking she had heard incorrectly. "Cora, what are you talking about?"

"You know perfectly well what I am talking about," Cora said, a tone of aggravation in her voice. Her nostrils flared.

Rachel knitted her brows together in concern. "No, I don't know. What's wrong? Why are you disappointed in me?"

"You told me that Dr. Nash was legitimate. I took you to my friends and we supported the paper running her letter. We believed you, Rachel. And she turned out to be a murderer and charlatan just as our dear departed Dr. Horgan said she was."

"Now hold it just a minute, Cora," Rachel began. "Henrietta Nash was no charlatan. She was a real doctor with a real medical degree. How was I to know she would murder Charles Horgan?"

"You worked with her, you should have known she was of poor character," Cora responded snootily.

"That's not fair, Cora. She wasn't of poor character. She was a good doctor and if Horgan hadn't demeaned her in the paper none of this would have happened. She was married to him and he used to beat her. Did you know that? Well I didn't, and I had no way of knowing what she would do. It was simply a tragedy, nothing more."

"A tragedy is right! But that does not change the fact that we had confidence in you, obviously misguided confidence. And now we have no town doctor. We hold you responsible for our being in this terrible situation."

"Seriously, Cora?" Rachel groaned. "How can you say that? This is no more my fault than it would be if the wind blew down a flagpole!"

Cora cocked her head up and glared back at Rachel. "Mrs. Bradshaw, it is your fault and nothing you say will change my mind. If I am sorry about anything, it is that I allowed you to rope me into your devious plot. You have embarrassed me amongst my friends."

"Cora-----"

"Good day, Mrs. Bradshaw. There is nothing more to say. Please do not call on me again as neither I, nor my friends, will welcome your visit." With that, Cora spun around and marched away, never looking back. Rachel watched her and saw Matt pass her in the wagon loaded with wood for the shelving. Matt took off his hat and nodded to Cora; she ignored him. He pulled the wagon in front of the house, hopped out and walked up to Rachel.

"What's up with her?" he asked, pointing his thumb backwards toward Cora.

"I just lost every friend I have in Santa Fe," Rachel responded despondently. "I'll tell you later. Do you need help bringing in the wood?"

Matt saw the look of unhappiness on Rachel's face. He bent over and kissed her on the cheek. "Tell ya what. I'll bring in the wood, you pour us a couple of glasses of that good bourbon and you can tell me about it."

Rachel nodded and headed into the house in search of the bourbon and glasses.

* * *

Rachel leaned against Matt's shoulder as they sipped their bourbon. She finished repeating the conversation with Cora and let out a soft moan.

262

"The worst part of it is that Cora is going to turn all the other women against me. I won't have a single friend left in this town," Rachel sighed.

"You don't need them," Matt tried to reassure her, rubbing her shoulder. "You have me, Catherine, James, Emily, Maddie and the twins."

Rachel smiled meekly. "True and I'm grateful for all of you. But it's also nice to have people who aren't family."

"Don't forget Cornelius," Matt added, trying to cheer her up.

"Oh yes, dear Cornelius. I wonder if he can use his magic to make people like me again."

"I doubt it. He's better at the big stuff."

"Yeah. Oh well. Not much I can do. If Cora is going to behave like this she never was a friend anyway."

"Now you're thinking with your head on straight," Matt said encouragingly. "Besides, by the time I finish your shelves and you're set up for patients, you won't have time for socializing."

Rachel picked up her head and looked at him quizzically. "Huh?"

"You're going to have the most beautiful shelves in town and all the sick people will want to see them and come pouring into our house to admire them."

"Hah!" Rachel laughed. "That's a good one!"

"My dear," Matt whispered into her ear, "you're going to have a nice little clinic going and truly, after a while, you won't mind not having all those friends who would walk away for the pettiest reasons." He kissed her on the side of her head. "And if Cora Sandoval or any of her friends get sick and come to you for treatment, you can refuse to help them."

"Matt!!!" Rachel quickly turned her head around and looked at him with horror. "I could never do that!" But she saw that Matt was smiling his devilish grin and she realized she'd been had.

* * *

A few days later Rachel was playing with Maddie when a knock sounded on the front door. She opened the door to find Señor Morales standing there holding a live rabbit. Rachel looked at the rabbit, then up at the man who now sported rosy cheeks.

"Señor Morales! How are you feeling? Please, please come in," Rachel said opening the door wide. She could feel Maddie holding onto the back of her skirt. She looked down to see her peering around the side, eyes wide.

264

The man stepped inside and held out the small rabbit by the ears to Rachel. "Mrs. Bradshaw, gracias for getting rid of the bruja. I am all better. I bring you this coñejo, as my thanks." He thrust the rabbit into Rachel's arms.

"This isn't necessary, Señor Morales. What am I to do with a rabbit?" she said looking down at the little animal squirming in her arms.

"Cook it of course. Rabbit is delicious!"

"No-o-o-o-o!" Maddie wailed and stepped in front of Rachel and held her little hands up to the animal. "I want wabbit!" she cried.

"That is very kind of you, but really, you didn't need to go to so much trouble. I was happy to help you," Rachel said hoping he would take back the rabbit before Maddie became attached to it.

"Mi placer," the man responded, bowed, tipped his hat and backed out of the house. "Gracias again." And he was gone.

"Mama, Mama, I want wabbit!" Maddie cooed, holding up her arms, a giggle in her little voice.

Rachel let out a sigh, realizing they had a new pet because there was no way she was going to cook Bugs Bunny. She led Maddie into the living room and set the bunny down on the floor. Maddie sat down immediately and began to pet the little creature. She lay down next to it and stared at the bunny, nose to nose. The rabbit wiggled its nose; Maddie wiggled her own nose in response. For several minutes, whatever the rabbit did, Maddie repeated, giggling with each movement. Rachel had never seen her daughter so mesmerized.

"What do you want to name it?" Rachel asked.

"Wabbit," Maddie responded, not missing a beat.

And so Wabbit joined the Bradshaw household and Matt was tasked with building a bunny house.

Chapter Fourteen

December 1884

"Matt, are you serious? You really think we can move back to Oak Valley next year? Is the house that close to being done?" Rachel was so excited she could hardly contain herself.

"That's what the architect tells me," Matt responded. "He thinks the house will be done by mid-year, unless you come up with any more 21st century modernizations that will hold up construction."

Rachel grinned, knowing that her insistence on indoor plumbing and closets and the other amenities she requested had caused numerous delays. The idea of an indoor toilet and being able to take a bath without hauling in buckets of water made her almost giddy.

"Are you going to miss living here?" he asked reaching over and running his hand behind her neck and drawing her close.

"Yes and no. I will miss Catherine and James and Emily. I will miss them terribly. Catherine especially has been my rock these past few months. I don't know how I could have gotten through without her. You were right. I didn't need those other friends, and I won't miss them snubbing me as they walk down the street. "

"And your patients?"

"Once the new doctor comes to town next spring I'm sure many people will start going to him with their ailments. My patients will have no choice after we leave. It would be awful to leave if there was no one here to care for them, but there will be. So I'll be able to go knowing I'm not abandoning them."

Matt bent over and wrapped her in his arms. She slipped her arms around his neck.

"Good, that's good," he responded, rubbing her back and speaking gently into her ear. "Now, if you can spare a couple of hours let's head up the mountain while it's clear and cut down a tree for Christmas."

Rachel broke out of his embrace with a big grin etched on her face. "Great idea! I'll go put a coat and hat on Maddie, and you bring round the wagon." Before he could respond Rachel was running up the stairs calling for Maddie.

An hour later they were walking through the woods in search of the perfect Christmas tree. It was a cold, clear day; the air was thin and sharp like jagged ice. The sun hung low, reflecting stillness all around; the living silence of the forest surrounded them. Matt held Maddie in one arm, the hatchet in the other.

"Dat one!" Maddie called pointing to a tree.

"Too tall, little one," Matt responded as he kept going up the hill.

"Dat one, Papa!" Maddie called out a few minutes later.

"Too small," Matt grunted, continuing on his way.

"Dat one?" Maddie tried again.

This time Matt stopped and walked around the tree, inspecting it from top to bottom. "I think you found the perfect tree, Maddie," Matt said turning to look her in the face. Maddie smiled. "Hold her, will you?" Matt asked, transferring her over to Rachel. Maddie squirmed to get down.

"Oh no, you don't," Rachel admonished her. "Papa has to cut down the tree. We'll stand back here so we don't get hurt, okay?" She stood back several feet giving Matt plenty of room to wield the hatchet.

The first crack of the hatchet reverberated through the trees. Matt hacked away at the tree until it was ready to topple. He looked over at his wife and child. "Ready?" he grinned.

"Ready!" Rachel called just as Matt pressed on the tree and let it fall. Maddie let out a squeal of childish joy and clapped her hands.

Matt reached over, picked up the end of the tree and dragged it back to the wagon where he loaded it in the back. On the way home Matt and Rachel sang Christmas carols, much to Maddie's delight. Just when they had sung all the songs they could remember, Rachel broke out with a new one.

"Rudolph, the red nosed reindeer, had a very shiny nose…" she began.

Matt looked over at her with a big question mark on his face while Maddie clapped her hands in glee through every verse. Rachel sang the whole song while Matt grinned and shook his head. When Rachel finished he remarked, "Let me guess, that's a 21st century carol?"

"Yep," Rachel answered cheerfully. "Actually it was written in the 20th century. It's one of my favorites. Maddie's red nose reminded me of the song."

* * *

Later that evening, after Matt set up the tree in the parlor and they had finished dinner, they found their box of Christmas decorations and began to decorate the tree. Unlike the years before Maddie's birth and the previous year when Maddie was too small to help, this year it took longer than ever. Maddie wanted to place every ornament on the tree. When they couldn't fit any more ornaments or bows on the tree, Matt and Rachel stood back and examined the tree.

"I'd say Maddie picked out the perfect tree," Matt mused, his arms crossed over his chest.

"I agree; our girl has talent," Rachel replied, walking around the tree.

"Speaking of our girl…." Matt jutted his chin toward the settee where Maddie lay fast asleep, a precious little smile etched on her strawberry pink lips.

"Tell you what, I'll put her to bed and you put another log on the fire, okay?" Rachel arched one eyebrow and turned her head slightly. The corners of Rachel's lips curved upwards, and her eyes sparkled with her best "come hither" look. But before Matt could respond she scooped up Maddie and took her upstairs.

She returned a while later dressed in an emerald green silk robe that barely covered her breasts. Matt looked up from the fireplace and grinned. He stood up and was at her side before she knew it. He turned her toward him and laid his hands on her breasts, massaging her nipples with his thumbs through the silk. Rachel threw back her head just as Matt bent down and began kissing her neck. He moved one hand down the front of her robe, untying it. His hand kept going down until he reached between her legs and began fondling her. Rachel let out a little cry of ecstasy; her legs began to falter but Matt caught her and lay her down on the rug. They made

271

love until they fell into an exhausted sleep serenaded by the crackling fire.

* * *

Christmas morning, Matt and Rachel gave Maddie her gifts to open first: a doll, a book and a doll house that Matt built for her. Her eyes widened with childish glee as she opened each gift.

"Where's Wabbit's pwesent?" she asked looking up at her parents.

Matt and Rachel looked at each other in a slight panic. "Here it is," Matt responded quickly, taking one of the ribbons and handing it to her. "This goes around his neck."

Maddie giggled, got up and walked over to Wabbit, sat down to put the ribbon on him. Matt joined her. "Like this Maddie," he explained taking the ribbon and tying the ribbon around the rabbit's neck. He knotted it so that Maddie wouldn't accidentally pull on it and choke the rabbit to death. "And you my dear," he said looking at Rachel. "Here." He handed Rachel a small rectangular box also tied in a colorful ribbon.

Rachel squealed as she opened her gift. Inside she found an elegant rosewood fountain pen inlaid with mother-of-pearl. In tiny letters it was marked,

272

Waterman. "It's gorgeous. And it's a Waterman. We have them in my time. Where did you get this?" she asked looking up at him.

"I found it on the utter-net," he responded dryly with all the seriousness of a preacher intent on saving souls.

Rachel bellowed. "It's internet, honey, not utternet! But seriously, where did you find it?"

Matt smiled sheepishly. "Oh, let's just say your friend Cornelius was most helpful."

"Of course, he would be," Rachel grinned, turning the pen over and over in her hand. "I had a collection of my grandfather's old pens. I loved them. He had a similar one, but not nearly as nice."

"You'll need this if you want to write with it," he said handing her another box.

Rachel opened it to find several ink wells and a dropper for transferring the ink from the well to the pen chamber. She beamed up at him.

"You know in my time, fountain pens are still around, but they're not that popular anymore. Most pens already have ink in them. We would throw them away when the ink ran out."

Matt grimaced, a look of disgust on his face. "Why would you throw away a perfectly good pen?"

"Because they aren't perfectly good anymore. The most popular pens are roller ball or ball point pens and they don't look anything like this. They're cheap. When the ink is gone there's no way to refill it."

"What a waste."

"True, but it's very convenient not to have to refill pens. The technology has made many people quite wealthy."

Matt's look of disgust disappeared. "Go on...."

"Think about it. People are dependent on the pens and have to buy new ones whenever they run out of ink. It's a constant turnover. Companies like Waterman, Sheaffer and Parker have made millions."

"From pens?"

"Yep, from little ole pens." She looked up from her pen to see the wheels turning in Matt's eyes.

"What are those companies again?"

"Why?"

"Several times you have mentioned companies that you know will be successful. Perhaps I should buy stock in one of the pen companies."

"Smart man. I knew I loved you for more than your charm and good looks." She got up on her knees, leaned in and kissed him. "As soon as I figure out how this thing works I'll write up a list." She looked down at the pen and held it gently in her hand, getting the feel of what it would be like to write with it. "Oh! Oh! I almost forgot. You have to open your gift."

Rachel leaned over to the tree and dragged out a box tied with a red ribbon. She held it out to Matt. He deftly opened the box and took out a new leather belt, tooled with a design of two horses pulling a wagon holding three people and adorned with a two-toned silver buckle depicting Rachel's hot air balloon that brought her to the 19th century. Matt looked closely at every detail.

"This is your balloon, is it not?"

Rachel nodded.

"And the wagon and horses, that's our trip up here from Oak Valley?"

Again Rachel nodded.

"Where did you get this? Or rather who made it?"

She smiled with pride. "You're not the only one who visited Cornelius. He obviously did well this Christmas. He made the buckle then he and I sketched out the design to go on the leather. He took the design and buckle to a leatherworking friend who tooled the design on the belt." She leaned inward to try to see the expression on his face. "Do you like it?"

Matt looked up at her with the most nostalgic look she had ever seen on his face. His sapphire eyes glistened; he momentarily seemed lost in his own world, in a place far from Santa Fe. Then he blinked and returned to the present. "Like it? Rachel, I will cherish it always." He stood up, removed his belt and replaced it with the new one. He looked down at it, fingering the tooling and belt buckle. "What made you think to have a new belt made?"

Rachel pointed to the one on the floor that Matt had removed. "You've been wearing that one since the day I met you. It's getting pretty ratty; I figured you could use a new one."

"Ratty?"

"You know what I mean. Nasty."

Matt looked down at the well-worn belt on the floor. "I know it's old, but is it that bad?"

Rachel laughed. "Yep, that's why I had a new one made."

At that moment Wabbit hopped over to the belt on the floor and began sniffing it; before they could stop him, he bit into the belt. Matt reached down and tried to keep the rabbit from chomping on the belt, but Wabbit wouldn't let go, letting out a rabbit growl that sounded more like a gurgle than a menacing snarl. "Guess it's his now," Matt smiled. "So much for having a second belt."

Chapter Fifteen

Spring 1885

Spring came early to Santa Fe. Along the streets and in the nearby hills flowers emerged, flushing the landscape in vibrant color. The higher temperatures enticed people to linger outside, taking in the warmer, but still crisp air. For Rachel, it meant she could gather her herbs earlier than usual and restock her supply of medicinals.

After lunch one day she dropped Maddie off at James and Catherine's home and headed into the hills with her basket, knife and scissors. She didn't have to go far before she found chamiso hediondo for pain, alamo for arthritis, mejorana for stomach ache, and numerous other plants. For several hours she took cuttings of all her primary herbs as well as ones she didn't use often, but nevertheless needed for unusual maladies. An hour later, her basket brimming with fragrant herbs and plant cuttings; she headed back down the hills to Santa Fe, taking a different route than the one she took earlier. The sun was mid-sky, descending toward the tops of the mountain peaks; clouds glowed rosy pink against the powder blue. She rounded a curve and heard a distinctive whimpering that stopped her cold. Rachel looked up and around thinking it could be the whisperwind, but it wasn't whispering, it was definitely crying. Slowly she moved toward the weeping until she came upon a very young boy, alone, huddled with his knees tight against his chest, and his arms hugging his knees. He looked to be about five or six years old. His black shiny hair was pulled back with a leather strap; hanging in a ponytail down his back. He wore clothing made of animal hide decorated with seed beads in diagonal stripes of alternating colors. On his feet he wore leather moccasins. Rachel accidentally stepped on a twig that cracked. The boy looked up, his dark eyes clouded with fear. He held up a hand to block Rachel coming closer. She stopped.

"It's okay, I won't harm you," she said softly. "Do you speak English?"

The boy nodded, continuing to hold up his hand. He watched her warily. Rachel kneeled down to his level and set down her basket.

"Why are you out here all alone?" Rachel asked as gently as she could.

"I sent away," he mumbled, looking down.

"From your family?"

"Only had mother; she died. Elders sent me away," he answered looking up at her, a tear seeping out the side of one eye. Long dark lashes circled his watery eyes. Although his skin was a smooth tawny color, his eyes were the pale gray of a wolf, with spokes of yellow circling the irises.

Rachel gasped. "Why would they do that?"

"Father was white man. Elders not let him live with Mother. Tribe says I am not a real *Tinde*. Am half breed."

"Is there an English word for *Tinde*?"

"*Tinde* mean the people. Mother say Spanish and Americans call us Jicarilla Apache."

"Jicarilla Apache? They live way up on the other side of the Sangre de Christo Mountains, far away. Who brought you here?" Rachel inched forward to see if the boy would let her come near. He didn't budge, but would not look up.

"Son of elder, Gian-nah-tah. Told me would be better I die," he said, his voice cracking.

"How long have you been here?" Rachel pressed.

"Two days," he sobbed.

"Oh my God, you poor thing." Rachel watched the young boy cry and felt her heart breaking. She inched toward him, gauging if he would move. He didn't. "What is your name?"

"Ish-kay-nay," he sniveled, rubbing his sleeve under his nose.

"Ish-kay-nay, I will not leave you here to die."

"I must. Gian-nah-tah say I do not deserve to live."

"That is not true. You do deserve to live." Rachel inched the rest of the way and sat down next to the boy and let him cry until he could cry no more. "Did Gian-nah-tah leave you with any food?" The boy shook his head. "You're very hungry, aren't you?" The boy nodded. She reached into her basket and took out an apple she packed earlier that morning. She offered it to the boy who looked up like a ravenous coyote desperate for food. He took the apple and ate it quickly. She watched him as he ate and saw a quiet strength in the young boy, an acute intelligence in his deep-set eyes.

"Ish-kay-nay, where is your father?"

The boy shook his head. "Don't know. He used to visit, but when mother died Gian-nah-tah took me away."

"Are you saying that your father doesn't know you are gone?"

Ish-kay-nay nodded.

"What is your father's name?"

"Papa."

Rachel sucked in a breath of cool air. She looked at the boy's bright eyes that were pooling with tears and felt a lump forming in her throat. She put her hand out to the boy.

"Come with me, Ish-kay-nay. I will take care of you." The boy shook his head. "Why won't you come with me?"

"Gian-nah-tah say I must die."

"Do you want to die?" Rachel asked. The boy shook his head. "I don't want you to die either. If you come with me, I will not let harm come to you." She stared at the boy's face; he looked up and met her gaze. In a moment of silence that passed between them they never wavered from watching one another. Rachel stood up and held her hand out to the boy. Slowly, cautiously, he got up and took her hand. Rachel bent down, picked up her basket and continued her way home, never letting go of his small hand.

* * *

"Rachel, do you----------" Matt walked into the kitchen but stopped when he saw Ish-kay-nay sitting at the kitchen table. He looked at the boy, then to Rachel who stood near him. The boy looked up at Matt like a scared animal, and jerked his head up at Rachel. She bent down and lightly laid her hand on his back. "It's okay, Ish-kay-nay, keep eating." She stepped over to Matt and motioned him to follow her into the next room.

"Rachel, who is that?" Matt asked, pointing back toward the kitchen.

"I found him in the hills, when I was collecting herbs. He's Jicarilla Apache. The tribe disowned him and abandoned him to die."

"Why did they abandon him?"

"He said his father is white. When his Apache mother died, the tribe threw him out. They could have waited for the father to come and take him, but instead they left him to starve and die on a hillside." Rachel's eyes misted over; she reached up and wiped away a renegade tear. "Oh Matt, I couldn't leave him out there. He's just a little boy."

"I understand, but what did you have in mind for when he's done eating?" Matt looked down into Rachel's eyes, searching for her usual level-headedness.

"Keep him?" Rachel suggested cheerfully.

"Rachel, he's not a puppy! That kid is a Jicarilla. Do you know much about how the Jicarillas feel about whites?"

Rachel shook her head.

"To put it bluntly, they hate whites, they hate the Spanish. That's probably why they didn't want him after his mother died. But we can't simply take him in. Have you any idea how hard it would be to raise a child like that in our society?"

282

"Matthew Bradshaw!" Rachel stood back crossing her arms over chest and looked at Matt coldly. "I'm surprised at you. This boy was cast out of his tribe and left to die, for God's sake. What am I supposed to do with him? Feed him and take him back to the hills to die with a full belly?"

"Rachel, you know I didn't mean it like that. Yeah, it's real unfortunate that his tribe cast him out, but is it our responsibility to save him?" Matt looked imploringly down at Rachel.

Rachel glared at Matt trying to quell the irritation rising in her chest. "Yes, Matthew, it is. I found him and I'm not abandoning him."

"I'm not suggesting you do, but may I suggest we ask the Sheriff if he has heard of any missing Apache boys? Maybe his story isn't true, maybe his father is looking for him. Did you consider that?"

Rachel's growing rage suddenly quelled as she realized he had a good point. "Hmmm, no I didn't," Rachel responded. "Okay, I'm willing to check with the Sheriff, but if he hasn't heard of any missing Indian kids, I'm keeping him."

"No need for you to go anywhere, I have to pass the jail on the way to send a telegram. I'll stop by and ask him."

"Thank you," Rachel murmured, and then looked up in alarm. "Oh, oh. Maddie!"

"What about her?"

"I was in such a rush to bring the boy back here that I forgot to pick up Maddie."

Matt shook his head, his brows knitted together. "Hope this isn't a sign of what is to come." Matt scowled at Rachel. He took his hat off the peg on the wall and placed it on his head. "I'll pick her up on my way back. In the mean time, don't do anything hasty. We will make a decision *together* about the boy once we have more information. Can you agree to that?"

Rachel glanced sideways then up at him. "Yeah, I can agree to that." As Matt headed to the front door she turned and went back into the kitchen where she found Ish-kay-nay staring down at an empty plate. Rachel spooned another serving of pot roast and mashed potatoes onto his plate. He dove into the food. Rachel sat down opposite him and watched him eat. She couldn't imagine how scared he must have been, abandoned, alone in the hills. And even though she knew she brought him to safety, she sensed he was probably still frightened.

An hour later Matt returned with Maddie and found Rachel tidying up in the kitchen. He looked around. "Where's the boy?"

284

"I don't think he slept the past few days. He nearly fell asleep in his second plate of food. I put him upstairs in the extra bedroom to take a nap." She reached out and took Maddie out of Matt's arms. "How's Mama's girl?" she cooed at the child who giggled and cooed back. She placed her in a chair outfitted with a pillow to raise her to the level of the table.

"We agreed to talk about this before you did anything."

"What? I can't let the boy take a nap until we talk? Matt, don't be unreasonable," she brushed him off. "The boy is exhausted and he's scared." She looked up at him, annoyed. She unconsciously held her jaw with a firm bearing; Matt saw it and knew that when Rachel set her jaw like that, she would not back down off whatever was bothering her. He was in for a long talk that would likely turn into an argument.

"So what did you find out from the Sheriff?" she asked as pleasantly as she could.

Matt looked down, the waves of his hair falling forward, and then held his head up. "Sheriff Garcia said that no one is looking for him, at least that he knows."

"What do you think we should do with him?" Rachel asked cautiously, not exactly bating Matt, but giving him an opportunity to start the discussion.

"Not sure," he responded slowly. "Perhaps the new orphans home."

"What new orphans home?"

"The legislative assembly enacted a new orphans home last year. It's under the custody of the Sisters of Charity of Santa Fe."

Rachel pulled her head back and looked at him squarely. "Are you serious?"

"Why wouldn't I be? He needs to be cared for somewhere."

"Yeah? So? Matt, the boy has been traumatized. He needs a home, not an orphanage."

Rachel turned to prepare a plate of food for Maddie.

"Jesus, Rachel, what is going on with you?" he snapped.

Rachel whipped around, her hands planted on her hips. "What's going on with me? I should be asking that of you. I can't believe that you would throw this young boy into an orphanage. Hasn't he been through enough? First, he loses his mother. Has no idea where his father is and then his tribe leaves him on a hillside to die. If you're suggesting that I hand him over to the Sisters, think again because that is not going to happen. Not on my watch. And if that is not what you are suggesting then you need to make yourself clear." She

286

sucked in a big breath of air before she finished. "I want to understand exactly what you are suggesting before you totally piss me off."

"It looks like I've done that already."

"Not quite. I'm actually trying really hard to keep my temper in check until I hear you out." Rachel drew in another large breath of air and held a lock on Matt's eyes; Rachel could see they were turning a deep shade of blue; a shade she knew only too well when Matt's ire was raised.

"All right," he said as calmly as he could, "I am suggesting we take the boy to the Sisters and ask them if they would take him in and care for him."

Rachel let out a whoosh of air. "Not going to happen! I am not about to take that scared little boy over to the nuns and pawn him off on them. This boy needs love and affection, something he won't get in an orphanage. Meanwhile, I'm trying to build his trust and make him feel safe. We take him to the nuns and he won't trust us at all."

"What trust? He just got here!" Matt shouted.

"Yeah, well, I'm still trying!" she shouted back.

The two of them stood in the kitchen glaring at one another. Maddie began clapping her hands; her newest way of communicating she was hungry. Rachel turned and looked at her, took her own hands and clasped them around Maddie's and rubbed noses with her.

"Yes, sweetie, dinner is almost ready."

Rachel looked up at Matt. "You need to do some soul searching, Matt. We have an opportunity to help a boy desperately in need. He needs charity and love and we are just the people to give it to him. To give him a family. Think about that."

Matt didn't utter a word, but continued to glower at Rachel, his face as pink as the shade the Sange de Cristo Mountains turn at sunset when the western sun rays hit at just the right angle. He turned and walked out of the kitchen and out the front door, slamming the door behind him. Rachel turned back to Maddie, a tiny grin of triumph on her lips. Maddie's eyes were wide, staring at something behind Rachel. She whipped around to see the boy standing there, tears running down his face. She realized he had probably heard much of the argument. Slowly she walked over, kneeled in front of him and wiped away his tears.

"Nothing to worry about. Come." Rachel stood up, placed her hand on his back and led him over to Maddie who was mesmerized by him. Rachel kneeled down next to the boy.

"Ish-kay-nay, this is our daughter, Maddie."

The boy leaned slightly forward to get a better look at Maddie who leaned forward to get a closer look at him. Maddie reached out and touched his face, and mimicking Rachel she brushed away a tear still lingering on his cheek.

"Ish," Maddie said.

The boy reached up and placed his hand over Maddie's. The two children stared at one another for a few moments until Maddie giggled and pulled her hand away then reached back and quickly touched his nose, followed by another giggle. For the first time Rachel saw him smile, a big radiant smile and big dimples, just like Matt's.

'*How ironic, that he has dimples,*' Rachel mused.

Rachel dished some pot roast and mashed potatoes onto a plate for Maddie, cut the food up into small pieces, pulled up a chair and began to feed her. Ish-kay-nay stood to the side shuffling from one foot to another and watching intently.

"Do you want to help?" Rachel asked him. The boy smiled shyly. "It's not hard, really, you can help feed her." Rachel reached over and gently took his hand and pulled him over. "Watch how I do it." She took a small spoonful of food and fed it to Maddie. When Maddie had chewed and swallowed Rachel put a little more food in the spoon and handed it to Ish-kay-nay. "Now you try it." Timidly he took the spoon and very carefully fed it to Maddie. He grinned at Rachel. "I told you it isn't hard. Give her another bite." He repeated the feeding and kept repeating it until Maddie had eaten her whole dinner. "Good job, Ish-kay-nay. Thank you."

The boy smiled shyly and looked at the floor. Rachel stood up and removed Maddie from the high chair.

"Let's go upstairs." With Maddie in one arm she took Ish-kay-nay's hand with her free hand and brought them both upstairs. She put Maddie in her bassinette with her bear and sang her a lullaby, noticing out of the corner of her eye that Ish-kay-nay was watching her intently. Maddie was not ready to go to sleep.

"More, Mama," she chirped.

Rachel sang another lullaby followed by another until Maddie nodded off to sleep. She covered her with a little quilt and led the boy out of the room. Back downstairs she pulled the metal tub out of its place under a cabinet and into the center of the kitchen. The boy sat on a chair to the side, his eyes large and round, watching her every move. She poured water from a very large jug into an equally large pot on the stove and began to heat it. As soon as it was warm, she poured the water into the tub.

"Let's get those clothes off of you."

Rachel reached toward him, but the boy backed away.

"Don't be shy, you really need to bathe."

The boy kept backing up until he backed into a wall. He froze in place like a deer caught in headlights.

"Are you scared of the water?"

He nodded.

"Nothing to be scared of. You will feel much better when you're nice and clean."

Rachel reached over and slowly began removing his clothing and the strap binding his hair. When he was undressed she lifted him up and put him in the tub. Once he was in the water and realized it wasn't too deep, the edges of his lips curled upward. Rachel reached into a cabinet and took out a bar of soap, a washcloth and a cup. She set a towel on a nearby stool. Using her hands she wet him down with cupfuls of water, then lathered up the cloth with soap and rubbed him all over. She scrubbed behind his ears, his face, feet, his hands and nails and massaged the soap into his hair. Working carefully she cleaned every speck of dirt off of him. The boy watched her with a look of wonder. She stood him up, rinsed him with clean water, lifted him out of the tub and wrapped him in the towel. She was drying him off when she heard the front door open and Matt's footsteps.

She looked up at him when he entered the kitchen, bracing herself for what might come out of his mouth in front of the child.

"That's a good idea," he said, his voice devoid of any emotion. "You can probably use this." He placed a package wrapped in brown paper and a string on the counter, turned and left the room.

Rachel reached over and opened the package. It was a small shirt, pants, underwear, socks and boots. Rachel smiled to herself, not sure what the demonstration meant, but figured she would find out soon enough.

When she had Ish-kay-nay dried and dressed, his hair combed and pulled back again with the leather strap, she took him into Matt's office to show him off. Matt looked up when they walked in.

"He has something to say to you," Rachel said carefully. She bent down. "Go on, tell him."

The boy looked up shyly. "Thank you, Mr. Bradshaw. I love boots." He quickly dropped his eyes, staring at the floor.

Matt turned his head to Rachel who caught his glance. She too smiled. Matt stood up, bent low and held out his hand. The boy didn't know what to do so Rachel placed his hand in Matt's and Matt shook it.

"You are quite welcome. I hope everything fit."

The boy nodded his head.

"He and Maddie met," Rachel said.

"Did they?"

"Yes, and they got along immediately, as though they had always been friends."

Matt furrowed his brow and looked down at the boy. Rachel noticed that Matt was no longer glaring, but wore a softer expression on his face. She would not have called it benevolent, but it was a big improvement over earlier in the day.

"Maddie is probably awake. Let's all go upstairs," she said taking the boy's hand. "Matt, you can see for yourself."

Rachel led the group upstairs and into the nursery. As soon as Maddie saw Ish-kay-nay she stood up in the cradle and stretched her arms toward the boy. "Ish, Ish," she called. He looked up at Rachel as though asking permission to approach. Rachel nodded and Ish-kay-nay walked up to Maddie who giggled and clapped her hands.

"Let's talk in the hallway," Matt said, placing his hand on Rachel's lower back and guiding her out of the room. He stood where they could still see inside the room, but not close enough to be heard over Maddie's laughter.

293

Matt looked down at the rug and put his hands in his pockets. "You're probably wondering why I bought the clothes and boots."

She nodded.

"I walked around town thinking about what you said, about being charitable."

Matt glanced into the nursery and saw Maddie bouncing her finger on the boy's nose. He was letting her and smiling in return.

"I found myself walking by the general store. Saw Tom Griegos buying some clothes for his boy who seemed to be about the same age as, as, as, what's his name?"

"Ish-kay-nay," Rachel responded.

"Yeah, same size as Ish-kay-nay and figured I'd get some duds for him. The clothing he came in was pretty dusty."

Rachel watched him and saw how he was struggling to make his point. She cautiously asked, "For what reason?"

Matt's eyebrows shot up to his hairline.

"He can't very well blend into Santa Fe and our home dressed like an Apache."

Rachel swallowed hard, grappling to keep her composure. "But he is an Apache, a Jicarilla to be exact, and as you pointed out his people don't like people like us. You said he wouldn't fit into Santa Fe society."

Matt nodded. "I know, but I thought a good deal about what you said. Maybe I was being too harsh. If not the orphanage, there is nowhere else for him to go unless we find his father, which isn't likely."

"No, not likely," she shrugged.

"So I figured I should get him some clothes and proper boots."

Rachel could see from the strained look on his face that Matt was having difficulty admitting that he had not handled the situation well. She wanted to ask him for an apology. She wanted to scream at him for his behavior earlier; instead she smiled slowly and decided to allow him his pride.

"He really liked the boots," she murmured. "You should have seen the smile on his face when I took them out of the package. He was genuinely excited."

Matt grinned a little.

"Are you saying you are now okay with him staying?" Rachel asked, wanting to make the arrangement clear.

Matt nodded. "Yeah, I'm okay with it." Matt nodded and glanced to the side.

"What's wrong?" Rachel asked. She could see he was still disturbed.

"I had hoped we would have a son, someone I could teach and to whom I could pass on my knowledge and skills and name. I just never thought that son would be an Apache."

Rachel sucked in a huge breath. "First off, he's a boy in need of a family. Who cares if he's an Apache? There's a reason I found him; maybe I was supposed to find him. Maybe we're supposed to help find his father. For now, we will care for this child and hope that we can erase the rejection he must feel at being thrown away by his tribe. Matt, they're the only people he has ever known. Besides that, I'm sure he is still grieving for his mother." Rachel reached over and ran the back of her fingers down Matt's cheek. "He needs all the compassion we can give him. Will he be the son you've always wanted? I don't know, but I hope you can treat him gently. Don't give up hope on our having another child. Now that life has settled down, perhaps I will get pregnant."

"Perhaps," Matt nodded unconvincingly. "But it has been a long time since Maddie was born...."

Rachel reached up and placed her thumb and forefinger on Matt's chin. "Yes, it has and if too much time passes I will visit the Medinas in Moralito and undergo the same treatment they gave Catherine. Of course, if I have the same physical reaction as Catherine, we could end up with twins."

Rachel saw a look of alarm in Matt's eyes; his pallor went ghostly pale. She laughed. "Look at the bright side. We'll have a lot of fun trying."

Matt's head shot up and his usual characteristic grin, dimples intact, spread across his face. Rachel stood up on her tiptoes and kissed him sweetly, wondering when Matt would notice that their new foster child had dimples just like his.

* * *

A few days later Rachel was in the kitchen preparing a meal when she felt a tug on her dress. She looked down to see the boy standing close.

"What is it, Ish-kay-nay?"

"Are we eating rabbit for lunch?" he asked.

"No, why?"

"Maddie showed me rabbit in cage. I like eating rabbit. Uncle hunted rabbit; it was good."

Rachel's eyes widened. "Goodness, no. That rabbit is Maddie's pet."

"What is pet?"

Rachel smiled, wiped her hands on a towel and bent down to Ish-kay-nay's level. "A pet is a member of the family. We take care of the pet and love it. We don't eat it."

"I had dog in my village. Is that pet?"

"Yes, a dog is a pet," Rachel answered cheerfully figuring that he was getting the concept.

"Am I pet?"

Rachel put her arms around him. "No, no, of course not." She pulled back and looked him in the eyes. "Children are not pets. Only animals are pets."

Ish-kay-nay took a moment to let this new information sink in. Rachel could see him thinking.

"Does rabbit have name?" he asked.

"Yes, his name is Wabbit. Maddie named him."

The boy smiled. "I named my dog."

"Really? What did you name him?"

"Dog," he announced proudly. "Mother said it good name."

Rachel cracked a smile and nodded. "Yes, your mother was right. A good name." She wondered what happened to Dog, but decided not to ask. If Dog lived in the pueblo or had died, either way talking about Dog might make him sad.

"Can I play with Wabbit?" Ish-kay-nay asked, a hopeful smile curling on his lips.

"Of course, I'll get him out of the cage. You and Maddie can play with him together."

Rachel walked into the back room where Maddie was playing with her doll next to the rabbit cage. She looked up and smiled upon seeing her mother. Rachel reached down, unlocked cage and took out Wabbit. She handed the bunny to Ish-kay-nay who carefully held him in his arms.

"Sit down next to Maddie and the rabbit will play with you."

Ish-kay-nay did as instructed and let go of the rabbit who hopped around the room sending both Ish-kay-nay and Maddie into fits of laughter. Convinced the rabbit would keep them entertained for a while Rachel stepped back into the kitchen to finish making lunch.

* * *

The next day after Matt left to meet his new group of security men for the Raton stage line, Rachel dressed and gathered up Maddie and Ish-kay-nay, and headed to James and Catherine's home to introduce the boy to other members of the family.

"Ish-kay-nay, what does your name mean?" Rachel asked as they walked.

"Boy."

"Excuse me?"

"Name mean boy."

"Why would your mother name you that?" Rachel asked, trying to keep her sense of aversion to the name out of her voice.

"All Tinde boys named Ish-kay-nay. Parents give proper name when older."

"Oh." Rachel let out a silent sigh of relief.

"My father not like name. He called me Wolf."

"Why is that?"

"He say I have eyes color of wolf."

"Your father was right about that. Do you like that name?"

The boy nodded.

"What name would you like us to call you? Wolf? Ish-kay-nay? Or we could shorten it like Maddie did, to Ish."

Maddie squealed. "Ish, Ish!" She reached out for the boy.

Rachel stopped and let Maddie pat the boy on the head.

"I like Wolf."

"Wuff!" Maddie giggled.

The boy looked up at Maddie then to Rachel.

"If you want to be called Wolf that's about as good as she can say it for now. Is that okay?"

Wolf nodded and grinned as they stepped through the garden gate at Rachel's in-laws' home.

Before they reached the door, it swung open. Emily stood there gaping at Wolf.

"Emily, sweetie, meet Wolf. He has come to live with us," Rachel said gently.

Emily froze in her place and shyly looked away.

"Emily, please welcome Wolf," Rachel repeated, this time giving Emily a stern look in the eye.

Emily stepped back and opened the door. As Rachel, Wolf and Maddie came through the doorway Emily looked at Wolf, scrutinizing his face. Wolf looked back, just as wide-eyed as Emily. As soon as they entered Catherine came down the hallway.

"What a lovely surprise!" Catherine cooed. She kneeled down to Wolf's level and smiled at him. "Is this the young man I heard has come to live with you?"

Wolf remained silent, plastered against Rachel's leg.

"It's okay, Wolf; she won't harm you," Rachel said softly. "Give her your hand."

Prompted, the boy extended his hand. Catherine took it into her own and shook it lightly. He never took his eyes off of Catherine.

"I am Mrs. Bradshaw," Catherine said.

Wolf looked up at Rachel. "But, you Mrs. Bradshaw."

Rachel nodded. "Yes, that's true. Mrs. Bradshaw's husband and my husband are brothers and we are both Mrs. Bradshaw."

"Not how Tinde calls wives," he announced.

"I'm sure it's not," Catherine agreed. "But here we do things a little differently. What is your name?"

"Wolf," he announced proudly, a tiny smile creeping across his lips.

"What a fine, strong name. I like it very much."

Catherine glanced over and saw Emily lurking in the corner. "Come," she called to Emily who shook her head. "Emily?" she said a little more forcefully. Emily walked over slowly, never taking her eyes off the boy. Nor did the boy take his off of Emily. Catherine put her arm around Emily's waist. "Can you please welcome our new guest to our home?"

"Welcome," Emily whispered.

"A little louder?" Catherine urged her.

"Welcome!" Emily said much louder, without a lot of kindness to her tone.

"Emily!" Catherine snapped at her. "That is no way to treat a guest. I will not tolerate your mistreating a guest in our home. You apologize and try again."

Emily set her jaw and stared down at the boy, who was still backed up against Rachel's leg. "Sorry," she said looking down. "Welcome to our home." Wolf continued to stare at her.

"That is better. Now Emily dear, will you take Maddie up to the nursery? I am sure she would like to see the babies. But be quiet; they are still napping."

Before Catherine could finish speaking, Emily grabbed Maddie out of Rachel's arms and headed up the stairs. Wolf looked up at Rachel, worried.

"It's okay," Rachel patted him on the shoulder. "Maddie visits here a lot."

"Would you like some hot chocolate, Wolf?" Catherine asked the boy who turned and looked at her.

"Do not know," he answered, looking back up at Rachel.

"He's probably never had it. Until now he's lived in his village all his life," Rachel said.

Catherine looked straight into Wolf's eyes. "Then you are in for a big surprise." She got up and headed to the kitchen, followed by Rachel and Wolf.

A while later Catherine poured the hot chocolate into several cups and set them on the kitchen table. She walked out of the kitchen and saw Emily descending the stairs with Maddie.

"Come, come," she waved to Emily. "I made your favorite."

Emily's eyes lit up. "Chocolate?"

Catherine nodded. "Now come, before it cools."

She took Maddie out of Emily's arms and walked behind her into the kitchen. Emily found Wolf and Rachel already sitting at the table. Rachel pointed at an empty chair indicating she should sit down, next to Wolf. Emily slid into the chair, turned slightly and saw Wolf staring up at her. Emily smiled shyly at him. He rewarded her with a big grin. Catherine sat down and held Maddie in her lap. She took a small spoonful of chocolate, blew on it and offered it to Maddie, who wrapped her rose-colored lips around the spoon. Maddie cooed as she swallowed the sweet liquid. Wolf watched her intently. After he saw how much Maddie liked it. he raised the cup to his lips and carefully took a little sip. As soon as the warm chocolate crossed his lips, his eyes flew wide open with wonder. He grinned a chocolately smile at Rachel.

"I take it that you like hot chocolate?" Rachel asked.

"Yes, yes!" he answered, tipping the cup back up to his lips. He loudly slurped the hot liquid. The noise made Maddie break out in giggles. Her laughter was so infectious it made everyone chuckle, even Wolf. Emily snickered so loud it made her snort very unladylike noises, which made the whole group cackle in hysterics.

"I never knew that hot chocolate could be such a good source of merriment," Catherine commented. "I will have to remember this the next time our house needs cheering."

Chapter Sixteen

Summer 1885

Matt burst into the house calling for Rachel. She ran down the stairs.

"What is it? What's happened?" Her heart was racing, but she realized it was with unnecessary worry because Matt was flashing his characteristic grin, dimples charging down the sides of his face.

"It's done. The house is done! And the new furniture has arrived and been placed throughout the house." He held out a telegram.

She took the telegram and read the note from the architect who telegraphed from Oak Valley. She looked up, a mixture of happiness and sadness brushed across her face.

"What's wrong?" He took her chin in his hand and looked down at her.

"I just can't believe we're finally moving back. It didn't seem like it would ever happen."

"I was beginning to have doubts too, but indeed it is done. Now comes the biggest job of all. It won't be easy to move the essentials and all of us down there. You ready?"

"This is one of those times when the 21st century definitely has an edge over the 19th century. A bunch of moving men could come in here, pack a truck and be down there in half a day, unload everything and all we would have to do is unpack."

"I'll grant you that. But given that we don't have such a luxury let's plan out the move." He ran his long arms around her and gave her a tight squeeze.

* * *

Over the course of the next three weeks Rachel packed everything but furniture, linens, some dishes, and a few kitchen utensils that they would keep in the Santa Fe house for when they would visit. Every other item that they owned was packed into wooden crates and trunks. Instead of using bubble wrap or the white plastic popcorn so common in the 21st century to protect fragile objects from breaking, Rachel used clothing, linens, hay, wood shavings – anything that would cushion against breakage during the long trip. Rachel was walking around the house trying to find something in which to wrap their dishware when she heard a knock on the door. Relieved with a distraction, she headed toward the knock and opened the door to find Catherine standing there holding a basket full of torn linens. She held out the basket to Rachel.

"I thought you could use these, for packing," Catherine offered.

"Bless you!" Rachel said. "I do need these. Thank you!" She took the basket from Catherine. "Come in. Let's have a cup of tea. I could use a breather."

"A breather?" Catherine asked. "Are your lungs bothering you or is that one of your terms for a rest?"

Rachel chuckled at herself. "Exactly."

She led Catherine into the kitchen. In a few minutes they sat down to a tea of manzanilla and yerba buena. Catherine took a sip and closed her eyes, smiling.

"One of my favorites," she whispered. "Madre would make it for me whenever I needed to calm down." She opened her eyes and stared at Rachel. "Are you all right?"

"Of course. I've been packing this place is all. It's a lot of work."

Catherine nodded, understanding. The two women sat in silence for several minutes, drinking their tea.

"I will miss you terribly, you know," Rachel said just above a whisper, looking down into her cup. "You have been more than a friend, more than a sister. More than I could ever have wished." She reached up and wiped the corner of her eye where a wayward tear was starting to fall.

Catherine set down her cup, reached over and took one of Rachel's hands into her own. Rachel looked up to see Catherine's eyes welling with tears.

"I will miss you too, but we will see one another when our family visits yours and you visit us here. This is not goodbye."

At that, Rachel burst into tears and was joined by Catherine. The two women leaned over and embraced until they heard a noise at the doorway. They turned to see Wolf standing there holding Maddie's hand. Both children's eyes ballooned with anxiety.

"Why Mama cry?" Maddie asked. Wolf nodded in agreement.

Rachel let go of Catherine and beckoned the two children to her. "Come here, you two." The children scurried over to her; she put an arm around each one. "Mama is sad because when we move we won't see Auntie Catherine so often anymore."

"Why we have to leave?" Wolf asked, looking up at her with sad eyes.

Rachel kissed him on the head. She could see that her tears worried him. "Like I told you before, we have a new home. You'll like it. You both will. But we won't see Auntie Catherine, Uncle James, or your cousins but a couple of times a year."

"Why?" Wolf and Maddie asked together.

"Because, it is far away."

"Can Emily come with us?" Wolf asked. "I like her."

Rachel and Catherine chuckled. In the beginning Emily was shy with Wolf to the point of being rude, but once she got used to him she included him in every activity when they got together. Wolf and Maddie had grown fond of Emily reading them stories. After Emily had read them every story book she had, she began making up tales which delighted the children even more, especially when she put the children into the stories as characters.

"I want Emwee come wif us!" Maddie announced.

"Oh sweetie, I wish she could," Rachel said. "Perhaps in a couple of years when she gets older she came come down and spend her summer school break with us." Rachel looked up at Catherine. "That is if Auntie Catherine and Uncle James will let her."

Maddie looked up at Catherine. "Pweeze, Auntie Catrine?" Wolf looked at her with eyes of longing.

"Of course," Catherine nodded at the children. "In a couple of years Emily will be almost an adult. She should be able to travel alone by stagecoach then." She looked up at Rachel. "But of course I will insist on training her to use Lillian and getting her one of her own to take along."

The reference to Lillian completely evaded the children. Rachel caught it and smiled accordingly. She wouldn't want it any other way.

* * *

The day finally came to take the stagecoach to Oak Valley. All the crates had been taken by wagon days earlier, and all that was left were traveling cases and themselves. James came to the house with a horse and wagon to help them take their bags to the line office. Rachel tucked Zoe into her large purse, just in case the need arose during the trip. Next to Zoe she packed little cakes that Catherine had baked, dried fruit, apples, and nuts for the journey to Oak Valley. As they approached the line office, Rachel saw Catherine with the babies and Emily. She felt her throat begin to constrict and her eyes begin to moisten.

"*No!*" she told herself. "*You are not going to cry!!*" She swallowed hard and blinked several times to dry her eyes. By the time they reached the little group her emotions were under control.

"Are you all ready for the big trip?" Catherine asked cheerfully, but Rachel could see the sadness in her eyes. Normally her eyes shone bright, but today they looked the color of a dust devil crossing a muddy creek.

"You bet!" Rachel answered in as upbeat a tone as she could gather. "Aren't we?" she asked bending down to the children.

Both of them nodded. Maddie held out her doll to Catherine and Emily. "Dolly going to ride inside."

"And so she should," Catherine said. "And you, Wolf? Are you taking anything inside to keep you busy on the trip?"

Wolf set his jaw proudly. He held up Wabbit's small cage. The bunny poked his nose out one of the holes. "Wabbit and my eyes."

Catherine shook her head slightly. "Your eyes?"

"He means that he will keep watch out the window for danger," Rachel interceded. "Wolf is going to help protect us, right Wolf?"

Wolf nodded, his pony tail tapping his back, pride beaming across his small face.

While the women and children talked, Matt, James and the driver loaded their belongings on top of the stagecoach, and secured them with ropes. Matt shook hands with his security man, Alejandro Serna, who regularly rode the Santa Fe to Oak Valley route and the driver, Philip Jones. Matt turned to the women and children.

"Ladies, and Wolf, we're ready to go,"

Everyone began hugging and kissing and promising to write. When Rachel felt tears burning behind her eyes she hustled the children into the stagecoach. The family took up most of the coach, leaving only enough room for a young man traveling to Oak Valley to seek his fortune in the mines. As soon as everyone was settled, the coach pulled out. Wolf held Wabbit's cage on his lap and stretched his arm out the window, waving to the other Bradshaw family until they were out of sight.

* * *

Over the course of the trip, Wolf glued himself to the window seat, scanning the countryside for danger. As soon as he got out of the coach at the first station where they stopped for lunch, Wolf began walking the grounds, searching.

"Wolf, come to lunch," Rachel called to him from the door well.

He shook his head. "Must make sure it safe."

"It is safe. We would not have stopped here if it wasn't. Come now," she waved to him to come inside.

Maddie, who stood next to Rachel holding one of her hands, let go and clapped her hands. "Come, Wuf, come!"

He turned around and flicked his eyes at Maddie. He smiled, his white teeth radiant against his bronzed skin. Rachel knew he couldn't resist Maddie's charms. Reluctantly he trudged over, crossed the door threshold, and sat down with the rest of the family. As soon as the bean enchiladas were served Rachel watched the anxiety on his face melt into joy. Next to hot cocoa, enchiladas were his favorite food. She couldn't imagine why he was worried and felt a need to inspect the area before he would come inside. It was her hope that when they settled into the Oak Valley house, his anxieties would cease.

After lunch they re-boarded the stagecoach. An hour into the trip, Maddie fell asleep in Matt's arms. Shortly afterwards, everyone in the coach, including Wabbit, took an afternoon nap, But Rachel was too excited to sleep. Besides, it gave her a chance to pursue one of her favorite activities, watching the terrain. As the day wore on and the sun began to descend toward the western horizon, she saw gray, angry summer clouds fill the sky.

'Just like the ticking of a clock, looks like we're in for an afternoon monsoon rain.' No sooner did the

thought cross her mind than raindrops began hitting the stagecoach, first softly, then with a thunderous pounding. She waited for the others to wake, but surprisingly no one did. She couldn't help remembering the first trip she took to Santa Fe from Oak Valley with Matt and Emily in 1880. It was that trip that brought Matt and Rachel together, but one she would prefer not to repeat. Even though the stagecoaches were far from comfy, traveling for three weeks in an open wagon with only two horses proved to be more grueling than she ever imagined. In comparison, this stagecoach felt like riding in a Benz. Late in the day, after the rains passed, everyone began to awake. Outside, the surrounding hills shimmered as the soft light of day passed into evening.

Matt raised his head, looked outside and over at Rachel. "Jesus, it's nearly dusk. How long have I been sleeping?"

"Hours. You fell asleep right after we left the lunch station. You all did." She reached over and ran her fingers along his jaw. "You must have been really tired."

"Yeah, I guess so," he said, sliding his hand through the chestnut waves of hair, pulling it back off of his face.

Maddie yawned and opened her eyes, searching for her mother. She smiled a little cupid grin when she saw Rachel looking at her. She reached out her arms and

315

Rachel took her into her lap. Maddie reached over and stroked a now-awake Wolf, who sat up straight and resumed his watchdog duties.

* * *

Over the following days the journey didn't change much until they began rolling into Oak Valley. Everyone sat tall in their seats trying to catch an outside glimpse. As they pulled into town, Rachel was stunned at the many changes that had occurred in her absence. Matt had witnessed them during his periodic visits to see the building of their home, but Rachel hadn't. The town was larger than she could have imagined. More streets, businesses and homes. She was delighted to see an array of new shops where she knew she would spend some time. The cobbler, seamstress' shop, a little café and a doctor's office were going to be her first visits. She hoped that the town's doctor would welcome her and not treat her as Horgan had. She shook her head, sorry she even thought of the man. Part of leaving Santa Fe was to also leave that episode in the past. She admonished herself for bringing it to mind.

As soon as they got off the stage and the luggage was unloaded, Matt walked over to a large, husky man with a wagon.

"Hello, Mr. Bradshaw," the burly man said. "You got here right on time. Here, let me help you with that." He reached down and began loading the luggage into the back of the wagon.

Rachel and the children stood to the side watching. The man wasn't just tall; he was huge, barrel-chested, with bowed legs and great spherical eyes. When the man finished loading he stepped over to Rachel. "You must be Mrs. Bradshaw. I am Luther Maxwell."

"Thank you, Mr. Maxwell. It will be good to get home."

They got into the wagon and headed to the house. They no sooner turned a corner, than the house loomed at them from the top of a street. Rachel gasped. Indeed it was the house they planned, right down to the wide porch circling the house. The wagon pulled up in front and everyone got out. Rachel looked everywhere. Roses were already growing in the front garden and rocking chairs sat on the freshly-painted white porch. She looked over at Matt.

"How did you know that I love roses and rocking chairs and wide porches? I didn't tell you."

He grinned, deep dimples intact. "You mentioned it one night in your sleep."

"I did?" Rachel gasped.

Matt nodded, reached over and pulled her to him; he kissed her lightly on the side of her head. "Let's go see this fancy house you wanted." He picked up a couple of cases while Luther Maxwell picked up a few more. Wolf proudly hoisted his own case and carried Wabbit's cage. As soon as they stepped through the front door well, a woman scurried down the hallway. It was Mrs. Trujillo, who used to work for Dr. Bradshaw, Matt's father. As rotund as ever, with thick, jet black hair braided and piled on top of her head in a large bun, her dark eyes gleamed with happiness. Rachel squealed.

"Mrs. Trujillo, it's so good to see you! I didn't know you were going to work for us!"

"When Mr. Bradshaw told me you were moving back I quit my other job. Now let me see the beautiful children." Mrs. Trujillo reached over and ran her hand over Maddie's head, who watched her with eyes as wide as marbles. Then she bent down low to Wolf. "What a fine looking young man." Wolf scanned her face, obviously not yet sure what to think of this jolly woman.

"Wolf, Mrs. Trujillo makes the world's best enchiladas," Rachel quipped. The boy burst out in an ear-to-ear grin. Rachel could not have said anything better to ease him into their new home.

The family walked through the foyer while Matt, Luther and Mrs. Trujillo carried the travel cases upstairs, followed by Rachel, Maddie and Wolf. The first bedroom they stepped into had a small bed covered in a sweet little pink and white quilt, and lace curtains.

"Look Maddie, now you will sleep like a big girl," Rachel pointed to the bed. Maddie's little mouth opened slightly; she turned and looked at her mother, a question on her face. "Yes, that's right, you're a big girl now and you get to sleep in a regular bed." She put Maddie down and let her walk over and inspect the bed. Across the room was an open toy chest, ready to be filled with Maddie's toys when they arrived with all their other belongings.

Next they went into another bedroom with a small bed, and a desk. With a quilt and curtains in blues and reds, the room was suited to a young boy. Wolf looked up at Rachel. "For me?" Rachel nodded. Wolf ran into the room and jumped onto the bed, clearly ecstatic at having his own room.

Finally Matt and Rachel entered their own bedroom. Rachel sucked in a breath of air and held her hands up to her mouth. The room was fit for a princess with exquisite cherry wood-carved furniture, floor to ceiling lace curtains, a large bed covered in a white quilt and large pillows, a dressing table, and chair. Off to the side she saw a door that, when opened revealed a large closet filled with wooden hangers. Rachel whirled around and threw her arms around Matt's neck.

"A closet! A closet! Matt, thank you!"

"That's not all." Matt took her hand and led her to the other side of the room and opened another door.

Inside was a toilet, a sink and a bathtub. Rachel broke out in giggles.

"What's so funny?" Matt asked, a perplexed look on his face.

"I'm just so happy, that's all. I am in heaven. Sheer heaven!"

Matt held his head back and blinked a couple of times. "Well, all right, if you're happy, that's all that matters. Come, I'll show you the rest of the house."

Matt led her from room to room, showing her the closets throughout the house and the downstairs bathroom. After pointing out the living room with its new furniture, he walked her into his office, explaining that he would run his security business from the house. He ended in the kitchen where Mrs. Trujillo was standing at a new cast iron stove. She stepped back when they entered the room.

"Mr. Matt has bought you a new stove. It is very nice," Mrs. Trujillo explained. "It uses coal, instead of wood. Much easier. You will like cooking on it."

"I'm hoping, Mrs. Trujillo," Matt began "that you can teach Rachel some of your dishes. Especially baking. She could use your help."

"Matt!" Rachel slapped him on the arm as he chuckled. "I'm not that bad. You know I'm not."

"No, but you could use a little improvement, and Mrs. Trujillo is just the person to teach you. Right, Mrs. Trujillo?"

"Don't you put me in the middle of this, Mr. Matt," Mrs. Trujillo admonished him. "I am happy to teach Mrs. Rachel, but only if she wants."

Rachel grinned. "Sure, I'd love to learn whatever you can teach me. But really, I'm much better than I used to be."

Mrs. Trujillo nodded. "Yes, I am sure that you are a fine cook."

Matt coughed into his hand. "That's overstating it quite a bit."

"Okay, Matt, you are outta here! Mrs. Trujillo will show me the rest of the kitchen."

Matt grinned, reached over and kissed Rachel on the cheek and left to put away what they brought with them on the stagecoach.

After showing her around the kitchen, Mrs. Trujillo led Rachel off to an ante room with ample counters, filled with shelves stocked with large dark brown glass jars. In the center of the room stood a desk and chair and two side chairs.

"Mr. Matt tells me that you are a yerbera now."

"Yes, that's correct."

"He had this room built for you to make your remedios."

Rachel walked around and inspected the room – the shelves, the jars, the bowls, a variety of utensils, even the new mortar and pestle. "This is perfect," she said looking all around. "As soon as I unpack the clothes I'll bring in the box of herbs that I brought with me, and set up everything."

"I hope it does not take too long."

Rachel turned around to Mrs. Trujillo. "Why?"

Mrs. Trujillo shyly looked down and fingered her apron. "When Mr. Matt told me about who you trained with I told everyone I know. The Medinas are famous curanderas. People around here have been waiting for your arrival. They want to come to you instead of the doctor."

"Oh! That's great, but I don't want to take away the doctor's patients. I had enough trouble with feuding doctors in Santa Fe!"

"Yes, Mr. Matt told me. Bad business. You will have many patients who will not go to a Western doctor. When you are ready, you tell me and I will let the people know that our new healer is ready to see patients." She patted Rachel on the arm as though to reassure her.

Inside, Rachel jumped with joy; she could not have begged for a better referral system.

* * *

Mrs. Trujillo proved true to her word. Rachel was no sooner set up in her treatment room than locals began visiting her for every imaginable ailment. For complaints such as broken bones, she sent them to the doctor in town. She didn't know how to set a broken bone and didn't want to make a mistake, plus she thought it might generate good will with the town doctor.

A few months after their return to Oak Valley a group of three Mexican men knocked on the door. They took off their hats when Rachel opened the door. The bandy-legged men looked as though they had been rolling in dust and weeds and hadn't combed their hair or shaved in a week. Their English was so poor that Rachel called for Mrs. Trujillo and asked her to interpret. Mrs. Trujillo frowned when she saw them.

In Spanish Mrs. Trujillo told them, "You are drunk with hangovers! Go sleep it off somewhere!" The woman glared at the scruffily dressed men.

Rachel could see that Mrs. Trujillo was perturbed with the men, but couldn't fully understand what she told them. Her harsh tone spoke volumes.

"What's the problem?" she whispered into Mrs. Trujillo's ear.

Out loud, Mrs. Trujillo told her that they were drunk and Rachel should not treat them.

"Mrs. Trujillo, I treat everyone. Even drunks sometimes need help. I would appreciate it if you would assist me."

Mrs. Trujillo frowned and glared at the men. She opened the front door wide and allowed the unkempt men to follow Rachel to the treatment room. As soon as they entered the room, Rachel pointed to chairs for the men to sit. They sat and held their hats in their laps. They watched Rachel with the eyes of a hawk.

"Mrs. Trujillo, please ask them why they are here."

"They have hangovers," she responded.

"Yes, I can see that. But there might be additional complaints. Can you please ask them?" Rachel was trying hard not to get frustrated with Mrs. Trujillo, who seemed to be acting as her manager.

Mrs. Trujillo asked them what the problem was. The men answered that they drank some bad tequila. They had never had such awful hangovers. Each suffered a colossal headache. When she repeated their answers to Rachel, along with her opinion that the tequila was probably fine and they couldn't hold their liquor, Rachel spun around and began making a tea, and filling a separate muslin bag with shredded bark. Soon after, she served each of the men a cup of cinnamon-scented tea.

"Please tell the men that this is canela tea. They must drink this tea three times a day on an empty stomach, before meals." She opened the little muslin bag and showed the men the cinnamon bark. "There is enough here for all three of you for today and tomorrow." Mrs. Trujillo repeated the instructions in Spanish.

As soon as the men finished their cups of tea, they stood up, and bowed their heads to Rachel. Both she and Mrs. Trujillo led the men out the front of the house. As soon as they closed the door Rachel turned to Mrs. Trujillo.

"What was that all about? I've never seen you treat anyone like that."

Mrs. Trujillo scrunched up her nose. "They are no good. A bunch of burros." She turned to go back to the kitchen. Rachel heard her whisper "pendejos" under her breath.

Rachel grinned as she watched Mrs. Trujillo walk to the back of the house. She never imagined she would hear that word coming out of her mouth.

Something caught her eye. Sitting halfway up the stairs was Wolf, watching her intently.

"How long have you been up there?"

"Who were those men?" he asked, not bothering to answer the question.

"Just some men with headaches. Like the other patients."

"I hope they no come back."

"Why, Wolf?"

"Bad feeling. They are no good. Bad men."

Rachel cocked her head sideways and scrutinized Wolf. "Why do you say that?"

"Feel it."

In the time that Wolf had come to live with them, Rachel learned that Wolf had extraordinary, intuitive talents. Several times he had known when a rattlesnake was lurking in the yard before anyone heard the rattling, shaking sound. Only a week before, he found a snake coiled, ready to strike. He stifled a scream and stared down the snake, calming it, until it slithered away. Another time he warned the family to go inside when the skies were clear. Moments later angry clouds filled the skies and a torrential rainstorm broke. But in his finest moment, during an afternoon walk in the hills, he warned the family that a pack of ravenous coyotes were descending on them from a stand of trees, even though they saw and heard nothing but a gentle breeze. He alerted them only moments before the animals came around a corner and charged with mouths open baring teeth sharp as daggers, saliva drooling off their jaws. Matt had his rifle with him and shot the lead animal, sending the others scurrying.

"What is it you feel, Wolf?" Rachel walked up the stairs and sat down next to the boy.

"They are wicked. Are going to do something very bad." Wolf bit his lip and looked up at Rachel with nervous eyes.

"Do you know when?"

Wolf shook his head; it was enough for Rachel. She reached over, put her arm around his shoulders and gave him a shallow squeeze. "Okay, we will be careful." Wolf nodded, got up and ran back upstairs, his braid flapping down his back.

Chapter Seventeen

Autumn 1885

One afternoon, while she was shopping in the general store, Rachel overheard two women talking.

"Yes, Lily, it is true. The railroad has requested money from the town council to finance building a line into Oak Valley," said a tall, sturdy woman who looked like she was built to weather any storm.

"Your husband is the mayor; so I imagine you would know. How are they going to vote?" asked a petite woman who looked no taller than five feet.

"Oh, they will vote against it, of course. Wilford says we don't need the railroad, but I am not so sure."

Rachel's felt elation swelling in her chest. This was it. This was why they came back to Oak Valley. She stepped over to the women.

"Excuse me ladies, I am Mrs. Rachel Bradshaw. Forgive me, but I could not help overhearing your conversation about the railroad."

The women nodded. "Yes," said the taller of the two, "it is an exciting proposition, but I highly doubt it will pass."

Rachel seized the moment. "That really is a shame, don't you think?" she asked the women, looking earnestly from one to the other. "The West is growing rapidly. If Oak Valley does not allow the railroad in, and should the mines dry up, people will leave. We will miss a great opportunity to grow our town."

The women chuckled. "The mines dry up? Absurd!"

"No, seriously, think about it. Mines have only so much mineral in them. I know the miners are looking for new veins. What if they don't find any? How will this town survive?"

The two women looked blankly at one another and back at Rachel. "You make a very good point, Mrs. Bradshaw," answered the taller woman. "You should attend the next council meeting and have your husband share your views."

"My husband? Why would he do that? I can speak on my own."

The women chuckled into their gloved hands.

"That is brave of you, Mrs. Bradshaw, but the men will not listen to a woman, especially regarding a subject as serious as this."

Rachel couldn't believe what she was hearing, but reminded herself that she was in the 19th century, an aspect of the 19th century that riled her sensibilities. "That is exactly why I should speak," Rachel said congenially. "I feel strongly about this. Don't you?" She looked earnestly at each of the women who glanced at one another and back at Rachel.

"Well, yes, I suppose so," the second woman agreed.

"Then I hope I will have your support at the meeting."

The women nodded.

"Wonderful! When is the meeting?"

"The 15th of November, a month from now," the small woman answered.

"I'll be there. Please forgive my manners," Rachel added. "What are your names?"

"Mrs. Dorothea Walton," said the tall woman. "My husband, Wilford, is the mayor."

"Mrs. Lily Hayes," said the tiny one. "Earl Hayes, my husband, is the town dentist. Yes, we will be there. If nothing else, it will be entertaining to watch a woman oppose the men on the council. They do not appreciate interference from women in town matters." Mrs. Walton nodded her head in agreement.

"Then all the more reason for me to speak my mind," Rachel responded, suppressing all but a small grin. "I look forward to seeing both of you there."

All three women nodded and went their separate ways. When Rachel was done shopping she asked the storekeeper to deliver the goods to the house. She wanted to find Matt and tell him that the reason for their return to Oak Valley had arrived. She was hell bent on fulfilling her destiny.

Rachel walked around town poking her head into different shops and businesses, looking for Matt. She saw a gaunt, wiry man she knew as Clem, sauntering down the wooden sidewalk. Rachel nodded to him.

"Hello, Clem. Do you remember me? I'm Rachel Bradshaw."

Clem removed his hat and bowed his head, all the while chewing on a long piece of straw sticking out of his mouth. "Sure Mrs. Bradshaw, I remember you from the last time you and Matthew lived here."

"Speaking of my husband, have you seen him?"

Clem looked down and kicked a splinter coming off the wooden sidewalk.

"Have you?" Rachel repeated.

"Yeah."

"Where is he?"

"Um, Mrs. Bradshaw, he's in the saloon. But you don't want to go in there."

"Why not?"

"It's not a place for a fine lady like yourself."

Rachel laughed. "That's kind of you to think of my reputation but I can handle myself. Bye!" she turned and headed across the street to the saloon. Clem put his hat back on, shook his head, and watched her go into the saloon.

Rachel stepped inside. It took a moment for her eyes to adjust to the dim light. Once they did she scanned the saloon. All the men who were sitting in chairs at tables went quiet and stared at her. Rachel heard some laughter and her eyes followed its source. She saw Matt sitting on a stool at the bar, his back to the door. Cozied up next to him was none other than Madame Bishu, the saloon proprietor, who was pressing her enormous breasts against his arm. The two of them seemed to be flirting and looking adoringly at one another. Rachel's mouth dropped as every ounce of blood drained from her face, leaving her pasty white with shock. She felt her knees weakening.

"Rachel, get a hold of yourself!" she whispered as she walked over to the oblivious couple. She stopped right behind Matt. Madame Bishu caught sight of Rachel and immediately pulled away from Matt who turned around to see why the woman had stepped back. When he saw Rachel the big smile on his face faded.

"You bastard!" Rachel seethed. She turned and rushed out of the saloon. As soon as she was outside she began running and didn't stop until she reached the house. Her mind flooded with memories of her devotion to her medical student boyfriend in the 21st century. She remembered how she believed that Bob Evans loved her, how they were building a life together, only for him to abandon her for his lab partner when he graduated. She had vowed to never love another man; she maintained that vow until she met Matt, who she thought was different. Rachel never imagined he would do this to her.

She ran inside and up the stairs. She took off her shawl, and threw her purse and gloves on the bed. She went back downstairs and into the treatment room. She knew she had to keep herself busy or she would start screaming. Mrs. Trujillo walked into the little room.

"Mrs. Rachel, are you alright?"

Rachel turned and looked at her. "No, no, Mrs. Trujillo, I'm not all right, but I don't want to talk about it. I don't mean to be rude, but please leave me alone."

Mrs. Trujillo's brow furrowed and the sides of her mouth sagged. "Maddie has been asking for you. May I bring her to you?"

"Yes, please do." Rachel was sure she would start crying when she saw Maddie, but she couldn't deny her daughter her attention, even in her anger.

Mrs. Trujillo was back downstairs with Maddie in moments. Just as she handed Maddie to Rachel, Matt burst into the treatment room.

"Rach----" he began.

"Out, get out," Rachel said, trying to stay calm.

"Rachel, I can explain."

"Oh no, you can't. I saw the look on both of your faces. I saw what you were doing. You can't deny anything and I don't want to hear it."

Matt took a step toward Rachel.

"Get out!!!" she screamed. "And I mean it!"

Maddie burst out in tears. Rachel wrapped her hands around the little girl's head. "It's okay, sweetie, it's okay," she cooed at the girl, running her hands down her head and back. She looked up at Matt. "Get out of here, now. I'm in no mood to talk to you."

Matt started to say something, but the fury on Rachel's reddened face stopped him. He turned and left. Mrs. Trujillo, who was standing off to the side, walked over and placed her hand on Rachel's shoulder. She squeezed it, turned and left the room. Rachel sat down at her desk and continued hugging Maddie until the little girl fell asleep in her embrace. Rachel carried her upstairs and put her in her bed for a nap. Wolf walked into the room, chewing on his knuckles. He had an unnatural stillness about him. Rachel could see that he sensed something was wrong. An agitation filled his eyes. She walked over and gave him a hug. "It's okay, nothing to worry about." But when she stood back she could still see the worry in his eyes. He knew it wasn't okay at all.

At dinner that night they all sat in silence. Matt attempted to catch Rachel's eye; she ignored him throughout the meal. The children tried to make conversation, but not garnering any responses, they also relegated themselves to silence. Wolf asked to be excused as soon everyone finished eating. When Rachel nodded he took his plate into the kitchen, and then bolted upstairs to his room. Rachel cleared the dishes to the kitchen. She turned around to bring in the rest and saw Matt carrying them in. He set the dishes in the sink and stood back.

"Let's talk," he said softly.

"Not on your life!" Rachel snapped, turning her back on him; she began rinsing the dishes.

"We need to talk," Matt tried again.

"Talk about what? Your infidelity? I don't think so."

"It's not what you think, what you saw. Will you give me a chance to explain?"

"No!" she answered with such finality that Matt backed off and left the room.

He stopped outside the kitchen, walked down the hall to his study and plopped down in a chair. He ran his hands through his hair and shook his head. He didn't know what to do. And he didn't know where to start. He had an urge to leave, but he knew that if he did, Rachel would think he went back to the saloon. If he was going to repair his marriage, he knew he needed to stay as far from Madame Bishu as he could. He stayed in the study until long past bedtime. When he went upstairs he turned the knob on the bedroom door; it was locked. He knocked quietly. No answer. He knocked again. No answer. Rachel wasn't going to open the door. He went back downstairs and tried to sleep in the study, to no avail.

In the bedroom, Rachel heard his soft knocks and ignored them. She lay on her back and stared at the ceiling.

'*What happened to us? Where did I go wrong?*' The words rolled around her head. '*Until today, wasn't everything fine? But, if it were fine why did he turn to another woman? And of all women, Madame Bishu?*'

It was hard enough that she found him with another woman, but even more humiliating that it was a woman he used to sleep with before Rachel landed in Oak Valley. She tried to think of what could have driven Matt to her; she could not think of anything. Suddenly she heard the characteristic hissing she had come to recognize as the whisperwind. She listened intently; the words came through though muffled. Finally she clearly heard the message. "Believe. Love will prevail." It did not comfort her. If anything it upset her more, because she lost her trust in Matt, a trust that was the foundation of their marriage. How could she believe in him?

By the time light began to seep in around the curtains, she was up and dressed. She glanced in the mirror and saw that puffy bags surrounded her bloodshot eyes. She felt like she had been to hell and back; her face revealed her painful journey.

"Oh great," she said aloud, leaning toward the mirror and patting the bags with her fingers. She didn't want Matt to see her looking as though she hadn't slept, even though indeed she had not slept at all. She checked on the children; both were still asleep. Quietly she descended the stairs and smelled coffee brewing. It was too early for Mrs. Trujillo. She found Matt in the kitchen. He handed her a mug of coffee. She took it. She didn't mean to look up at him; out of habit she did and saw that he looked as ragged and raw as she did. In fact, she surmised that he looked worse, with even bigger bags under his eyes and a sallow tint coloring his skin.

"Are the children still asleep?"

Rachel nodded.

"We have to talk."

Rachel looked down into her coffee. She took her time responding. Her throat was so dry she could hardly swallow, much less speak. Fatigue clouded her mind, grief etched along the rims of her eyes. She took a sip of the coffee to wet her throat.

"I want you to move out," she whispered, not looking up.

"Move out?" he asked in a slightly louder voice.

"Yes, the sooner the better."

"And why would I do that?"

"Isn't it obvious?" she looked up at him, hurt searing across her face. "Our marriage is over."

"What the hell?" he barked.

Matt set down the coffee cup and stepped over to Rachel. He reached to put his arms around her.

"Don't touch me!" she snapped at him, backing up.

The muscles in his body tensed, fixed as stone. He jumped back. "Rachel, don't be unreasonable. This isn't worth ending our marriage." A small, involuntary muscle twitched on the side of his face, a thin, vertical line ran between his brows.

"No?" she looked up at him. She could feel tears welling behind her eyes. She shut her eyes against the burning tears. "*Damn,*" she admonished herself. She didn't want him to see her cry, didn't want him to interpret her tears as weakness. She wiped at a tear seeping out of one of her eyes. She held her head high, trying to control the furious energy rising in her chest. "I take fidelity seriously. I have never even looked at another man since I met you. You have been my rock, my world. I thought I was yours, but obviously I was wrong. Very wrong."

"You are my world, you know that," he said, a quiet note of common sense in his voice.

"I truly believed I was, up until I walked into that saloon yesterday. At that moment I realized that I had been living a lie." She jutted out her chin defiantly. "I'm just curious, how long have you been unfaithful to me? It doesn't really matter. I just want to know how long I've been made a fool. Did it start here? Or were there others in Santa Fe?"

"Rachel, don't be ridiculous."

"Don't! Don't say I am being ridiculous. And don't brush me off. At the very least, you owe me an explanation." She set down her mug. Suddenly, the coffee tasted rancid as it mixed with the bile she swallowed to keep it from rising in her throat.

Matt turned around and laid his hands on the counter. He looked out the kitchen window. "I have never been unfaithful to you, Rachel. And I never will."

"Then what do you call that little display in the saloon yesterday? Nothing?"

"Exactly!" he bit out angrily, quickly turning toward her. "Nothing happened, Rachel. I have been faithful to you."

Rachel laughed haughtily. "You expect me to believe that? I saw you. I saw how you were looking at her and how she was looking at you. You were flirting for God's sake!"

"Okay, so I was innocently flirting a little, but did you see me touching her?"

"You didn't have to; she had her watermelons plastered against your arm. The two of you were ready to go up to her room."

"We were not! I would never have let it go that far."

Rachel put her hands on his hips. "Oh really? Didn't look that way from my viewpoint. You both looked ready to hit the sack."

"Well, you're wrong. How can I prove it to you? How do we get back what we had?"

Rachel was the one to turn away now; she couldn't look at him. "I'm not sure we can. I have loved you more than I ever thought possible. And I thought you loved me the same way. But I was wrong. If you truly loved me you would never have let that woman touch you." She glanced back at Matt. He stood stone faced, his fists tight at his sides. "Matt, love is based on trust. Yesterday, you lost my trust."

He bent his head low, raised it and looked at her, nearly looking through her. "How do I earn it back?"

"I don't know what you have to do to gain my trust again. But for now, you should find another place to sleep because you are not welcome in my bed." Rachel walked out of the kitchen and up the stairs. As she entered Maddie's room she heard the front door open and loudly slam shut. She was grateful he was gone but at the same time she wanted him home. She couldn't imagine how they would get back the life they had before yesterday.

Over the next few days, a foreboding silence overshadowed the household. Meals were particularly grim as each parent tried to engage the children in conversation to keep from talking to one another. The children didn't buy into it. Rachel wasn't sure where Matt was sleeping. One morning Mrs. Trujillo came up behind Rachel and coughed. Rachel looked around at her.

"Yes?"

"Shall I wash Mr. Matt's bed linens?"

"What bed linens?"

"The ones Mr. Matt is using in the study where he is sleeping. They could use some freshening."

341

"Sure, whatever," Rachel answered distractedly.

A part of her was grateful to learn he had been sleeping at home, but another part of her wished he wasn't. With each day she missed Matt more and more. Even so she couldn't forgive him. She was sure he had been more than flirtatious with Madame Bishu, and she wished he would simply come clean with an admission of guilt.

Around noon there was a loud knock on the front door. Rachel opened it to find Madame Bishu standing on the porch in one of her fine gowns, studded with rhinestones and edged with lace. Rachel tried not to show her shock; she held her head high and gave her a visual check from head to toe. She was even prettier than she remembered from when they met briefly in 1880. Not only did she still look like a 19th century Christie Brinkley, but had matured into an even better looking woman, replete with golden blonde corkscrew curls, high cheeks, sensuous lips, and a long slender neck that opened to an impressive bosom peeking out under the lace.

"If you are looking for Matt, he isn't here," Rachel said in a flat voice devoid of emotion.

"Mrs. Bradshaw, I am not here to see him, I am here to see you. May I come in?"

"I think not," Rachel responded curtly. "What do you want? If it's Matt, you've already got him."

"It is not Matthew that I want. He's yours and has been from the moment he laid eyes on you when you first arrived in Oak Valley. I came to speak to you. To tell you that there has been a grave mistake."

"What mistake?" Rachel knitted her brows together.

"Your husband has been faithful to you, Mrs. Bradshaw. I know the men of this town and believe me I know which ones are not true to their wives. Matthew is not one of those men."

"Didn't look that way when I saw the two of you together in the saloon."

"That was my fault. I was joking around with Matthew. Trying to get him to loosen up a little, just like I do with all the men. But he wasn't interested. I was foolish to keep trying."

"You were pressing your breasts against him," Rachel stated matter-of-factly as though she was remarking on the changing weather.

"Yes," Madame Bishu nodded. "I was, and as you walked in he was telling me to stop, but I kept it up saying that I thought he liked it. He had just said that he preferred yours when you walked up. That's what we were laughing about. I was acting hurt, because I'm sure you know that before you, Matthew paid me regular visits when he came to town."

"Yes, I know that," Rachel responded, this time her voice a little softer.

"Don't be angry with your husband and ruin your marriage over this. It is not worth it. If you are going to blame anyone, blame me. I am at fault, not him."

Rachel stood there staring at the woman. She didn't know what to make of it.

"How do I know that Matt didn't ask you to come here and tell me this story so I would take him back?"

"You will have to search your heart for that answer, Mrs. Bradshaw. I can tell you that he did not tell me to come see you. In fact, I have not seen him since that day you came into the saloon. Then I saw him on the street today. He looked terribly sad. I asked him what was wrong and he told me that you are angry with him because you think I took him into my bed. I have known Matthew a long, long time. Not much bothers him, but he is as distraught as I have ever seen him. No, he did not tell me to come here. Your heart will tell you what to believe. I can only urge you to not let a mistake on my part ruin your marriage. You have something rare with Matthew."

Madame Bishu picked up her ruffled skirts and went down the stairs, across the yard to the street, never stopping to look back. Rachel watched her walk down the street until she could see her no more. She turned back inside and nearly stepped on Wolf.

"How long have you been there?" Rachel asked.

"Since you opened door."

"It is very rude to eavesdrop on other people's conversations," Rachel said firmly.

"She speaks truth."

"And you know this…..how?"

The boy shrugged. "Not know how. Just know. Papa Matt is good man."

Rachel looked the boy through and through. She knew he was right and she knew she should have allowed Matt to explain, but she was so hurt her heartache wouldn't allow her to do anything but shut him out of her life. She didn't know if she could bring herself to apologize to Matt for her treatment of him. She knew she had to try.

"Come, it's getting cold," she said as she closed the door and led him toward the kitchen. "Let's get something warm to drink."

As soon as they entered the kitchen she saw Mrs. Trujillo.

"Are you done washing the sheets from the study?"

Mrs. Trujillo nodded.

"When they're dry please put them away in the linen closet. Matt won't be sleeping in the study anymore."

Mrs. Trujillo's eyebrows rose, a slight smile on her face. "No?"

"No," Rachel answered definitively. "Now let's find that tin of cocoa, shall we, Wolf?"

Wolf ran over to a low cabinet, opened the door and drew out a container. He handed her the tin of cocoa with a big toothy smile plastered across his face. As Rachel began making the hot cocoa, she asked Mrs. Trujillo if she had started making dinner yet.

"No, Mrs. Rachel. Is there something in particular you want?"

"Roasted chicken with boiled potatoes tossed in melted butter, beans in red chile sauce, and flan for dessert, if it wouldn't be too much trouble."

"No trouble at all," the woman responded, a little smile darting out the sides of her lips, because she knew it was Matt's favorite meal.

* * *

Dinner was quiet as had become the pattern the previous few days. When they finished, Wolf asked to take Maddie upstairs. When Rachel gave him permission, he quickly took Maddie's hand and ran up the stairs with her. Matt watched with a look of curiosity on his face. He looked over at Rachel who was smiling at him. His eyes widened with surprise.

"I think it's time to put our argument behind us," she began, absentmindedly playing with one of her curls. Her thick hair was loose, cascading down her shoulders and back.

Matt slid back in his chair, his arms crossed over his chest. "That would be wise. We can't continue living like this."

"No, we can't. I had a visitor today who shed some light on what happened that day in the saloon."

Matt's eyes narrowed, the vertical crease resurfacing between his brows. "And who was that?"

"Your friend, Madame Bishu."

"She came here?!" Matt said almost shouting. "Why?"

"She came to apologize and say that you had nothing to do with encouraging or accepting her advances."

"I didn't accept ANY advances from her!"

"I know that, now. But I sure didn't know it then. From my vantage point it appeared that you were encouraging her. She assured me that you were not. At first I thought you put her up to coming here, but I soon realized that you didn't and her concern was genuine."

"I tried to tell you that when I followed you home that day, but you wouldn't let me."

"Matt, I was too hurt to listen to you. Nothing you said would have quelled my anger or grief. I couldn't fathom what I had done to drive you to another woman, much less to your previous lover. I truly am sorry I didn't give you the opportunity to explain yourself. But, do you understand it wouldn't have done any good? I was devastated."

He slid a little further down in his chair and ran his fingers over his mustache, never taking his eyes off of Rachel. "Yes, I suppose, even if you were dead wrong. How could you think for even a moment that I would seek favors with another woman when I have the best woman in the world at home?"

Rachel stared at him, not able to murmur a word.

"We have something that other people envy, something I never knew was possible. You say you love me, but you obviously have no idea the depth of my affection for you, Rachel. If you asked me to die for you, while I wouldn't like it, I would do it without question.

Is that a love that a brothel madam can even dream of breaking?"

A lump formed in her throat; her eyes began to burn with tears. Rather than speak, she got up and walked over to his chair. He rose and took her in his arms. She ran her hands about his waist and laid her head on his chest and held him, melding them into one. Tears of relief silently spilled down her cheeks. After a few moments, Rachel pulled her head back and looked at him, looked through him to the place where she knew his soul lived. Matt rested his forehead on hers and held her head in his hands, wiping at her tears with his thumbs. He bent down and kissed her – first gently, then passionately, deeply, nearly swallowing her. She responded, kissing him back as though it was the first, the last and the finest kiss of all time.

"Does this mean I am welcome in the bedroom?"

Rachel nodded, smiling.

"Good, because sleeping in the study chair is killing my back."

"I'll work out your back kinks tonight," she grinned suggestively, arching one brow. Her green eyes lightened to the color of new grass, as joy permeated her being. "Listen, I am mentally exhausted from all of this and I'd like to turn in early tonight. But first I need to put food away and clean up the kitchen. If you help me I can finish faster." She wiggled her eyebrows at him.

The edge of Matt's mouth turned upward; his eyes danced. "Yeah, sure. Guess I should have known something was up when I saw what you served for dinner."

Rachel rose up on her tiptoes and kissed him lightly, then removed herself from his embrace and began clearing the table, Matt at her side. As soon as they finished cleaning up and putting away food they ascended the stairs, hand in hand.

"Gotta put the children to bed," she said when they reached the landing.

He followed her into Maddie's room where they found Maddie already in her nightgown, asleep in her bed. Next they went into Wolf's room where he too was already in his pajamas and sleeping soundly, his arm wrapped around Wabbit who snored bunny breaths. They tiptoed out and didn't see Wolf smiling as he watched them go.

* * *

The middle of November, Rachel put on her best dress, hat, and gloves. She wrapped herself in a warm shawl and went downstairs to the study where Matt was filling out some paperwork.

"Are you ready?" she asked.

He looked up. "Let me just sign these papers. I need to mail them on the way to the council meeting."

Matt finished the paperwork, inserted them into an envelope, grabbed his hat and leather coat and escorted Rachel to the door. In minutes, they mailed the envelope at the post office and headed to the council chambers where they found many of the town's citizens already seated. They sat in the last two seats.

"Uh-hum!" a voice rang out. "Calling this meeting to order!"

Several men sat at a long table at the front of the room. The man speaking sat to the side of the long table. He identified himself as the clerk and read the minutes of the last meeting.

At the long table sat four men. A placard in front of the man at the far left end indicated he was Mayor Wilford Walton, Dorothea's husband. Rachel looked around the room and spotted Dorothea who saw Rachel at the same time. She was sitting next to Lily and her husband Earl Hayes, the dentist. The three of them nodded to Rachel. Next to the mayor sat Hubert Brown, Bartholomew Monroe and Jack Clayton.

"The purpose of this meeting is to discuss the request made to the council by the El Paso and Northeastern Railway," Mayor Walton began. The crowd murmured.

"As you know the railroad runs along the trail, west of town. They are offering to build an extension line into Oak Valley, if the town funds the construction that would start in the next decade. The railroad is requesting $10,000 and is giving us 10 years to come up with the money."

The room erupted in a buzz of conversation.

"Quiet!" the mayor called out. The room silenced. "We are here to discuss the merits of accepting or rejecting the railroad's request. Who would like to begin?"

"I would," said Hubert Brown, the light-haired councilman nearly as round as he was tall. He stood up, leaned back and tucked his thumbs into his front vest pockets. "This expenditure would be a very poor use of our limited funds." He shook his head causing his jowls to wobble from side to side. "While indeed we are growing, we can ill afford to saddle ourselves with an exorbitant expenditure. If the railroad wants to come into Oak Valley, I say let them fund it." As soon as the man sat down the room erupted in chatter.

"Silence!" yelled Mr. Walton over the noise. When the room quieted he asked if someone would offer an opposing view.

Rachel was just about to stand up when a man in the audience beat her to it. She had seen him about town, however didn't know his name. He looked big city, elegantly dressed in tailored clothing made of fine cloth.

"With all due respect councilman, that is an absurd opinion. First, it is to our benefit for a line to run into Oak Valley, not the railroad's. The West is growing rapidly. If we do not fund and allow the railroad into Oak Valley, the expansion that is sweeping across our region will pass us by, and I say we cannot allow that to happen."

Before the man sat down, Bartholomew Monroe, an older, distinguished-looking man, stood at the council table. "The rail line is already planning to follow the El Camino Real. They will likely build a station out there, a ways west of here. Why should we pay for an extension when we can simply run our wagons over to the rail line? Spending $10,000 for that short a distance does not make good fiscal sense." The man sat down and again the room erupted in conversation.

This time Mr. Walton waited for the noise to simmer down on its own, then asked if there were any other opposing views. Rachel jumped up. "Yes, I have one," she called out across the room. The people turned to look at her. No one could mistake the looks of amusement on the councilmen's faces.

"Just for argument's sake, let's say you don't fund the extension. And for argument's sake, the mines run dry. It could happen you know; it has certainly happened to other mines. What would happen then? We would have no industry, no mines, and no modern transportation to bring new business to Oak Valley. Don't you think it is being rather short-sighted to assume you can operate a town without modern transportation, especially if the mines cease to provide an income to the town?"

"That's ridiculous!" retorted Jack Clayton. "The mines aren't going to dry up. We're exploring new veins as we speak."

"She's right," said another man in the audience who stood up. "I supervise at the mines. We figure that in 10 years the silver'll be fully mined out. We're lookin' for other veins, but we haven't found any yet. If the mine dries up, without other bidness, and no railroad, this town'll be a ghost town in no time."

Rachel shuddered as she remembered seeing the sign outside of Oak Valley in the 21st century that told of how the town refused the rail line. When the mines went dry, indeed it turned into a ghost town. She saw it for herself.

The man sat down and another person who opposed the expenditure stood and voiced his opposition. And so the afternoon went. One opposed, followed by one in support. Finally, Mayor Walton called a halt to the discussion.

"It is very obvious to me that this issue is not going to be resolved at this meeting. Therefore, I move that we table a vote and decision until after the New Year. At our January 1886 meeting we will resume the discussion and hopefully come to a mutual decision. Will anyone move to agree to this postponement?"

Councilman Jack Clayton raised his hand. "I move to postpone the vote until the January meeting, even though I don't agree with it."

The mayor glared at him. "Now Jack, you know you can't offer an opinion while making a motion."

"Okay, fine," Mr. Clayton grumbled. "I move to postpone the vote on the rail line until the January meeting. Period."

Mr. Monroe seconded the motion and Mr. Walton closed the meeting. The crowd broke out in conversation. The noise was so deafening that when Matt tried to say something to Rachel, she couldn't hear him at all. She waved him to move outside. As they emerged they were met by Dorothea Walton, Lily and Dr. Hayes.

"Well done, Mrs. Bradshaw," the dentist said.

"I agree," Mrs. Walton added. "You have a lot of gumption going up against the council, especially my husband." She grinned at Lily. "Did you see the expression on Wilford's face when Mrs. Bradshaw stood up to speak, and then how shocked he was at her comment?"

"I did," Mrs. Hayes answered, looking back over at Rachel. "I congratulate you. I would never have had the nerve to do what you did."

"Well, somebody had to bring up the issue of the mines," Rachel responded. "It's silly really to put all your eggs in one basket and shoot down every chance of landing on the moon."

The two women and the dentist looked at Rachel as though she were speaking Greek.

"What my wife meant to say," Matt jumped in, "is that if the town does not diversify and continues to count on the mines for its sustenance, if they fail and there is no railroad to bring in new business, the town will surely die."

"Of course, of course," nodded Dr. Hayes. "I quite agree."

Mayor Walton emerged from the hall and met up with his wife. He glared at Rachel, took his wife's arm and led her away. The Hayes chuckled and bid Rachel and Matt farewell.

"I'm proud of you," Matt whispered into Rachel's ear.

"Are you? Was I okay?"

"Absolutely. No one else was thinking beyond next week and their current bank accounts. If nothing else, you got them thinking."

"Yes, but do you think I got the council thinking enough to overturn their bias to vote down the rail line? I didn't get the feeling that the council was going to vote for the extension. It seemed like they were giving people a chance to voice their opinions, but have no intention of honoring the majority opinion if it differs from that of the council."

"You're probably right. We'll have to see what happens at the January meeting."

"Oh Matt, it can't wait until then. We have to do something now. We have to influence the naysayers now."

"And how do you propose to do that?" Matt peered down at Rachel.

"Give me a bit, I have an idea and need to think it through."

"This wouldn't be like your first plan in Santa Fe to go to all the wives and urge them not to have relations with their husbands unless the newspaper ran Henrietta's letter, is it?"

"No, not exactly," Rachel responded. "Actually, I think I have an even better idea. But I'll sleep on it and think through the details."

Matt glanced down and shook his head. "I've got a funny feeling about this; when you get that look in your eye…"

"Oh let's not talk about it now," Rachel quipped. "I'm hungry, where are you taking me to lunch?"

Matt bug eyed at her. "Lunch? Well, okay. The café." He put his arm around her and led her to the restaurant that was already crowded with people who had attended the meeting. A few people frowned at Rachel while others smiled. Seeing no open tables, they left and headed home where they dined with the children on Mrs. Trujillo's green chile stew and fresh warm tortillas.

* * *

The next morning after breakfast, the children occupied playing ball, Rachel stepped into the study where Matt was recording his monthly finances in a ledger. She grinned. He was using the solar powered calculator she had given him; something she had with her when she traveled from the 21st century. She walked over to him.

"It's still working, is it?" she said, looking down at the calculator.

"Yep, as well as the day you gave it to me. I don't know what I'm going to do when this thing stops working. It's a godsend."

Rachel bent down and kissed him on the cheek. "Some new device will become available, I'm sure. In the meantime, this one should last for quite a while longer. Listen, would you mind keeping an eye on the children? I have to run an errand; I'll be back in a few."

"Yeah, sure," he nodded, never taking his eyes off his ledger.

Rachel walked out and stood in front of the hallway coat rack, put on her heavy shawl, hat and gloves, and headed out the door and toward the saloon. She stepped inside to a near-empty room. Madame Bishu was standing by the long wooden bar, talking with the bartender and one of her working girls. She turned to see who walked in, and when she saw it was Rachel she dismissed the girl and quickly walked over to Rachel.

"Matthew is not here, I promise you," Madame Bishu began. Underneath her face powder her cheeks flushed red.

Rachel smiled as sweetly as she could. "Matt is at home. I'm not here about him. I consider that business behind us."

"Then what are you doing here?" the madam pressed, arching her brows and waiting for a response.

"I want to talk to you about something important, something that affects the future of this town."

Madame Bishu nodded and led Rachel to a table in a back corner where she wouldn't easily be seen if any customers walked into the bar. She gestured for Rachel to sit.

"Would you...would you," she stammered, "like something to drink?"

Rachel grinned. "Sure, a good bourbon if you have it."

Madame Bishu nodded, went behind the bar, took down a bottle of amber liquid and poured two drinks into short glasses. She returned to the table and handed one glass to Rachel.

"I don't usually drink in my establishment, but something tells me I may need it for this conversation."

"I would like to think that the subject of our conversation will not be upsetting," Rachel grinned at her. "In fact, it might even be fun."

"Fun?" Madame Bishu blinked several times as though eye movement would help her understand Rachel's use of the word.

"I'll get right to the point. Yesterday the town council held a meeting to decide on whether to pay the railroad a large fee to fund the construction of an extension into Oak Valley."

"Yes," Madame Bishu nodded as she sipped her bourbon. "Last night several customers were talking about it."

Rachel took a sip of her bourbon and continued. "So, here's the deal. If the railroad came into Oak Valley, wouldn't you benefit? See a lot more customers for your business, well, both of your businesses?" Rachel looked straight at the Madame and showed no embarrassment.

"Yes," Madame Bishu answered cautiously, narrowing her eyes a bit.

"At yesterday's meeting, it was very apparent that the council members don't want the extension. Although they asked the public for input, it was appallingly obvious that they are going to vote against it at the next meeting, regardless of what the public thinks.

Many people who stood up and spoke yesterday, myself included, think that it would help the town."

"Why are you here telling me all this?"

"The point I made at the meeting yesterday is that if, and I only mean if, the mines dry up, and we don't have another source of industry or the railroad extension to bring in new business, that Oak Valley will turn into a ghost town."

Rachel watched Madame Bishu's face. She could see she was thinking, taking in her statements.

"That is possible. But again, how do I factor into this?"

"Let's be honest, Madame Bishu. You are the only saloon in town and the only brothel. I have to assume that a number of the council members seek the services of you or your girls." Madame Bishu nodded. "You could be very instrumental in getting those council members to change their vote."

Madame Bishu turned her head slightly. "How so?"

"Well, for example, you could tell the council members that they are no longer welcome in your establishment for either of your businesses. Considering you are the only saloon and brothel in town, that would create quite a predicament for them. The other idea is more extreme."

"And what is that?"

"You could tell the council members who frequent your girls' rooms that you are going to tell their wives if they don't vote for the rail line."

Madame Bishu had just taken a sip of bourbon and when she heard Rachel's second idea, she choked on it. She coughed and coughed, and slapped her chest to clear her throat.

"That is extortion, Mrs. Bradshaw, and quite extreme. Why would I do this and risk being thrown in jail for blackmail?"

"Well, first, it would be for the good of the town. Second, you would ultimately benefit from the people who will come in on the new rail line. Third, I highly doubt you would be arrested for extortion because it would mean the council members exposing their adultery with your working girls, which I really doubt they would want to happen. And finally, you owe me. You nearly broke up my marriage."

Madame Bishu frowned. She sucked in a large breath of air and with it her enormous breasts rose high in her lace bodice. "Yes, I do owe you, I'll admit that. But what you are asking.....it is a significant request. It could damage my business or it could help it. I am curious. Why do you care so much about this town? You and Matthew could live anywhere. Why here?"

"Oh, let's just say I have a special connection to this place and I wouldn't want to see the town die."

Madame Bishu regarded Rachel skeptically, watching her face for several moments before she spoke. "I will grant you cleverness. I consider myself to be a shrewd businesswoman, however, I must admit, I would never have thought of this."

Rachel gulped down the rest of her bourbon. "So, will you do it?"

Madame Bishu stared at Rachel a full minute before she knocked back the rest of her drink and answered. "Yes, I will. Your points are well made and, as you say, I stand to benefit in many ways if the rail line comes into Oak Valley."

Rachel smiled and stood up. "Thank you. I appreciate your support."

"I will send word when I have completed my conversations with the gentlemen in question. They frequent my establishment regularly. I should be able to speak with all of them within a week or two."

"Fine," Rachel grinned. "And by the way, I meant it when I said that what occurred before is behind us. We both have vested interests in this town. Working together we can make Oak Valley the jewel of New Mexico."

Madame Bishu bowed her head slightly and escorted Rachel to a back door to leave discreetly. As soon as the door closed behind her she all but skipped home. As soon as she opened her front door she ran into the study to share her good news with Matt. When he heard what she did, he burst out laughing, a deep guttural belly laugh that made his shoulders shake.

"What's so funny?" Rachel asked, confused, not knowing if she should be mad or happy at his reaction.

"You, my dear, you are unbelievable! Just weeks ago you were ready to end our marriage over that woman and now you are conspiring with her to sway the rail line vote. You are definitely the sharpest woman, with the most gumption, that I have ever known."

Taking large steps he strode over to Rachel, bent down and gave her a big kiss. They were interrupted by a cough. They pulled apart to see Mrs. Trujillo standing in the doorway, a young woman at her side.

"Mrs. Lucero is here to see you, Mrs. Rachel. Her belly hurts."

"Of course," Rachel backed away from Matt. "Please take Mrs. Lucero into the treatment room. I'll be right there."

As soon as they were gone, Rachel gave Matt another small kiss, turned and hurried out of the room. As he sat back down, Matt couldn't help grinning.

* * *

The January 1886 meeting of the council chambers was even more crowded than the previous month. This time Matt and Rachel got there early enough to sit near the front. People chatted loudly until Mayor Walton banged his gavel on the table, bringing the meeting to order.

"We convene this meeting to further discuss the merits of bringing the railroad extension into Oak Valley," the man began. "Clerk, please conduct the roll call and read the minutes from the last meeting."

Rachel leaned over to Matt. "Did you hear what he said? He said only merits, not drawbacks. That's positive, don't you think?"

Matt smiled, reached over and squeezed her hand. A spry man with neatly combed, blonde hair and a large mustache that grew over his mouth conducted the roll call and read the minutes from the previous meeting. As he spoke, his mustache wiggled, making it look like the mustache was speaking instead of the man. When he finished reading, he looked to the mayor who coughed into his fist to gain attention.

"Let us resume our discussion of the rail line proposal we began at the last meeting and let us begin with those opposed to the extension. Who would like to speak?" the mayor asked.

A tall, muscular man with an acne-pocked face stood up. "I'm Horace Villareal."

"Yes, Mr. Villareal?" the mayor nodded to the man.

"The wife and I have been discussin' this and we're wonderin' what this is gonna cost each citizen?"

Wilford looked over at Hubert Brown. "Hubert, I believe you have those figures. Will you answer the question?"

"Well, to be fair to everyone, considering that we currently have about 3,000 residents it would cost approximately $3.33 per person," Hubert answered.

"What about those who can't pay?" Horace pressed. "This hasn't been a good year for my store."

Bartholomew Monroe barked at him. "For crying out loud Horace, you'll have 10 years to save up to pay it! That's .33 cents a year each for you and your wife. Don't tell me you can't afford to save .66 cents a year? If you can't, drink one less beer a week!"

Horace turned a bright shade of scarlet. "Well, if you put it that way, I suppose so." He sat and slunk down in his seat.

"Any other questions or opposition?" Wilford called out, scanning the room with his eyes. No one stood or made a sound. "All right, what about supporters?" Several people stood up immediately, talking all at once. "Silence! One at a time!" yelled the mayor. He pointed to a man wearing a jacket a couple of sizes too small. Wide, bushy sideburns stuck out from the side of the man's face. "Frank, you have the floor."

"I could use some outside business. There's not enough customers in town for me to make a living," the man said.

"That's probably because you make those high-falutin' saddles covered in silver studs that nobody can afford," Jack Clayton, the third councilman, called to him. "Bring down your prices or make a cheaper saddle and you'll get customers."

The room broke out in laughter; the man sat down with a frown on his face.

Wilford pointed to another man in the back who stood holding his hat across his chest. He was thin and lanky. "I think it's a good idea," the man said.

"And why is that?" Bartholomew Monroe asked.

"I dunno know, I just think it is." The man sat down amidst chuckles from the gallery.

Several more speakers stood and made similar comments, all in support of the rail line. As the last speaker sat down someone came in the door. The mayor and the councilmen stared at the back of the room, their faces reddened, and beads of sweat popped out across their foreheads. Everyone turned around to see Madame Bishu standing at the back of the room, smiling.

Rachel giggled and grinned at Madame Bishu, who catching Rachel's eye, grinned back. They both looked to the front of the room. Rachel whispered toward Matt. "This is gonna be fun. Look at them, they're sweating."

"Gentlemen, I think it is time for a vote on the rail line extension, don't you agree?" a flustered Wilford asked the councilmen. They all nodded and avoided looking at Madame Bishu.

"Jack?" Wilford asked.

Jack Clayton answered "I vote for the rail line."

"Hubert?"

"Yes vote."

"Batholomew?"

"Yes vote."

"I vote yes too, that makes it a unanimous vote to approve the rail line coming into Oak Valley," Wilford stated.

The room erupted in cheers with a few hats being thrown into the air. Rachel looked up at Matt.

"You did it, Rachel, I'm proud of you," Matt said cupping her jaw in his hand. "After the first meeting

I wasn't sure it could be done, but you were a force to be reckoned with."

"Come on, it wasn't that hard. Faced with losing their privileges at Madame Bishu's or her informing their wives of their indiscretions, well, it was a no-brainer, Matt. This vote couldn't lose." She grinned as though she learned she had won the lottery, and in her mind, it was pretty much the same thing. Rachel looked to the back of the room for Madame Bishu, but she had already left. "I'd say this calls for a celebration. Let's go." She took Matt's hand and led him out of the building.

"Where to?" Matt asked

Rachel grinned slyly. "You'll see." She headed straight to the saloon and before Matt could stop her, she bolted inside. Madame Bishu stood at the bar. Her jaw dropped slightly at seeing Rachel and Matt, but recovered her composure quickly and nodded her head. She headed over to the center table where Rachel sat down.

"Are you sure you want to be seen in here?" Madame Bishu said in a hushed voice.

"Absolutely. I have nothing to be ashamed of and we have you to thank for saving this town."

"It was not all my doing, Mrs. Bradshaw. It was your idea."

"Yes, but you executed it – and brilliantly, I might add." Rachel patted the chair next to her. "Won't you join us for a celebratory toast to Oak Valley?"

Madame Bishu looked at Matt who had been watching silently and back at Rachel. "What would you like to drink? It's on the house."

"That's very kind, but we will pay," Rachel responded.

"No, I insist, it's the least I can do. What will it be? Whiskey? Champagne? Wine?"

"You have champagne?"

"We do, a fine bottle from France. I've been waiting for a good enough reason to open it. Seems to me that this is as good a reason as any, maybe even better."

Madame Bishu strode over to the bar, and spoke to the bartender who reached under the counter for three champagne glasses that Madame Bishu brought over to the table. A moment later the bartender returned with the chilled bottle of champagne and opened it tableside, pouring it into their glasses.

"To Oak Valley then?" Madame Bishu asked looking at Rachel and Matt both of whom nodded and swallowed their champagne in a single gulp.

Chapter Eighteen

Summer 1887

"Wolf, you ready?" Matt called out to the boy up the stairs.

Rachel walked down the hallway. "Ready for what?"

"I'm taking Wolf up the mountain today and showing him how to shoot." Matt no sooner finished speaking than Wolf barreled down the stairs.

"Shoot? Really? Don't you think he's a little young?" Rachel knitted her brows together and crossed her arms over her chest.

"Mama, I'm old enough now. Aren't I, Papa?"

"Indeed you are," Matt reached over and affectionately roughed up the top of his head. He bent down and kissed Rachel lightly. "Don't worry, I'm just showing him the basics. It's time he learned and who better to learn from than his father?"

"All right, just don't be too long. Wolf, remember that your cousin Emily is coming in on the stage later today. You don't want to miss that."

The boy leaned over and gave Rachel a hug. Matt picked up the small rifle he bought for Wolf and a box of bullets and headed to the door, followed close behind by Wolf, who skipped rather than walked.

Rachel marveled silently at how Matt had gone from reticently accepting Wolf into their home to treating him as his son. She watched them through the front window. They walked out the front yard, Matt with his arm around Wolf who looked up at Matt, beaming with pride and joy.

* * *

Later that day Rachel, Maddie and Wolf milled around the stage line office, waiting. The children played tag while Rachel repeatedly looked up the street. Finally, she caught sight of the stagecoach and pulled the children onto the wooden sidewalk. As the stage neared, they saw Emily waving happily out the window. When the coach stopped, Emily emerged out the door and into Rachel's arms. Maddie jumped up and down, whimpering.

"Maddie, look at how you've grown!" Emily said, reaching down and hugging the little girl, trying to lift her. "I can hardly pick you up anymore."

"Talk about who has grown, look at you!" Rachel said in awe of her niece. "You are quite the young lady."

Emily smiled demurely, her long brown lashes sweeping across her cheeks. And indeed, she had grown a great deal since she last saw the Oak Valley family. Now 15 years old, she had blossomed into a beautiful teen with rose-colored cheeks, cherry lips and blonde hair, threaded with highlights of gold. She still wore it in a braid down her back.

"How are you, Wolf?" Emily turned to the boy. "You're quite a big boy! Turn around so I can see all of you."

Wolf proudly spun around on his boot heel, his arms outstretched and his braid flying as he turned. When he stopped he stood as tall as he could.

"I can't believe how long your braid is now. It's almost as long as mine."

Wolf grinned, his two front teeth missing. Emily giggled.

"Where are your front teeth?" she asked.

"Mama says the tooth fairy took them. I put them under my pillow and the tooth fairy paid me for them. I opened a bank account with the money."

Emily looked over at Rachel, her eyebrows raised in question.

Rachel wrinkled her nose. "It was a tradition when I was growing up," Rachel stated matter-of-factly.

Emily looked back at Wolf. "Your English is much improved. You sound like me now."

Again, Wolf took her statement as a compliment, a big grin showing his appreciation. "Will you stay with us all summer?" he asked.

"Yes, until I have to go back to Santa Fe for school in the fall." Emily turned to Rachel. "That is, if it is still all right with you and Uncle Matt."

"Absolutely! Well, let's go home, shall we?" Rachel asked the children. "Mrs. Trujillo baked a caramel cake for your arrival, Em. We've had a hard time keeping Wolf from eating it."

Wolf grinned, a devilish twinkle in his dark eyes. "Race you home," he said to Emily. "Whoever gets there first gets the whole cake!"

"Uh-uh, it's my cake!" Emily squealed taking him up on the challenge, running behind him as fast as she could, their braids flying in the wind.

* * *

A couple of weeks into her visit, Emily walked into Rachel's treatment room where Rachel was processing her latest batch of dried herbs. Emily was holding Maddie's hand.

"Auntie Rachel?"

"Yes, sweetie?"

"We finished straightening our rooms. May I take Maddie with me to go shopping?"

Rachel looked over at the girls. "Of course, what do you need?"

"Some new ribbons for my hair. Mine are getting tattered."

"Hold on a minute and let me get my change purse to give you some money."

"That's not necessary; I brought some money with me."

"Well, okay, but don't be long, lunch will be ready in an hour." Rachel leaned down and kissed the two girls. "Now you, young lady," she said to Maddie, "you mind your cousin, okay?"

Maddie smiled a sheepish grin and held her head down low. "I will, Mama."

"Can I go too?"

The three of them looked to the door to see Wolf standing there.

"Have you tidied your room?" Rachel asked. Wolf shook his head. "You know the rules. No play until rooms are neat and orderly. So, no, you can't go with them." Wolf lowered his head to his chest, slunk out of the room and up the stairs.

"Awww, can't he go with us, just this once?" Emily asked, her Bradshaw blue eyes doe-like, pleading.

"Nope. I know it seems mean, but it's important to keep to a routine. If I let him off this time, he will try to get out of it again. I don't want to set a precedent."

"Mama, what's a pressi, a, pressi-sent?" Maddie asked.

"It's precedent, honey. And it means setting a pattern for behavior that he will think is okay to do again."

"You mean kind of like when I won't eat my vegables and you won't let me have dessert until I eat them?"

"Exactly. Now you two move along, I have work to do in here. Have fun!"

The girls turned and left the house. Within minutes they reached the center of town, where they headed to the general store for ribbon shopping.

Emily and Maddie looked at every spool of ribbon, drawing out long pieces to see the colors and feel each one. They giggled and laughed dragging the ribbons over their faces and wrapping them around their wrists. Finally, Emily carried their choices to the man at the counter and asked him to cut lengths of each one. Emily paid him, and taking Maddie's hand led her out of the store. They stepped off the curb just before a group of Mexicans galloped up and stopped in front of them. Emily glanced at them and stepped back onto the curb, pulling Maddie with her. The man on the front horse grabbed Emily, causing her let go of Maddie's hand. The man behind him scooped up Maddie and followed the first man, the third man one racing on their tail. As the men roared out of town the girls screamed, bringing stares from the townspeople who watched the men carry away the girls.

* * *

Wolf returned to the treatment room. "I cleaned my room. Can I go to town now and join Emily and Maddie?"

"You sure it's neat and tidy?" Rachel eyed him. Wolf nodded. "Okay then. Remind them to be back by lunchtime." Rachel turned back to her herbs and heard the front door open and close.

Wolf strode toward the general store where he saw a large group of people milling around in front, talking in loud, animated voices. As he approached, a man held a bag with ribbons sticking out the top. He stood next to a woman that Wolf recognized as a friend of Rachel's.

"What's going on Mrs. Hayes?" he asked.

"Oh, Wolf. Something terrible has happened. Are your parents at home?"

He nodded. "What happened?"

Luther Maxwell, who was holding the bag of ribbons, stepped over to Wolf. "Miss Emily and Miss Madeleine were kidnapped. A group of Mexicans rode into town and grabbed them right off the sidewalk. One of the girls dropped this bag of ribbons."

Wolf gasped. "I'll go after them."

"No, Wolf. We're putting together a posse. Go home and tell your parents that the posse will leave in 20 minutes."

Wolf didn't wait a moment. He ran as hard as he could all the way home, bursting into the house.

"Mama, Papa?" he yelled as loud as he could. "Help!!"

Rachel, Matt and Mrs. Trujillo converged on Wolf at the same time. "What is it, Wolf?" Matt asked kneeling down to the boy's level.

"Maddie and Emily, they've been kidnapped! The town is forming a posse to go after them and said they're leaving in 20 minutes." Big tears seeped out of his eyes; he wiped away at the moisture on his face.

"Wait, wait, calm down, Wolf," Matt said in a serious tone. "Who kidnapped them? When?"

"A few minutes ago, in front of the general store. Mr. Maxwell said some Mexicans grabbed them off the sidewalk." Wolf looked up at Rachel. Her face had gone white with shock.

"How many men, Wolf?" Matt asked.

"I don't know."

"Rachel, I'll go, you stay here and take care of Wolf."

"Like hell, I'll stay here. I'm going with you, and Wolf can stay here with Mrs. Trujillo."

"No, Mama, let me go. I can track them," Wolf pleaded.

Rachel and Matt looked at Wolf. "What do you mean, you can track them?" Matt asked. "Since when can you track?"

"My uncle taught me. Let me go with you. I can find them!"

Matt looked up at Rachel. "I don't want to waste time arguing with either one of you. This is going to be hard ride, but if you want to go, Rachel, get your gun and mine and plenty of bullets. Change clothes and get Wolf ready. I'll saddle up the horses. Meet me in front of the house in 10 minutes."

"Mrs. Trujillo, can you pack us some food to take on the ride?" Rachel asked. Mrs. Trujillo nodded and raced to the kitchen.

Before Matt left the house Rachel and Wolf were sprinting up the stairs. Wolf ran to his room as

Rachel ran into hers. Not having the time or patience to deal with her 19th century fashions, she ripped off her clothing and dressed in one of Matt's shirts and a pair of Matt's pants that were several sizes too big. She cinched the waistline with a belt and wore a pair of her own western-style boots. She pulled her hair into a pony tail to accommodate the cowboy hat she found in Matt's side of the closet. In one hand she carried a bag with her gun and ammunition and Matt's rifle and, in the other hand, a hat for Matt. She found Wolf downstairs in his jeans, boots and hat. As they headed to the door Mrs. Trujillo handed Wolf a bag of food and water. They stepped outside just as Matt brought around the horses. Matt placed the food and water into his saddles bags. Rachel swung up onto one horse, Matt put Wolf onto another, and he got onto a third. They raced the horses to the middle of town where they found a large posse massing. Matt took the lead.

"Which way did they go?" he asked looking around at the men.

"We're not sure, Matt," Luther Maxwell answered. "We'll follow the tracks out of town as best we can." He looked over at Rachel and Matt. "Are you sure you want them with us? This is going to be a rough ride."

"Not a negotiable point," Rachel snapped. "Now, let's stop wasting time!" No one protested. They clucked horses and galloped out of town. As she rode she said aloud in a soft voice, "Whisperwind, if ever I needed you, it's now. Help us find the girls. Keep them safe until we get there." No sooner did she finish speaking than she heard a faint whistling, similar to the first time the whisperwind spoke to her outside of Chimayó. She listened carefully and finally heard the answer to her prayer.

"The girls live. Will protect them."

Rachel wiped away a tear, comforted that the spirits would watch over the girls. The posse rode toward the main road, what Rachel knew to be Highway 54 in the 21st century. As they galloped, they periodically slowed down to check for whether tracks veered off. They didn't. Once they reached the main road, they looked for multiple hoof tracks matching the number of horses seen riding off with the girls. Wolf spotted them first and pointed south. The group let their horses rest for a few minutes then resumed the ride southward. After a couple of hours they came upon an old miner ambling along on a donkey.

"Old timer," Matt called to him. "Have you seen some Mexicans with a couple of girls?"

The man whose weather-beaten face was like tanned leather looked up at Matt and nodded. "Could be. Saw a group of Mexicans go by here a while ago with a couple a young-ins. Saw dresses flailing in the wind. Wasn't my business."

"Which way did they go?" Rachel asked.

The man eyed her suspiciously.

"Well?" Matt asked impatiently.

"Same way you're goin'. South."

The posse picked up speed and kept heading south. After hours of hard riding, they slowed as the sun descended toward the horizon.

"Let's set up camp here," Matt called to the group.

"Matt, let's keep going. There's still daylight. We'll lose time," Rachel implored him.

"Rachel, it's going to be dark in an hour. They're going to have to stop too. Their horses, like ours, will need to be fed and watered. We'll pick it up at daybreak and that's all I'm going to say about it."

He got down and took gear off of his horse, Rachel's and Wolf's. In short order the posse set up camp and began cooking a simple meal of beans and rice. The men set the horses to graze and water. As soon as dinner was over, the group bedded down to rest for the next day's ride. Rachel lay between Matt and Wolf.

Matt fell asleep right away, but Rachel couldn't sleep. Staying focused on the trail had allowed her to keep her fears at bay. Now, in the silence of the night, her worst fears rose and consumed her mind. She envisioned Maddie and Emily being subjected to all sorts of abuse. She tried not to think about it, but couldn't help herself. She began to whimper quietly, loud enough for Wolf to hear. The boy rolled over and laid his head on Rachel's shoulder and put his arm around her.

"Don't worry, Mama, we'll find them."

Rachel stroked his head. "I sure hope so, Wolf, I sure hope so."

"The wind said they are alive and it will protect them."

Rachel turned her head to look at him, a quiver in her voice. "You heard the whisperwind?"

Wolf nodded.

"How long have you been able to hear the wind?"

"Since I came to live with you."

Rachel ceased her crying and finally fell asleep with Wolf's arm still wrapped around her. Right before dawn Rachel awoke with a start. She nudged both Wolf and Matt. "Let's go."

Matt rose and woke the others to get ready to ride.

"What about breakfast, Mr. Bradshaw?" one man asked.

"If you're still hungry after all those beans you ate last night, Rachel has some jerky you can eat," he snapped at the man.

Rachel reached into her food bag, took out several pieces of jerky and handed them to the man. She gave several pieces to Wolf and Matt and a couple of other men who watched her with hungry eyes. She also passed out biscuits that Mrs. Trujillo packed. She decided to hold back on the rest of the jerky, cookies and dried fruit should they need them later. As soon as the horses were ready, they mounted and resumed their ride. This time Wolf kept getting nudged to the back of the pack and he couldn't see the tracks in front of him. A couple of hours later, they slowed to inspect whether they were still following the hoof tracks and realized they lost had them. They circled back to retrace their steps, this time at a slower pace. Wolf pulled to the front, watching with hawk-like precision.

"There's the tracks," he called out, pointing east.

Indeed, several sets of hoof tracks headed into a grassy area toward rising mountains. Although it appeared forbidding, it didn't deter the group. They advanced at a steady pace, Wolf in front, watching for a change of direction. A short while later the tracks disappeared altogether, about the time they came upon an orchard. An old man with long white hair and a white beard emerged from the orchard, holding a basket of fruit.

"Do you live around here?" Matt asked him.

The man nodded. "Up there," he pointed to a hill where they saw an old adobe perched on top. His voice carried a distinct French accent. "I'm Frenchy Rochas. This is my land. What do you want?"

"We're looking for some Mexicans who have a couple of girls with them."

"Would they be your girls?" Frenchy probed.

"It's our daughter and niece," Rachel responded. "They kidnapped them yesterday from Oak Valley."

"Their tracks turned in here," Wolf added.

The old man looked at Wolf from under the broad rim of his hat, scrutinizing him from head to toe, then turned back to Matt.

"Doesn't surprise me. All kinds of vagrants hide out in Dog Canyon until it's safe to continue their journeys. But you say the young ladies were kidnapped?"

Everyone nodded. "And the kidnappers, they were Mexican?" They nodded again. "Been a lot of kidnappings of young girls in these parts. The Mexicans come up here, grab them and take them to the brothels in Mexico. They pay good money for them down there."

Rachel cried out, "No! They're only girls. My little one is just four and a half years old!"

"Was the other girl older?"

Rachel nodded. "Our niece, she's 15."

Frenchy nodded. "She was probably the target and your daughter got picked up because she was with her. Happens a lot."

Rachel eyes burned with tears building behind her eyes. She swallowed hard to keep herself from crying. "Did you see them come this way?"

"When I was in the back of the orchard I heard a bunch of horses go by; couldn't see anything. Might have been them."

"And which way would they have gone?" Matt pressed.

Frenchy pointed toward the hills. "The canyon goes in quite a ways; the trail winds up the mountain. They could be hiding anywhere."

"Thanks," Matt called to him and motioned to the group to proceed. They moved at a slow pace, Wolf in front, looking for tracks. Hours went by and although several complained of hunger, they pushed on, rising higher up the mountain.

"Wait!" Wolf called out and slipped off his horse. He kneeled down and inspected the earth and grasses. He pointed to a set of towering granite rocks. "They went this way."

One of the men in the group disagreed. "Those rocks are perched right against the hill. There's no room to hide back there. We should stay on the course we're taking."

"No, they went this way!" Wolf stood his ground. "Look!" He pointed to several broken branches on a bush a few feet in the direction of the tall rocks. Matt got down off his horse and inspected the broken branches. Wolf pointed to a layer of grass a little further ahead. "The grass is flat, Papa, they went that way."

"He's right," Matt announced, remounting his horse.

The group turned and as they approached the rocks, they heard gunshots, forcing them off their horses. They set the horses to grazing while they snuck quietly through the tall, willowy grasses. As soon as they reached the first boulder, they plastered their backs against the flattest area and stepped sideways, silently moving ahead. Matt was in front and when they reached the end of the rock, he peered around and jerked his head back.

"They're in there," he whispered. "And they're trapped. This is the only way out."

"Are the girls with them? Are they all right?" Rachel asked.

He nodded. "They seem to be."

"Mr. Bradshaw, what is the plan?" whispered another posse rider.

"Not sure," Matt said quietly. "If we barge in there they may shoot the girls."

"No, they wouldn't," Rachel said. "The girls are bounty for them. They wouldn't risk both losing their bounty and their lives. Besides, there are more of us than them. If we go in there, maybe they will give them up, seeing that there is no way out."

"Possibly," Matt said. "But who knows what they will do?"

"I say your wife is right, Mr. Bradshaw. We should just walk in there, guns raised," another man offered.

"Matt, we don't have a lot of options," Rachel pressed.

Matt stood stone faced, listening to all the suggestions. Finally he nodded. "Okay, let's go in, but Rachel, you and Wolf stay in the back. I'll not have the two of you hurt."

The men massed and headed around the corner, guns raised, closing off the only exit out of the canyon crevice. The Mexicans were sitting around playing cards. The girls were sitting a few feet away, their hands and feet tied and bandanas stuck in their mouths. Emily and Maddie saw them first, their eyes flashing wide. Moments later, the Mexicans jumped to their feet and drew their weapons. A mixture of surprise and fear bloomed across their faces as they saw how many people they faced, each pointing a gun at them. One man ran over to the girls and aimed his weapon at them.

"Leave, or we shoot!" he called to the posse. "Leave!"

"Like hell we will!" Rachel called out moving to the front of the group, the bead of her gun on the man's head. "You let go of them. I swear to God, you harm them and I'll kill you." She lowered her aim to the area below his waist. "But first I'll shoot your balls off and let you suffer worse than a wild dog."

The man's mouth opened slightly. He dropped his gun and said something in Spanish that Rachel couldn't fully understand, something about being sick.

"He says you cured him," a man in the posse said.

Rachel stepped forward still aiming her gun at the man. She narrowed her eyes, focusing and looking at him carefully. "I remember you…….Yes. You came to my house. I helped you when you were sick. And this is how you repay my kindness? By kidnapping my daughter and niece?"

"Mrs., I sorry. Did not know was your familia," the man said, holding up his hands. He glanced over to the others and waved his hand indicating they should drop their weapons. They did so without being asked twice.

"You pendejo!" she screamed at him and ran over to the girls, dropped to her knees and began untying them. Matt and Wolf raced to her side. In moments they released the girls, who began sobbing hysterically, holding onto Rachel, Matt and Wolf. Meanwhile the posse used the ropes to tie the kidnappers' hands behind their backs and their feet together. They stuffed the kerchiefs into their mouths and hoisted them up onto their horses, laying them belly-side down across the saddles, and led them out of the crevice.

"What will you do with the bad men?" Wolf asked.

"These bad boys are going to jail," Luther Maxwell answered, laying one of his large hands on Wolf's shoulder and giving it a gentle squeeze of reassurance.

Matt, Rachel, Wolf, Maddie and Emily walked out of the crevice and mounted the horses. Emily rode with Wolf while Maddie rode with Rachel, face-to-face, not letting go of her mother. The family rode separately from the posse so the girls wouldn't have to look at the Mexican kidnappers the whole way home.

The next day, both groups arrived in Oak Valley, an hour apart. As the family strode into town, they were met with cheers by people who stopped to watch them ride by. They didn't stop, instead heading straight home. As soon as they got to the house, Mrs. Trujillo ran out and helped the girls off the horses, giving each one of them a bear hug. They trooped up the stairs into the house. Rachel asked Mrs. Trujillo to run hot baths right away. As soon as everyone was bathed and dressed, they sat down at the kitchen table for a big helping of Mrs. Trujillo's chicken tamales and beans and chocolate cake. Mrs. Trujillo didn't have to ask if anyone wanted seconds, they all took another helping, cleaning their plates twice.

An hour later, townspeople began knocking on the door carrying food, flowers, and gifts for the girls. Mrs. Hayes handed Rachel the bag of Emily's ribbons.

"Thank you, Lily, you're a gem," Rachel took the bag from her. "Believe it or not, Emily was asking about the ribbons on our way back. I assured her that

392

someone would return them and that, if not, I would buy her every last ribbon in the store."

Lily turned to go down the porch stairs and was met head-on by Madame Bishu, who stepped to the side to let her pass. Lily stopped and glared at her, then looked straight ahead as though she wasn't there, proceeding out the garden. Madame Bishu looked up at the open door.

"Is it all right if I come in?"

"Of course," Rachel waved her inside.

"I know you've all been through a good deal. I brought you something special to help you and Matt calm your nerves." She held a bag out to Rachel who took it. Matt emerged from the back of the house, stood at Rachel's side and looked inside the bag. "No parent should have to bear what the two of you have endured. Drink this with my fondest wishes."

"Thank you, Madame Bishu," Rachel murmured.

"Ruby, it's time you called me Ruby," she smiled, reached over and squeezed Rachel's hand.

"Okay, then it's also time that you called me by my name, Rachel."

Ruby smiled, nodded, turned and left.

They watched her saunter through the garden gate and down the street.

"What's in the bag?"

Matt reached in. "Your favorite." He pulled out a large bottle of Jack Daniels Tennessee Whiskey. "Ninety proof, sweetheart. If this doesn't make you forget the last couple of days, I'm not sure anything will."

* * *

That night Wolf pleaded with Rachel to sleep with the girls. "I have to protect them."

"Wolf, they're okay now. Really, they are."

But Wolf's anxiety wouldn't be quelled and Rachel relented. He brought his blanket and pillow into the girls' room and made a bed on the floor. All three children got into their beds and insisted Rachel tell them a happy bedtime story. Rachel's heart sang. Routine was returning to their household. She started to tell them a story of two brave girls and a strong boy who went up against and defeated an evil goblin. But only moments into the story, all three children fell asleep. Rachel kissed them all and tiptoed out of the room, content that they were well and safe. She went downstairs to find Matt in the living room pouring Jack Daniels into glasses.

"Only a little bit for me, please," she said as he poured into her glass.

"Why? You love this stuff."

"I've got my reasons," she smiled at him. She sat down next to him and he handed her the glass. They clinked their glasses and each took a large swig. Rachel laid her head on Matt's shoulder.

"Will our lives ever be normal?" Rachel asked.

"That depends on your definition of normal," he answered running his arm around her.

"You know," she sighed, "normal, boring stuff. No murder, no kidnapping, no drama. Plain old boring."

"Was your life in the 21st century boring?"

"Compared to my life here? Absolutely."

Matt leaned down and kissed her tenderly on the head. "I think the worst is behind us, darlin'. From here on out, let's work on boring and our little family. Which reminds me, isn't it about time you visited the Medinas and have them give you whatever they gave Catherine? Before the kidnapping, Wolf was asking me if he could have a little brother."

Rachel leaned up and gave Matt a kiss on the cheek. "Not necessary, Matt. His little brother or sister should be coming along in seven months or so."

Matt whirled around, his face bursting with unabashed joy. He wrapped his arms tightly around

Rachel and buried his face in her thick hair. She felt his shoulders shake slightly. Rachel pulled back. A solitary tear coursed down his cheek.

The End

For information on other books by Jeffree Wyn Itrich, please visit:

www.jeffreewyn.com

www.facebook.com/JeffreeWyn

www.amazon.com/author/jeffreewynitrich

www.goodreads.com/goodreadscomJeffreeWyn

Made in the USA
San Bernardino, CA
26 August 2013